Unexpected
LOVE

Cover Image: Masterfile/ Budget Royalty free

ISBN: 978-0-9862933-9-9

PINK GIRL Publishing

To my first loves
God
Mommy and Dad

Acknowledgements

Thanks to my friends Barbara Byndon, Beverly Evans and Cheryl Winborne, for giving me their honest opinion on these new characters and series. I'm so glad you all liked it. A shout out to my ARGroup...thank you.

As always, thanks to my Editor Jeanne Cadeau for being so patient with me.

About the Author

A California native, novelist Tracy Reed pushes the boundaries of her Christian foundation with her sometimes racy and often fiery tales.

After years of living in the Big Apple, this self proclaimed New Yorker draws from the city's imagination, intrigue, and inspiration to cultivate characters and plot lines who breathe life to the words on every page.

Tracy's passion for beautiful fashion and beautiful men direct her vivid creative power towards not only novels, but short stories, poetry, and podcasts. With something for every attention span.

Tracy Reed's ability to capture an audience is unmatched. Her body of work has been described as a host of stimulating adventures and invigorating expression.

Unexpected
LOVE

TRACY REED

Preface
Fiona

I can't believe I'm spending my wedding anniversary with my divorce lawyer. Instead of celebrating our love for each other, my husband and I are fighting on how to put an end to something that probably never should have been. That statement makes it sound like I'm sad, which I'm not. In fact, if I hadn't yielded to a little thing called lust, I wouldn't be here fighting for something that lying, manipulative sack of s!*# knows I created.

Every time I think about how my husband lied and deceived me, I get angry. I really should have listened to that little voice that said, "stab him", but I really don't look good in orange. And I'm not a fan of having the state control my schedule. But when I think about my marriage, how would jail have been any different from how I was living?

When I saw my soon-to-be ex-husband, Rhys Edward Walters, it was love at first sight… I thought. Looking back now, maybe that jolt I felt wasn't love, but the breakfast burrito I had just eaten.

As I was saying…It was my sophomore year of college. I was sitting in the library when I saw this fine guy walk in, and our eyes locked.   I was done. As far as I was concerned, God had answered my prayer. Not only was I going to graduate with my degree in Marketing, I was now hoping to leave with my MRS. degree as well. Mrs. Rhys Walters, that was my new minor.

Too bad no one told God that was the plan. I spent the next three years hoping Rhys would ask me out. We were constantly around each other, and every now and then he would throw me a bone and say "Hi", followed by a warm, blinding smile. Once he even sat next to me at lunch, and I was so nervous I almost peed myself .

And then one day a friend told me there was a guy she wanted to fix me up with. I thought why not. The guy I was pining after didn't seem to realize I even existed. When I asked, "Who?" she replied, "Rhys Walters", I almost passed out. I just knew it was a sign from God, and this was confirmation that He had gotten my request and had chosen my friend as the channel by which to fulfill my request.

I waited patiently for my fix up with my dream guy, but it never happened. Instead, he had the tenacity to hook up with some freshman floozy. I was done with love. I sped through college and vowed to leave any memory and fantasy of life with Rhys behind. I don't think I even saw him at graduation.

Unexpected Love

I moved to New York after college and went to work for this cool beauty start up as a Marketing Coordinator. In a matter of three years I had moved up to Director of Marketing. I like to think it was because I was very good at my job. But the truth is, it was easier to get a title upgrade and stock options than a salary increase. That interesting employment package later proved to work to my advantage. About a year later, the company took off and my stock options were worth more than the raise I had requested.

A few years later, while I was at Barney's waiting for the elevator, I looked out the corner of my eye and spotted a familiar face.

"Fiona Jeffries". The deep voice was just as I had remembered it.

I looked in the direction of the voice and staring at me with a wide smile, was the guy who had broken my heart. Okay, so technically, he didn't know he was guilty of such a treasonous act.

"I'm sorry, do I know you?" Of course I knew him. He was only the star of my dreams for three years of college. He looked the same. Tall, beautiful honey-colored skin. Warm eyes and from the way his suit was hugging his body, he still had his amazing physique.

He smiled. "Rhys Walters."

I played it real cool. I wanted to see how far he was willing to go to make me remember him. "The name is vaguely familiar." I turned my attention back to the descending elevator.

"You're kidding, right? We went to college together. You were friends with Chantal Richards."

"I can't say that…"

"Average height, dark shoulder length hair, a little curvy…," he sighed. "She tried to fix us up, but…"

Bingo. So he did know about the date. I turned to face him. "Oh yeah, I remember her, but I don't recall anything about a date."

Ding. The elevator arrived, the doors opened and we stepped aside and waited for everyone to exit. Once it cleared, we stepped inside.

"What floor?"

"Three. Thank you."

He pressed the button and then looked me up and down. I know I looked good, and I was so glad I had chosen today to wear my favorite red and white DVF wrap dress. The one that makes my breasts look amazing and accentuates my hips and behind in a good way. I refer to it as my, Ego Booster Dress. I looked at him surveying me. Yep, you had a chance at all of this and you passed on it. The elevator stopped and I waited for the doors to open and then I started to exit.

He grabbed the door and stopped it from closing. "Are you free for coffee?"

"Excuse me?"

"Coffee? Are you available for coffee?" He smiled.

Even if I wasn't available, I was about to be. This was Rhys Walters, and there was no way I was not going to have coffee with him.

I looked at my watch and then back at him. "A quick coffee."

That was over ten years ago and now I'm asking myself, how could I have been so foolish?

Chapter 1
Fiona

My husband Rhys is a selfish liar. Two traits he kept well hidden. In the beginning of our courtship and marriage, he played his role perfectly. But as we got more comfortable with each other and settled into our roles, he changed.

Good old Rhys always had an excuse for the things he didn't want to do and didn't do. And an even better lie for the things he got caught doing.

We vowed to be together 'til death. If I had known then what I know now, I would have included the phrase, "Or until I have had my fill of your lies."

It's amazing how naive some college educated people

are. We became so committed to our goals that we forgot about our marriage.

I don't know when it happened. We were on different work schedules and eventually different life schedules. I was ready to start a family and he wanted to build a publishing empire. Someone was going to have to make a sacrifice. We tossed an emotional coin and I lost.

When we met that fateful day at Barneys, I was so caught up in believing God had finally answered my prayer, that I never bothered to do a proper due diligence. Rhys fed me some trumped up story about being an editor on a political magazine.

I later discovered he was a junior copy editor slash ad sales assistant on a political blog. He had a dream of starting his own magazine. His concept sounded great. He wanted to target the changing face of politics. To be honest, it bored me. I spent the encounter staring at his beautiful lips.

We got married fairly quickly and he started his magazine. A year later he started a second one and two years later, two more were born. It seemed like everything he touched turned to gold.

Last year, after a somewhat romantic dinner, Rhys made an announcement that changed our lives.

"I've been thinking, this isn't the year to start a family. I know you've been patient about obliging my schedule. However, I…what's the rush? It's not like we're old."

"I See." Somewhere along the way, I had been left out of the board meeting of our marriage. "So tell me Rhys, where do you see us in the next five years?" I asked. I needed to know when I could make family plans. My biological clock was blasting.

"Launching another magazine, taking the company global and expanding our digital footprint."

I nodded as I cleared the table and walked into the kitchen. "That's not us. That's the company. What about us?"

"The company is us," he said. "And, I see us with a larger apartment or maybe a brownstone."

"A larger place?" I placed the dishes in the sink and turned to face him.

"Yes, we'll need it."

"We will?" I got excited because it seemed like he was actually making plans for our future, for our family.

"Of course. Our place is nice but it's just not big enough for our needs."

"We can stay in the loft the first year because they usually sleep in our room for the first few months."

"What are you talking about?"

"The baby."

"What baby?"

"Our baby. The reason we need a bigger place. "

He smiled. "We don't need a bigger place because of a baby."

"Then why?" I asked.

"For entertaining clients." He sipped his wine. "This is good."

"Uh-huh." I folded my arms in front of my chest and asked the question I should have asked over ten years ago. "Do you want children?"

"Not really."

His answer blindsided me. Right now, I wanted to kick myself in the head. How could I not know this? With a little more courage and the pieces of my heart and world lying at my feet, I asked another difficult question. "At what point did you decide you didn't want children?"

"I never did." He proudly announced.

I felt like I had just been punched in my stomach. In one casual sentence, he had stolen my future. I closed my eyes and told myself not to jump across the counter and put that butcher knife in his throat. I wouldn't cut off his penis, because if I kept him alive, I'd harvest his sperm and get the child he refused to give me.

"But you knew I wanted children. In fact you said it would be wonderful. Was that just talk to get me to agree with your revised plan?"

"Yes, but let me explain."

"What's there to explain? Congratulations, you've just hit the trifecta of relationship mistrust. You lied, deceived and betrayed me."

"I know it seems like I've just committed treason against our vows, but—"

"Why did you marry me?" I felt I should know why he had stolen the last ten plus years of my life before I took his and escaped to a remote island.

"I needed a showpiece. Someone I knew would be there for me. A partner. Baby, we're a team."

"A team?"

He walked around the large white quartz topped island to where I was standing. He gently rubbed my arms. The gesture almost caught me off guard. But then I looked into his eyes and realized why I was so angry.

"Yeah. I'm the coach and you're the quarterback. I send in the plays and you execute or implement them, based on our meetings."

"I see. And sometimes as the quarterback on the field, I will overrule or ignore the instructions of the coach for the greater good of the team."

"Exactly." He kissed me on the forehead and started to

walk back around the kitchen island to the other side.

"As quarterback, I'm executing my own play."

"That's what I'm talking about."

"We're a team, right?" I refilled our wine glasses.

"Right."

"And for all practicality, the magazines are our children."

"I never thought of it like that, but you're right. They're our children." He sipped his wine. "This is good."

"I'm glad to hear that, because when we go to court, I want to make sure the judge understands that." I sipped my wine. "You're right. This is good."

"What are you talking about?" He put his wine glass down on the marble counter.

"The magazines, our children. Most courts issue custody of the children to the mother. Especially if she's been a devoted mother, like me."

"Are you insane?" he shouted.

"No. I'm just looking after the well-being of my children."

"What are you talking about?"

"I'm talking about our new game plan." I had done to him what he did to me. I destroyed his future with a few impromptu words. That was more painful for him, and more gratifying for me.

"Game plan?"

"Yeah, sweetie. You know the one where I take over the magazines."

"I don't think so. There's no way I'm giving you my magazines," he shouted. Now he wanted to act like a father.

"But I thought they were our children?"

"Are you insane?"

"Could be, but I think it's a fitting settlement."

"And if I refuse to relinquish control?" he asked.

"Then we let a judge decide."

"Then, so be it."

"I'll see you in court." I finished my wine.

⁂

I was sitting in the living room of our loft overlooking the busy streets of Tribeca enjoying a cup of my favorite French roast coffee, when the elevator door opened. I turned my head slightly to verify it was Rhys. I took another sip of coffee and continued editing DOWNTOWN. DOWNTOWN, is a lifestyle magazine named after the chic new neighborhoods that have sprung up throughout the country in the downtown and industrial areas across the country. I came up with the idea for this magazine when we first moved to Tribeca. I thought it would be good to highlight great downtown living areas in other states. Rhys agreed. I did the research, and two years later DOWNTOWN was born.

My instincts proved to be on point. People were excited about seeing other transition neighborhoods. Not to mention the boom the mag brought to the local businesses we featured.

I've always given Rhys credit for starting this magazine, but it was really my idea. I quit my job and went to work on DOWNTOWN permanently as Editor-In-Chief. Second to CHIC, our fashion publication, it's our other major money maker. Also my idea.

It burns me that Rhys refers to the magazines as his, when the top two revenue makers were my ideas. Some team… I've been doing just as much, if not more of the work, and letting him take all the credit. These are my babies and I refuse to let him or anyone else step in and take them.

"I got a call from my attorney informing me that all production is to cease until the court rules who gets control of the magazines. What are you doing?"

BARK! BARK! BARK! BARK!

He stopped in his tracks. "What the HELL?!...What is that?"

"That's my baby."

BARK! BARK! BARK! BARK!

He stepped closer. "Your what?"

BARK! BARK! BARK! BARK!

"Call it off."

"Bentley, come to Mommy." The beautiful black pit bull trotted over to me, sat next to my foot and I patted his head. "Good boy. Mommy loves you." I handed Bentley a treat and continued sipping my coffee. "You were saying?"

"When did you get that thing?"

"Just goes to show how often you're here. Bentley has been here almost three weeks." I patted his head again. "As you were saying?"

"What is going on with you?"

"What are you talking about?" I returned my attention to my work and coffee.

"You know exactly what I'm talking about."

"Grrr..." Bentley growled.

"Call off your mutt."

Bentley ran over and stopped in front of Rhys. BARK! BARK! BARK! BARK! BARK! BARK!

"Would you do something about that thing...call your dog off."

"Bentley...Bentley...Bentley...come to Mommy."

The pit bull stopped barking and stood his ground in front of Rhys. "Oh well. Typical man. Does things his way."

"What possessed you to get a dog?"

"I wanted a committed male in my life."

"What's that supposed to mean?"

"What do you want Rhys?"

"I want to know why you're acting like a female Bentley."

I looked at him and smirked. "Clever, but I'm just doing what any good mother would do."

"What?"

"I'm fighting for my children."

"What will it take to get you to stop this insane game?"

"Child support."

"Now I know you're crazy."

"Unless you want to see this thing played out on your competition's pages and websites, and them making a mint off your unwillingness to settle with your wife—"

"Fine. How much?"

I walked into the kitchen and Bentley followed me. I reached into a clear glass jar and handed Bentley another treat. "Here you go, baby."

"Those are dog treats?" Rhys asked with raised eyebrows.

"Yes." I looked at Rhys and smiled. "Did you eat one?"

"I thought…never mind."

I laughed as I refilled my coffee cup and added a little sugar. "Well, the pet bakery said they were a favorite of most dog breeds." I smiled and sipped my coffee.

"Not funny. I could have gotten food poisoning or…"

"Clearly you didn't because you're standing here annoying me."

"Are you finished?"

"You're the one that wanted to talk."

"What will it take to put an end to all of this?"

"One-third controlling interest in the current and all future publications. Plus, fifty percent of all the property and real estate holdings." I sipped more coffee. "I will retain my health benefits and life insurance."

"Are you nuts?" He walked over to the edge of the counter and braced his hands along the counter.

"That comment just added a board seat to my list."

"Are you——"

"Would you like to make it sixty percent of your secret cash account?"

"You're insane."

"I'm going to have to ask you to stop calling me insane, or I'll sue you for defamation of character and take the Hampton's house."

"WHAT?!"

BARK! BARK! BARK! BARK! BARK! BARK!

"Shut that thing up."

"Calm down, Bentley. Mommy's okay."

Rhys turned around, composed himself and turned back around. "What if I buy you out of the magazines?"

"With what?"

"I'll get a loan."

"Good luck with that. Hey, the thought of working with you everyday doesn't appeal to me either, but I don't trust you." I took another sip of coffee. "I want the loft. As well as fifty percent of all the cash and stocks. And I want forty percent of the money in your secret Caymans account."

"All because I don't want children?"

"No, because you lied. I would have preferred you

cheated on me. At least that's something I could see and fight. But this, this is a mark against your character and an assassination of my trust."

"What if I say I don't want a divorce, that you can have your baby?"

"What makes you think I would want to have a baby with you, knowing how you feel?"

"Because you love me."

I laughed out loud, took a key out of the drawer and walked over to the elevator. "That's funny. I think that's what they call an audible play, dear. Too bad, I'm not listening." I pushed the elevator button. "I've had all of your things moved to a loft downstairs."

"Where did you get the money to do that?"

"The college fund we setup for our children." He stood still with a blank look on his face. "Here you go." I handed him the keys and the elevator doors opened. "Good bye."

He boarded the elevator. "We're not done with this."

BARK!…BARK!…BARK!…BARK!…

"Seems we are."

Chapter 2
Ty

"Good morning, Fiona. Have a seat."

BARK! BARK! BARK! BARK!

I immediately looked up. "What was that?"

"Calm down, baby. Once Mommy handles a little business, we'll go to the park," she said to the black Pit bull sitting next to her foot.

My gaze went from the dog to her beautiful legs. I have always been enamored of Fiona's legs. I have to admit, I've often had fantasies about those beautiful smooth caramel colored thick thighs wrapped around my waist as I made love to her. But poor timing made me a prisoner of my fantasies. If only I had met her first, she'd be mine and not my ex-best friend's wife.

I put my pen down and cast my attention onto the woman I have measured all others against. And not one of them, not even my current girlfriend compares to her. I shook my head and smiled. "Now I understand what Rhys meant."

"What did he say?" she asked as she uncrossed and crossed her legs.

"He said you had gone insane and bought a killer dog."

She laughed. "I told him if he continued to call me insane, I was going to sue him for defamation of character." She patted the dog on the head. "As you can see, Bentley is a sweetheart."

"He said the dog…"

"Bentley." She quickly corrected me.

"Bentley." I rolled my eyes and smiled. "Why did you name your dog after a car?"

"It's another thing Rhys promised me."

"Rhys promised you a Bentley?"

"Not in so many words." She smiled.

"How many words exactly?" I folded my arms across my chest.

"He said when I turned forty, he would get me whatever I wanted."

"And you wanted a Bentley."

"Exactly."

"Fiona, Rhys is right, you're nuts."

"Never mind what he thinks. Where are the papers? I promised Bentley we'd go to the park this afternoon."

"About that, Rhys has changed his mind."

"About what?"

"Everything."

"What?!"

"He said he'll give you five million and that's it."

Bentley stood up and growled at me. "Calm down,

baby. Mommy likes this man. He's on our side." She patted Bentley's head and he relaxed.

"I need Bentley in all of my negotiations."

"Last time I checked this was a community property state." She stood up and started pacing. "What are my options?"

"You're kind of stuck." I found it a little difficult to concentrate on her question while watching her walk. The sway of her hips and her parfum invaded my mind and confused me. "Uhm, you never really had a legal agreement with the company."

"I'm his wife. It's not like I needed one. I helped him start that company."

"He's saying the concept for the magazines were all his, and you were merely a consultant."

"That's a bunch of crap. Ty, you were his attorney. You know how hard I worked to help him."

"Of course I do, but the court doesn't want to hear that. You need something in writing."

"Okay, what about the personal property. I know I'm entitled to…"

"Yes, you are. However, he doesn't agree to your terms."

"So, what are my options?"

"We start over. Give me a list of what you want and I'll present it."

"That lousy piece of…not only did he lie to me about wanting to have children, now he's trying to deny me half of what's mine."

"It's a decent offer."

"But is it a fair offer?" she asked.

I exhaled. "I've known you over ten years and I've known Rhys much longer than I care to mention. And to be honest, this is a lousy deal." I walked around and leaned against the front of the desk. She stopped next to me chair and my entire body got hard. I couldn't physically handle being so close to her. "What he's doing to you is disgusting." I folded my arms across my chest.

She looked at me and I recognized the hurt. That's how I looked when I realized my childhood friend no longer had any use for me or my firm. He cut me off without a millisecond of a thought. Lousy piece of garbage didn't even have the guts to tell me to my face. Instead, he had his new attorney send me a letter terminating our working relationship. Then the snake had the nerve to call and ask if we were still boys. I was done with him.

"I don't know why I'm surprised. He's basically trying to do to me what he did to you," she said. "He has no loyalty."

"That's not true."

She looked shocked at my statement. "Excuse me."

"Rhys is loyal to Rhys," I joked.

"You're right." She smiled and sat down in front of me.

What I wouldn't give to wake up every morning to that beautiful smile.

"Exactly. I mean, how do you fire the attorney that helped you set up your company? If it hadn't been for your connections, Rhys would still be working at that blog. Ungrateful son of a…"

"That's enough about my ex-best friend."

"Tiberius, you are a lot better person than I am. If I didn't think he'd have me arrested, I would sneak into his loft and…"

I covered my ears. "Please stop. I can't be privy to the rest of that statement just in case you act on it." I smiled.

BARK!…BARK!…BARK!…BARK!

"Bentley, I'm charging you with keeping your Mommy out of trouble."

BARK!…BARK!…BARK!…BARK!

"Exactly."

"Excuse me, Bentley's my dog."

"But like most guys, we speak the same language." I smiled.

"Anyway. What's my next move?" She leaned forward and grabbed my knees. My breath caught and I lost focus momentarily.

"Uhm…are you sure you want out?"

"Yes." She didn't hesitate to answer.

"Okay, I'll put my best…"

"Ty, please don't give this to anyone else." She started to get a little anxious.

"Fi, I'm not…this isn't my area." I looked at those gorgeous dark brown eyes and got pulled in. Just like I did when she said she didn't care what Rhys did, she was still my friend and insisted we have lunch once a week. "Okay, I'll handle this."

"Thank you." She smiled.

"But if it starts to get too far out of my range, I'm handing it over to my family law guy. Okay?"

"Okay. Thank you." She hugged me and I knew the rest of the day I'd carry the memory of her soft body pressed against mine.

I felt something brush up against my leg and looked down. "What is Bentley doing?"

"He either likes you or he's about to hump your leg. Which means he really likes you."

"Let's hope it's the first one." We laughed as we pulled apart.

Chapter 3
Fiona

Rhys and I have been battling a few months and we still haven't come to an agreement about our divorce. I'm tired, but I refuse to give in. I'm going to fight this to the end.

Bentley and I settled in for an evening of Netflix and takeout. I picked up my phone and pressed the number to my favorite Chinese restaurant when the buzzer rang.

Bark! Bark! Bark! Bark!

"I heard it." I smiled at Bentley, walked over and answered the buzzer. "Hello."

"Mrs. Walters, your attorney is here."

"Who?"

"Your attorney. Tiberius Wells."

"Oh, send him up." I hung up the receiver and looked at Bentley. "Seems we have company. Once your Uncle Tiberius leaves, I'll order dinner."

Bark! Bark! Bark! Bark!

"You like Ty. Is that why you're doing your happy dance?" I smiled.

Bark! Bark! Bark! Bark!

Bentley trotted over to the elevator and sat down. I had to laugh. He was so cute standing watch for his new friend.

A few minutes later the elevator dinged.

Bark! Bark! Bark! Bark!

"Calm down."

Bark! Bark! Bark! Bark!

The elevator door opened and Bentley ran over to Ty.

Bark! Bark! Bark! Bark!

"Bentley, settle down."

Bark! Bark! Bark! Bark!

"Hi, Bentley." Ty stepped out of the elevator. "Where's your Mommy?"

I heard Bentley's little feet trotting across the mahogany floor towards the kitchen.

"I'm over here." Bentley ushered Ty over to the kitchen like a drum major. I reached in the glass treat jar, pulled one out and placed it in his mouth. "Thank you for answering the door for Mommy." I rubbed Bentley's neck.

Ty stood there shaking his head. "You two deserve each other."

Bentley walked over and brushed up against Ty's leg.

"Excuse me, look who's talking." Ty looked down at his leg.

"What can I say, he has good taste in people," he teased.

"That would explain why he growls at Rhys." We laughed. "What's with the bags?"

"Dinner."

"Let's eat." He placed the bags on the counter and started pulling out Chinese takeout boxes. "You read my mind. I was about to order takeout."

"Great minds think alike." He smiled and took a long brown wrapped item out of the woven bag. He opened it and placed the large bone on the floor in front of Bentley. "I even got a little something for Bentley."

"You're scaring me." I smiled.

"Hey, I gotta keep both of my clients happy." He smiled.

Then he pulled out a bottle of champagne. "Okay, what's going on?"

"I heard from Rhys' attorney."

"And…"

"He agreed to everything."

"What?" My eyes got wide.

Ty started to open the bottle. "We need glasses."

I pulled a couple of glasses out of the cabinet and placed them in front of Ty.

"He agreed to everything? I don't believe it."

Pop! "That's what I said." He filled both glasses. "What should we toast to?"

That was too easy. "Even the money in the Caymans?"

"Yep." He raised his glass. "Come on Fiona. Let's celebrate."

"What about the loft?"

"Yours."

I didn't want to burst his bubble, but it seemed too pat and perfect.

Bark! Bark! Bark! Bark!

"I know Sweetie, something doesn't seem right."

Ty put his glass down. "Okay, what's the problem?"

"I know Rhys. He wouldn't just cave like this, he'd fight." I sipped my champagne.

"It's been four months, Fi."

"Exactly. I've seen him in negotiations that have lasted much longer."

"Do you want me to reject the settlement?"

"Yes…no…where are the papers?"

He reached inside his bag and pulled out a thick manila folder. "Here."

I fanned the papers. Then took half of the pages and handed the other half to Ty. I needed to make sure I wasn't missing something. We opened the food containers and started reading. With half a dumpling aimed at my mouth, I spotted something that caught my eye.

"That son of a---"

"What?" I handed the page to Ty.

"Right there." I pointed.

"Mrs. Walters or Fiona Harris will receive thirty three percent of the print profits of all current and future publications both domestic and foreign. That's what you asked for."

"No, I said I only wanted the rights to CHIC and DOWNTOWN." I started pacing back and forth. "That sneaky, lying bas---"

"So, he's giving you more. What's the problem?" Ty bit on his egg roll.

I looked at Ty. "Print profits."

"I'm sorry, Fiona, I don't see why that's a problem."

I braced my hands on the counter. "At one time, Fairgate Communications offered to buy CHIC and DOWNTOWN. They were starting a lifestyle channel and said those two mags would be the perfect foundation. There was even talk about some product branding…books, housewares and fragrances. But we turned the deal down."

"Oh, I get it."

"That statement must mean the offer is back on the table. That's why Rhys agreed to everything I asked for and cleverly didn't say anything about branding."

"How much was the deal?"

"Six times the settlement he agreed to."

"What the——"

"Exactly." I started pacing and rubbing my hands. "I started those magazines. I conceived the formats and assembled the staff. Those are my babies."

"So what do you want to do?"

"Tell him the only mags I want are CHIC and DOWNTOWN."

"And if he says no?"

"Then we go to court."

"I thought you didn't want to go to court?"

"I don't, but I'm not going to let him take my babies." I sipped my champagne. "Get my babies, and I'll spring for the champagne."

☙☙☙☙☙☙☙☙

Bentley and I were out for our afternoon walk enjoying the sunshine. We were sort of banned from the doggie park for a little while. Seems Bentley had developed a little reputation for humping all the female dogs. The sneaky little devil. I didn't realize he had made it his mission to hump every female dog in the park.

I think we might have been fine if it hadn't been for that prize winning poodle he was caught mounting. The look on her mother's face when she saw Bentley and her little Madeline. I know I should be ashamed. Thank God, Bentley's been fixed. Otherwise, I might be a grandma several times over. One of the other doggie moms told me prize winning Madeline wasn't all that innocent. Seems she's been had by half the dogs at the park.

Now we limit our walks to the neighborhood until I find a new dog park. We walked back to the loft and were greeted by a surprise on the kitchen counter. I let Bentley off his leash. "Go check out the house for Mommy." He took off surveying the loft. I walked over to the intercom and called downstairs. "Hi, Solomon."

"Hello Mrs. Wal—I mean Miss Fiona. What can I do for you?"

"Did you leave an envelope for me?"

"No. I didn't. Hold on, let me ask Bruce." There was silence for a few seconds. "Mrs. I mean, Miss Fiona, Bruce said he left the envelope."

"When…why?"

"He said the messenger from Mr. Walters' office said you were expecting it and to leave it in your loft. Is there a problem?"

"No. In the future, please leave anything from his office at the front desk."

"I'm sorry. We were just following instructions."

"No need to apologize. Bye."

"Bye."

I hung up, pulled my phone out and pressed Ty's number. After the second ring he picked up. "What's up?"

"Can you come over?"

"Why, what's wrong?"

I looked at the large manila envelope. "I came home and found a large manila envelope from Rhys' office and…"

"Don't touch it. I'm on my way." Click.

Bentley and I paced the length of the loft. I was nervous, anxious, and petrified. What if it were Anthrax or a letter bomb? Now I was sounding like an idiot. Rhys wasn't smart enough to send me a letter bomb. Maybe a dead rat or snake, but never anything as complicated as a bomb. I exhaled.

I walked over to the counter and creeped up on the envelope trying to size it up. Why would Rhys send me anything? He knows all communication is to go through our attorneys. Then it occurred to me, maybe it was papers regarding CHIC and DOWNTOWN. I did tell Ty to tell Rhys I wanted my babies. I exhaled. That's probably what it is. Now I felt badly about having Ty come over. But if it were about the magazines, Rhys would have had his people contact Ty. My anxiety level quickly shot back up.

I opened the window and let in some air. I needed to keep a clear head. I looked down at Bentley and he seemed to be smiling.

"Your Mommy's hallucinating, right?"

Bark! Bark! Bark! Bark!

"When your Uncle Tiberius gets here, he'll straighten out all of this."

Bark! Bark! Bark! Bark!

The phone rang. I jumped and Bentley ran over to the phone.

Bark! Bark! Bark! Bark!

"Mommy's coming." I picked up the phone. "Hello."

"Miss Fiona, Mr. Wells is here. Shall I send him up?"

Unexpected Love

"Yes." I hung up the phone and looked at Bentley. "Your Uncle Tiberius is here."

Bark! Bark! Bark! Bark!

Bentley started dancing in circles.

"That's right. He's going to fix this for us."

Chapter 4
Ty

The elevator door opened and I stepped out.

Bark! Bark! Bark! Bark!

"Hey, Bentley." I patted his head and continued into the kitchen. "I see you're looking after Mommy."

Bark! Bark! Bark! Bark!

I took my jacket off and dropped it on the back of the stool. "So, what's the problem?"

Fi pointed to the envelope on the counter. "There it is." I picked it up not giving any thought to what could be inside. "What are you doing? That could be anthrax, a snake, a bomb, the plague, or I don't know what."

I started laughing. "The plague…really Fi."

"Hey, I wouldn't put it past Rhys."

I shook my head smiling. "First off, Rhys isn't that street smart." I opened the envelope, pulled out the papers and started reading. A few moments later I put the papers down and looked at her. "This was here when you got home?"

"Yes. Sitting right where you found it."

"Where's your copier?"

"Down the hall." I took the papers down the hall with Bentley following behind me.

I stood in the middle of the room skimming over the documents. I couldn't believe what I was reading. I reached into my pocket, pulled out my phone and pressed the button for my office. I started to press the call button and then I got an idea. This divorce was really more of a corporate partnership break. That was right up my alley.

I made copies, put the originals back into the envelope and walked back to the kitchen with Bentley following behind me.

I looked straight ahead and saw Fi pacing. "What was it?"

I didn't respond and walked over to the intercom and pressed the number for the concierge desk.

"Hello, Solomon. Would you please come up to Miss Harris' loft?"

"Yes, sir," he replied.

"Thank you." I hung up the phone and walked back to the kitchen counter.

"What's going on? What was in that envelope?" Fiona asked. She looked more terrified now than she did when I got here.

I placed the envelope on the counter never taking my

hand off of it. I was trying to contain my excitement.

"Can I have some water?"

She opened the refrigerator, pulled out a bottle of water and handed it to me.

"Here."

"Thanks." I opened the bottle and took a big sip. "That hit the spot."

"Now that you've quenched your thirst, tell me what was in the envelope." She walked around the counter and tried to take the envelope.

"Stop it." I picked up the envelope and stepped away.

The elevator dinged.

Bark! Bark! Bark! Bark!

Bentley walked over and stood in front of the elevator waiting for the door to open. The door slowly opened, and the tall middle-aged gentleman in a black suit and light gray shirt stepped out.

"Hi, Bentley," Solomon said as he walked into the kitchen. "Hello, Miss Harris…Mr. Wells. What can I do for you?"

"Have a seat," I said as I pointed to the black iron and wood stool.

"I'm fine standing."

"Solomon, who signed for this envelope?" I asked.

"Bruce. Maybe he should be here inste—"

I held up my hand. "That won't be necessary."

Solomon looked a little nervous. "Did we do something wrong because we—"

"You did nothing wrong. I need you to call the messenger and tell them this was delivered to the wrong address. It was supposed to go to Mr. Walters' office."

"Oh." Solomon seemed to relax a little. "Why don't I just take—"

"No. I uhm…it would be better if…"

Solomon hesitated a moment. "I understand." He looked at Fi. "This isn't the first divorce in the building we've had to deal with. There was a couple on the second floor that was…they were brutal on a level not of this world." He smiled. "Me and the boys never liked Mr. Walters. He doesn't smile or tip."

I smiled. "Thank you, Solomon."

"Miss Harris, me and the guys are at your service." He looked at Fi. "Tell me exactly what you want me to do."

"I need you to call the messenger service," I said.

"I can't do that," Bruce replied.

"But I thought you said you would help Miss Harris?"

"I will. But the envelope is correctly addressed," Bruce replied.

I paced a few moments. "I can't…"

"I could call the sender and tell them, Mr. Walters isn't here and we aren't allowed into his apartment when he's not home."

"Perfect. Do it."

Solomon reached into his pocket for his phone and dialed the number that was on the delivery ticket. "Hello, Collin Lawson's assistant…thank you…yes…this is the concierge at Mr. Walters' building…yes we did…oh…okay…it will be at the concierge desk…no problem…you're welcome…bye." Solomon pressed the button ending the call.

"What did she say?" I asked.

"She said she was glad I called, because the envelope was mis-delivered. She's sending someone over now to pick it up."

"Perfect." I handed him the envelope. "I don't want you to lie, but I also don't want you to let on that this was left in Miss Harris' apartment."

"Yes sir."

I reached into my pocket, pulled out a hundred dollar bill and handed it to Solomon.

"Sir, this is too much." He tried to give it back to me.

"Consider it a back tip from Mr. Walters," I said.

"In that case, thank you." He took the money and put it in his pocket. "Will there be anything else?"

"Make sure no one says anything about that envelope being delivered to Miss Harris."

"Yes, sir."

"Thank you, Solomon," Fi said and walked over and hugged him.

"Miss Harris, it's my pleasure to help you."

Bark! Bark! Bark! Bark!

Solomon rubbed Bentley's neck. "And you too, Bentley." He walked over and pressed the button for the elevator. The door opened immediately and he stepped inside and left.

Once the door closed, Fi looked at me. "What's going on?"

I ignored her, dialed my phone, and looked at her smiling. "Hello, Tiberius Wells calling for Collin Lawson... yes, I'll hold...thank you."

"What are you doing?" Fi asked.

"Hello, Collin. My client has changed her mind about a few things."

"No. I haven't," Fi protested and I brushed her off.

"Are you and your client available to meet tomorrow afternoon?...your office will be fine...we'll see you at three... bye." I pressed the button and ended the call.

"Are you insane?" Bentley walked around and sat at my

42

feet. "What was in that envelope? Was it about the Fairgate deal?"

"Something even better," I replied.

"Tell me."

"I would prefer you hear it tomorrow when Rhys does."

"How do you expect me to sleep, knowing there's…"

I walked around the counter and grabbed her shoulders. "Trust me. If this goes as I believe it will, you'll be a free woman."

"It's that good?" she asked.

"Even better. Trust me."

She sighed and her shoulders relaxed. "Okay."

Chapter 5
Fiona

I think Bentley and I walked over ten thousand steps in the loft. We both finally gave in to sleep around three this morning. But it was a short nap. We were both up at six thirty.

I put his leash on and we went outside for Bentley's morning poop stroll. I needed to clear my head and pray. This whole thing with Rhys had been draining. I know one thing, once it's over, I'm swearing off men for a while, except for Bentley, Ty and my brother, Mercer. Those are the only men I want in my life.

I grabbed a coffee and a bagel and a doggie snack for Bentley and we went back to the loft. When I stepped off the elevator, I had an intruder.

"What are you doing here? Did you forget you live downstairs?"

"Not funny."

"It wasn't meant to be." I sipped my coffee

I walked around him to the other side of the counter. "Anything you have to say to me can wait until our meeting this afternoon."

"What do you want?"

"What are you talking about Rhys?"

"What are these new terms you're demanding."

I put my cup and bagel on the counter. "I have no idea what you're talking about." I tried to keep my cool.

Bark! Bark! Bark! Bark! Bentley trotted over and stood in front of Rhys. Bark! Bark! Bark! Bark!

"Call off your mutt."

Bark! Bark! Bark! Bark!

"Bentley baby, come to Mommy."

Bark! Bark! Bark! Bark!

"I know he's a horrible man." Bentley trotted back to me and stood firm.

"Not only are you insane, but so is your dog."

Bark! Bark! Bark! Bark!

"I told you not to call me insane." Bentley ran over, lifted his leg and peed on Rhys' shoe, then trotted back to me.

"What the…these are custom John Lobb and…"

I laughed.

Bark! Bark! Bark! Bark!

"This isn't funny. Do you know how much these shoes cost?"

"I told you not to call me insane. Bentley and I are very sensitive to that word." He walked over to the elevator and pressed the button. "Send me the bill for the clean up."

"I definitely will." Ding.

Bark! Bark! Bark! Bark!

"Shut up." He stepped onto the elevator and left.

I got down to Bentley's level and rubbed his neck. "Mommy loves you. Thank you for getting rid of that mean man." He licked my cheek and I laughed. "Thank you for the kiss." I stood up, reached into the glass jar, pulled out a treat and handed it to him. I looked at my watch. "After your move, I don't think I should take you with me this afternoon. How do you feel about a spa day?"

Bark! Bark! Bark! Bark!

"Okay. I'll get dressed and drop you at the spa before I head over for round two with Rhys. I hope whatever your Uncle Tiberius has planned will put an end to this nightmare."

Bark! Bark! Bark! Bark!

❦❦❦❦❦❦❦❦❦

"Ty, whatever this is you have planned better be good."

"Trust me, it's better than good." He smiled.

I was too nervous to sit down. I paced back and forth waiting on Rhys and his attorney. I should have known he'd be late. It was just another one of his little games. I wish I knew what Ty had planned. I wish I could have seen what was in that envelope.

I sat down, but got right back up.

"Would you relax?" Ty said.

"How can I? It feels like my life has been on hold for the past six months waiting on this snake to…"

"Fi, in the scheme of things, this is a quick divorce."

"Quick?"

"I've seen divorces drag out for years."

"God, please don't let that happen to me. I can't do that."

"Fi, sit down." He pulled the chair out and I sat down. "Want some water?"

"Yes, please."

He handed me a bottle of water. I opened it and took a few sips.

"Better?" He asked as he sat down.

"Not really." I looked around the conference room. "You'd think at the rate Collin is billing Rhys, there would at least be some nuts on the table."

"Let them have the nuts, we want the cheddar." Ty winked.

"Cheddar? Listen to you trying to sound tough." I smiled and sipped some more water. "It had better be a lot of cheddar. Otherwise, I'm letting Bentley deal with him." We laughed.

The door opened and it seemed like all the air and life exited. I looked up and saw Rhys and his attorney, Collin Lawson. Leave it to my soon-to-be ex-husband to get a television attorney. That's not fair. Collin wishes he was as good as one of those Law & Order attorneys.

I looked at both of them and they looked like matching bookends. Both in dark gray suits and light blue shirts. I didn't know it was bring your twin to divorce deliberation day. I leaned over and whispered to Ty," Were we supposed to be dressed alike?"

He looked down at his papers, stifling a smile. "Shhh…"

"Really." I looked down at my black and white Oscar de la Renta dress. "I mean, I could have worn a navy suit or dress to match you."

Ty nudged me. "Behave."

Collin and Rhys, sat down across from us. Collin placed his file and notebook on the table and leaned back in his chair. "What do you want?" Collin asked smugly.

Ty opened his folder and pulled out a stack of paper sand turned it over. "Mrs. Walters is prepared to tear up the amended agreement and sign the original one."

"No. I'm not." I tugged on his jacket sleeve. "Are you insane?" Ty brushed my hand away. "What are you doing?"

"Excuse me a moment." He pulled me up out of the chair and walked me over to the corner.

"Are you out of your mind?" I said through clenched teeth. "That original agreement stinks. You said so yourself."

"Do you trust me?"

"Yes, but…"

"Then, let me do my job."

I sighed. "Ty, if you screw this up, Bentley will be eating a meaty treat tonight and it won't be a steak."

"Trust me."

"Does this have anything to do with that envelope?"

"Come on, let's get this over with." He winked.

Ty escorted me back to my chair and I sat down. "Thank you."

"As I was saying. Mrs. Walters is prepared to sign the original agreement."

"I don't understand," Collin said. "I thought…you know what, I'm not going to question it." He reached into the folder and pulled out the original settlement papers and handed them to Rhys.

"What's going on?" Rhys asked.

"Don't question it," Collin said. "Just sign and I'll have your office send the check over after the meeting."

Rhys signed all the copies and handed them back to Collin. He reviewed them and handed them to Ty. Ty placed them on the table and when I reached for them, he pulled them back. "One moment, Fi."

"What's going on?" Collin asked.

"Funny thing." Ty took a small stack of papers out of his briefcase and turned them face down. "My client insists that she was the one that came up with the concepts for CHIC and DOWNTOWN."

"We agreed that she came up with the concept. So what's the problem?" Collin asked.

"She also said, she hired the staff."

"Again, this is nothing new. The financial settlement compensates her for that." Collin sounded irritated.

"Interesting thing. I came across a document that says her involvement was a little more detailed."

"What are you talking about?" Rhys asked.

Ty pushed the document across the table to Collin. He skimmed it and looked at Ty. "What do you want?"

"What are you doing? She agreed to the settlement," Rhys said.

"That was before this." Collin handed Rhys the document.

Rhys started reading and his eyes got wide. "What the sh—-where did you get this?" Rhys asked.

"Seems someone didn't think CHIC and DOWNTOWN were going to succeed. So to avoid a loss, those two magazines were put into a separate corporation with Mrs. Walters as the sole owner," Ty announced.

"WHAT THE CRAP!" I jumped up and covered my mouth with my hands.

"Fi, please sit down."

I fanned myself with my hands. This was the best gift Rhys had ever given me. "I'm sorry."

"I'll allow my client to sign the original agreement, because the things she wanted already belong to her." Ty handed me the documents.

"My client and I need a moment," Collin said.

I looked at Ty and he was stone-faced. I had never seen Ty in action. The way he took charge and defended me was very sexy. Oh, where did that come from?

"Take your time. Your client is paying for my time."

"What?!" Rhys said.

"That was part of the original agreement. You offered to pay all of Mrs. Walters' legal fees."

"Ty you're as nuts as your client," Rhys shouted.

"Settle down Rhys," Collin said. They got up and walked over to the corner for a mini conference.

I wish I could hear what they were saying. But from the look of Rhys' body language, he wasn't happy with Collin's advice. After conferring, they returned to the table.

Ty looked at his watch. "In a hurry, Ty?" Collin asked.

"My client and I have all the time in the world."

"Here's the thing, we're going to fight," Collin announced.

Ty nodded. "I thought you were going to say that." He reached inside his folder and pulled out another piece of paper.

"Next, this guy is going to pull a rabbit out of his folder," Rhys joked.

"I got your rabbit," I lunged toward him.

"Ty, you better get your girl," Rhys said sarcastically.

"Fi, please sit down," Ty said.

I sat back down, sighed and shook out my neck. "Finish this."

Ty patted my hand. "I believe one of the reasons for the divorce is fraud."

"Fraud," Rhys shouted. "Now you're just grasping at straws," he smiled.

"My client said you didn't want to start a family until your company was on solid footing."

"That's correct," Rhys replied. "Good thing we didn't have kids, because that would have tied me to her for life."

"Rhys, please don't answer anything without asking me," Collin said.

"Then I need you to explain this." Ty handed Collin a slip of paper and then he handed it to Rhys.

"What the—" Rhys started to speak.

Collin shook his head. "What do you want?"

I pulled on Ty's jacket. "What?"

He brushed my hand away. "We're taking CHIC and DOWNTOWN, thirty-five percent of all the profits of the other titles as well as any future titles the company produces. By all profits, that means any media outlets applied to the titles. She's keeping the loft and she will allow him to buy out her half of the Hampton's property. She retains all of her benefits and retirement. If the company is sold, she will be paid forty-five percent of the total sale." He handed Collin another slip of paper. "Here is a list of the assets we're taking."

"Is that all?" Collin asked.

"We'll split all the cash and that includes the Caymans account and half of the stocks. As a good faith gesture, we'll need a payment of five million dollars by the end of the day."

"Is that all?" Collin asked.

"Is that all?" Rhys asked sarcastically. "That's more than she deserves."

Ty looked at me. "Is that all?" I nodded. "Yes. Seems my client is happy."

I don't know what just happened, but apparently, I got everything I wanted.

"I'll send the check over before the end of business today," Collin said.

"Thank you." Ty handed me a pen and a different stack of papers. "I took the liberty of drawing up an amended agreement to reflect what we just discussed."

"How efficient of you," Rhys said smugly."

"Sign the papers, Fi." After I signed the papers, he handed them to Collin for Rhys to sign.

"I guess you got everything you wanted," Rhys said as he signed the papers.

"And then some," I answered him.

"I wasn't talking to you. I was talking to Ty."

"All I did was my job," Ty replied.

"Keep telling yourself that." Rhys handed the papers to his attorney, stood up and buttoned his jacket. "Collin, I'll have my accountant send the check over." He looked at me. "Fiona."

"Rhys."

He walked out.

Collin stood up and looked at Ty. "I have to say that was very well played counselor. If you ever get tired of the minor leagues, I'm sure we could find a place for you here." He extended his hand to Ty and they shook.

"Thank you for the offer, but I like being my own boss."

"How did you know about Teresa?"

"It was a blessing that fell out of the sky," Ty smiled.

I stood up. "Collin."

"Fiona."

Ty put his hand on the small of my back and guided me out of the conference room. The heat from his palm sent a surge that traveled the length of my body.

We walked to the elevator and stepped inside.

"What just happened?" I asked.

"You won."

"What was on that piece of paper and who is Teresa?"

"Teresa is Rhys' daughter."

"His what?!"

Chapter 6
Ty

"I'm sorry, did you say Rhys' daughter?" Fiona asked.

I spent most of the night trying to figure out how I was going to answer this question. I knew as soon as Fiona heard about Rhys' secret she was going to want details. The truth is, I didn't have any, only what I saw in that envelope.

Before that envelope arrived, I wasn't sure how to get Fiona everything she wanted.

"Fi, please be quiet."

"What?"

I placed my hand on the small of Fi's back and guided her out of the building. She seemed to be in a trance, just going through the motions as we walked. We continued out onto the sidewalk walking towards the parade of black Mercedes sedans parked at the curb, but the black Maserati stood out. I looked straight ahead and spotted my driver.

"There's the car." I tipped my head at the tall, young man in a black suit, light gray shirt and black tie. We continued over and stopped at the car. The driver opened the rear passenger door.

"Good afternoon, Mr. Wells."

"Good afternoon, Aidan. I see you're helping your dad out today."

"Yes, sir. Good afternoon, Miss…"

"This is Mrs. Wal…I mean, Miss Harris," I answered.

"Hello," Fi said.

"Hello, ma'am." He smiled.

"Thank you." She replied as she climbed into the back of the car, rested her head against the headrest and closed her eyes.

I walked around to the other side and got in. "Fi…Fi… Fi, I know you're not asleep," I said. "Put your seat belt on."

She opened her eyes and stared at the ceiling of the car as she buckled her seatbelt.

"I can't believe what just happened. "Why didn't you tell me?" She lowered her head and looked at me with those doe-shaped eyes sending a jolt to my core. I was her captive.

"I needed you to be genuinely surprised."

She shook her head. "That's an understatement." She sighed. "I may not like it, but I think you did the right thing by not telling me."

"I'm glad to hear that."

"I think if I had known any of this before hand, I probably would have snuck into Ryhs' loft and killed him."

I laughed. "I think you're being a little dramatic." I took my phone out and began typing a text.

She turned toward me slightly. "I'm serious. I'm pretty sure I would have done him physical harm. A daughter? Would you stop looking at your phone and talk to me?"

I continued typing. "Fi, can this wait until we get to your place?"

"Fine." She sighed, sat back and folded her arms across her chest.

About twenty minutes later, the car stopped. "We're here, Mr. Wells," Aidan announced.

I lifted my head up and looked out the window. "Aidan, would you please get Miss Harris' dog. He's a black pit bull named Bentley. I told them you'd be picking him up. Thank you."

"Yes, sir."

Aidan climbed out of the car and closed the door.

I looked at Fi and she gave me a sharp look. It felt like I'd just been stabbed with an ice pick. "I need you to not talk about what happened until we're alone. You and I have attorney client privilege. I know Aidan won't say anything about our conversation, but we need to keep what happened between us."

"But—"

"Fiona," I grabbed her hand. "I know you have questions and I'll do my best to answer them. But, I would prefer we had our conversation without an audience. Understand?"

She looked up, met my gaze and nodded. "Okay."

"Good." I patted her hand.

The door opened and she turned around. Bark!... Bark!...Bark!...Bark!

"Bentley." She rubbed his neck. "How was your spa day?"

BARK! BARK! BARK! BARK!

"Mommy missed you, too." She pulled the large black dog into the car and set him between us.

BARK! BARK! BARK! BARK!

I rubbed his neck and patted his head. "Hey, Bentley."

BARK! BARK! BARK! BARK! He licked my hand and rested his head on my thigh.

"Should I be jealous of you and Bentley?" Fiona teased.

"What can I say? Bentley is a good judge of character."

The front door opened and Aidan climbed in behind the wheel, closed the door and locked his seat belt. "Where to, Mr. Wells?"

I looked at my watch. "Miss Harris' apartment. Do you have the address?"

"Yes. My dad gave it to me."

"Perfect. Thank you."

Chapter 7
Fiona

We exited the elevator and I let Bentley off his leash. "Go play while Mommy talks to Uncle Ty."

I unbuttoned my jacket and started to slip it off and was startled by a second set of hands. That same heat I felt when Ty placed his hand on the small of my back as he guided me out of the building was there again.

"Here you go," Ty said as he folded my jacket and handed it to me.

"Thank you." I took my jacket and placed it on the back of the sofa.

My mind was full of questions. Some about the meeting, the others about those new feelings I was having towards Ty. Neither set of feelings made any sense.

He took his jacket off and laid it on the back of the sofa next to mine. "Okay, let me have it." He brushed his tie and smiled.

Have it? I folded my arms in front of me and leaned against the kitchen counter. "What happened? I mean apart from me getting everything I wanted and then some."

He pulled out a stool and sat down with his hands clasped in between his legs. For some reason my eyes went straight to his belt and then traveled further down. What was happening to me? I walked around the counter so I couldn't see below his waist. How was it possible that I was being turned on by my friend?

Ty turned around and rested his hands on the counter. Those large, slightly rough, strong hands I imagined traveling the length of my body searching for...

"The envelope that was delivered to you was supposed to go to Rhys. It really was an accident that it was delivered to you. I think what happened is no one bothered to tell the mailroom that Rhys had moved."

I rubbed the back of my neck and folded my arms in front of my chest. "You're right. It was a blessing that fell out of the sky."

"When I skimmed the documents, I knew things had shifted in our, I mean your favor. It wasn't until I read them when I got back to my office did I know how much they had shifted."

"What was..."

"Rhys never intended for CHIC and DOWNTOWN to be part of his...let me rephrase it. He was just pacifying you. CHIC and DOWNTOWN were supposed to be pet projects to keep you occupied....tax write offs. He never thought you would actually succeed. So to protect himself, he set up a separate company under your name."

"But I have staff for both magazines."

"You lease your staff from Rhys."

"What?"

"Technically, the only employee at both magazines is you." He shifted on the stool. "See, he made you appear to be a small business that was leasing staff, space, office and production needs from his company. Technically, he was double dipping. Not only was he earning money off those leases, he retained all the sales and doled out a salary to you."

"That son of a—"

"Calm down, Fi."

I rested my hands on the counter and stared at Ty. "So, what's next?"

Ty's phone dinged and he looked at the screen, picked it up and started typing. "Sorry about that. What did you ask me?"

"What's next?"

"You tell me. You can keep the magazines or sell them to Fairgate. I will caution you, if you choose to sell, I'm pretty sure they will insist on a non-compete."

"Meaning?"

"They could demand you not start another magazine similar to CHIC or DOWNTOWN. They could require you to stay out of any form of media for an unspecified number of years."

"What?"

"I've seen agreements that even said no blogs, books or podcasts. Fi, this is big business and it can get vicious."

I covered my eyes with my hands. "Ahhhhh…."

"Fi…Fi…"

I heard footsteps and then I felt his hot hands on my

shoulders as he turned me toward his chest. And then the tears came. During this entire process with Rhys, I had yet to cry, but here I was crying.

"Shhh…shhh…shhh…" Ty gently rubbed my back. "Let it all out. I know this has been a lot to absorb." He pulled me closer and suddenly the tears stopped and my mind went back to that place where those new feelings for Ty were.

I lifted my head and looked up. Staring back at me wasn't my attorney or friend, but a hot man. A man with a strong squared jaw, eyes like sparkling chocolate diamonds and teeth so bright they could guide ships in the night. A man whose body melded perfectly with mine and whose touch not only comforted me, but aroused me as well.

I couldn't take my eyes off his mouth, because it was so damn sexy. I wanted those beautiful, strong, full sexy lips to travel the length of my body. I bet he knew exactly how to use his mouth. A chill ran through me. I couldn't blink. Otherwise, I would remove myself from the fantasy my mind was having. I sucked on my bottom lip and felt his body react to the simple gesture. Could it be he and I were feeling the same thing? I splayed my hands on his chest and it felt like I was touching hot, carved stone. I swallowed hard and my mind went some place it had never gone before with Ty…and I liked where it was. I know I shouldn't be having salacious thoughts about him, but his obvious erection pressed against me wasn't really helping deter them right now.

I really wanted him to kiss me. I bet he was a good kisser. He had to be with lips like that. It would be a shame to be blessed with a mouth like that and not know how to use it. I can't believe I thought that, but I did. I wondered how his mouth would feel sucking that gap between my breasts or along the inside of my thigh.

My knees buckled slightly at that thought. Man, it had been a while since I'd been kissed. I mean a real, make your knees buckle and the hairs on the back of your neck stand up kiss. The kind of kiss that makes your heart race and your body betray you. A kiss you feel deep down in your core. A kiss so intense it pushes you to the edge of reason and says, "I know we shouldn't, but I need you like I have never needed a man before."

We locked eyes and he lifted my chin. The heat of his body surrounded me as he slowly lowered his mouth closer to mine. My heart started racing and my body was doing things I had never felt before. At that moment, I wanted Ty to take me over to the sofa and let me work out all the anger and frustration I had been feeling the past few months.

His hands slid further down my back. I wrapped my hands around his neck and pulled him closer to me. His hands slid further down caressing my behind. There was a sudden strangeness surrounding me. I couldn't quite describe it, but it made me feel…daring. It seemed as if all the air had disappeared. I started breathing harder.

Ty opened his mouth slightly and lowered it closer to mine. I was eager to meet his mouth if only to get air. His large hot hands pulled me closer to him as his mouth got closer. I imagined what his tongue would taste like inside my mouth. The thought of his large, warm tongue dancing with mine, pushed me over the edge. I pressed his head down, eager to…

BARK! BARK! BARK! BARK!

We quickly pulled apart like two teenagers caught making out. I patted my chest.

BARK! BARK! BARK! BARK!

"Bentley walked over to the counter where his treat jar was, sat down and looked up.

BARK! BARK! BARK! BARK!

"Okay…okay…Mommy will get you a treat." I reached inside the treat jar and handed Bentley a treat.

I looked at Ty. "Do you want something to eat? What am I saying? I promised you dinner and champagne, if you got my magazines." I smiled. "So where do you want to go? Let's do it up right. I'm sure I can get us a table at…"

He covered my hand with his. "I can't tonight."

"Got a hot date?" I teased.

"I wouldn't say that." He walked back around the counter.

"I didn't know you were seeing anyone." Now I was embarrassed. But he almost kissed me. "I didn't…why didn't you tell me?"

"It just never came up."

"Who is she?"

"Her name is Julia." He smiled.

I nodded. "Very proper society name." I teased. "How did you meet?"

"A friend introduced us."

"What does she look like?"

"Why?"

"In all the years I've known you, I've never seen any of your…I mean you're a great guy, and you deserve to be with someone who appreciates you."

"Thank you."

"So, what's she like?"

"You aren't going to let this go, are you?" He smiled and folded his arms across his chest.

"No."

"If you must know. She's pretty, smart and funny."

"And…" I smiled.

"She's a lobbyist and lives in D.C."

"D.C.? So when do you see each other? How long have you been together? I'm sorry. I'm all up in your business."

"Yes, you are," he teased. "We see each other every other weekend. She comes here or I go there."

"So this weekend…that's why you passed on dinner tonight. I'm sorry."

"Don't be. I need to get as much work done tonight as I can, because she'll be here tomorrow."

"Wow…I never would have pegged you as the distance type."

"What does that mean?"

"You just strike me as the type of guy who is very committed. Please don't take this the wrong way, but you come off very settled."

"I don't follow."

"When I see you, I see the guy who is there at a moment's notice. Like yesterday with the envelope. You are very much the protector. The boyfriend who rushes over to his girlfriend's place with a hammer, trap, and peanut butter when she calls in the middle of the night because she saw a mouse."

He laughed. "I am, but I wouldn't bring a hammer. I'm not that sadistic." He smiled.

"But your girlfriend lives in another state."

"It's D.C., not California."

"I know, but I never would have guessed you were that guy. Is it serious?" I smiled.

"What's with all the questions?"

"Just curious." And now very jealous. There's a chick in D.C. who gets to kiss those sexy lips. Who gets to have those large, strong hands wrapped around her. Who gets to rest her head on that hard chest. Who gets Ty as her earthly protector. What the crap! I've fallen for Ty.

Chapter 8
Ty

I knew she was here, because her spicy, scintillating parfum filled every inch of my apartment and my mind. I dropped my keys on the credenza, took my jacket off and placed it on the back of the black velvet sofa. The space was filled with the seductive sounds of our favorite lovemaking songs. Seems she'd taken a page out of my playbook tonight.

I loosened my tie as my eyes adjusted to the darkness. Then I heard the sound of stilettos connecting with the mahogany wood floor, tapping out a slow tribal beat that stirred something primal inside me.

I walked towards the approaching footsteps looking straight ahead. Coming out of the darkness into the candlelit hall like something out of a dream, was the director for the evening.

The way the wind caught the hem of her robe as she walked, revealing her smooth mocha legs, was hypnotic. Her strides were like those of a beautiful, long legged, brown mare prancing before a crowd.

She continued towards me with all the sass and sexiness of a woman on a mission. The closer she got to me, the more excited I grew. I had been picturing this moment for quite a while. But my fantasy in no way compared to what I was experiencing.

The silk of her robe was losing its battle to conceal her nakedness. My eyes traveled up her body and my eyes went to the amethyst pendant sitting in between her full breasts. The light blue stone on a simple platinum chain paled in comparison to her beautiful breasts.

She stopped a few inches in front of me and I felt like a nervous virgin, eager to experience a woman's touch for the first time. She stepped closer and there was barely room for air to pass between us. She looked at me, tilted her head to the side, and sucked on the corner of her bottom lip.

"Seems I'm a little over dressed."

"That you are," she confirmed.

I started to undress and she never took her eyes away from me. When I removed my last piece of clothing she stepped closer and I knew if either of us inhaled, our bodies would touch and the moment would be ruined.

She circled around me inspecting me. When she reached my back, I felt her delicate hand graze my ass and my body hardened. I felt like a young buck being readied to service the mistress of the manor.

She pressed her hot full lips against my back and my

breath caught. This foreplay was torture. She continued back around and stopped in front of me. She looked up with those doe-shaped brown eyes, and I was under her spell.

She untied her robe, never removing her gaze from me. I was hoping she would invite me to slip her robe off, but she didn't. She was in charge and my job was to be patient and follow her lead.

She slipped out of her robe, stepped to the side and started to walk past me and our fingers barely touched. Not looking up, she said two words, "Join me." She started walking down the hall and I willingly followed her like Adam did when he followed Eve into temptation. I knew it was wrong, but I was willing to suffer the consequences of my decision.

She continued down the candlelit hall with the soulful, seductive music dragging me deeper into her lair.

The way the light highlighted her beautiful mocha body was very tantalizing. I wasn't sure what she had planned, but my body sensed it was something I wanted to experience.

We stopped in front of a large set of double doors that magically opened to reveal a scene set for love. Candles on every surface and a fur throw at the foot of the bed.

I followed her inside and she leaned against one of the bed posts. She looked up and asked a simple question, "What do you want?"

What I wanted was to make love to her until time stopped or my body became numb from our intense lovemaking.

I stepped closer, never losing eye contact with those gorgeous dark brown eyes. She dragged her delicate finger down the front of my chest stopping right below my navel. I inhaled deeply anticipating where her finger might go next.

Then I remembered, I hadn't answered her question. I growled and spit out an answer. "I want what you want."

Her finger slipped further. "How do you know what I want?" she purred.

I knew what she needed. She needed to know what all consuming lovemaking felt like. She needed to be left breathless. She needed an orgasm so hard it would leave her body sated and drained. She needed to be touched and tasted from head to toe. She needed to be loved by a man who loved her.

"I know you."

"So you say." She rolled away from the bed post and walked to the side of the bed with her back to me.

I stepped to her, lowered my mouth to her ear. "Let me love you the way you should be loved."

She fell back against my chest and I scooped her up into my arms and placed her in the center of the bed. She was beautiful. I was torn. My mind said to take it slow, but my body said, take her hard and fast.

I climbed into bed next to her and dragged my finger along the center of her body and watched as she writhed and danced. I found my answer in her deep moans. Taking it slow was what she wanted.

She pulled me on top of her and whispered, "I want every beautiful inch of you now."

"Your wish is my command, but first…"

I dragged my index finger along the inside of her hot thick thigh and she began to moan. I kept my eyes locked with hers as my finger inched further up her thigh and she started to breathe harder. I nuzzled her neck and eased my finger inside her warmth, and she let out a sexy moan.

I took my time teasing her and watched as her body began to react to my touch. Her skin became hot and pebbled. I added another finger and she clutched the sheets as she arched against my hand. She looked beautiful slowly coming apart for me. I lathed my tongue across her hard nipple and she began to tighten around my finger.

"Uhmm…I…I…" She was close.

I moved my mouth between both her breasts and she grew more excited. I stopped moving my fingers and let them rest in her warmth. The way her body was moving was the most erotic thing I'd ever seen. I know she didn't know how sexy and beautiful she looked on the threshold of crashing.

I dipped my tongue in her navel and she cried out. I kissed my way back up to her breasts as my fingers started to taunt her again. "Please." She covered my hand.

"Please what?"

"Please…don't…stop."

I knew she was right on the verge of crashing. I slowly removed my fingers and watched as her heavy breathing made her breasts rise and fall. Her panting was an invitation I wanted to accept.

I nestled my hips in between her thighs, pinned her hands against the bed and slowly slid inside her warmth. God, she felt good. The way our bodies got in sync was incredible. I didn't want to hurt her, so I was prepared to go slow and easy until she adjusted to me, but she became aggressive and demanding.

"Harder," she cried out.

I looked at her and was surprised by her request. I braced myself and fulfilled her request. Her body started to tremble and shake the harder I pushed, and then I felt her tighten around me and she cried out.

I let go of her hands and she grabbed my ass pushed me deeper. I crushed my mouth against hers and drove my tongue deep inside her mouth with the rhythm my body was sharing with her. Then I felt her tighten again. I couldn't believe she was on the verge of another orgasm. That excited me. I bore down on the bed and buried myself deeper inside her.

"More baby…I—I—I want…I want…I want it all."

I felt my orgasm rising. I couldn't break, not yet. "You feel so good."

I looked down at her gorgeous full breasts bouncing. God, she's beautiful. She started breathing harder and bucking. Her cries quickly turned into a sweet and sexy wail.

I lifted her hips and buried myself deep and hard into her heat. She was tightening around me and I knew she was close to another…

"Oh, my God…" she cried out.

She grabbed my ass and pushed me deeper inside her heat. I desperately wanted to come with her. I grabbed her nipple between my teeth sucking and pulling and felt my orgasm building. "God, you feel good."

"Baby…I…I…uhmmm…"

"Not yet, hold on."

I felt the pressure building and knew I was close. Oh, God…she dug her fingers into my ass, bit my shoulder and my body gave in to the crazy animalistic beat. I buried myself deep and hard inside her heat pushing us both to the edge of…

"YES," she cried out as the wave of orgasm took over her body.

"OH, GOD…OH, GOD… OH, GOD…" I came hard and collapsed on top of her.

I lay there until my body stopped shaking and then I rolled over onto the other side of the bed. I pulled her delicate body to my side rubbing her back until we fell asleep.

I lay still with my eyes closed replaying the best sexual experience I'd ever had. I didn't want to wake her, but I selfishly wanted to experience her again.

My phone rang and I ignored it. I closed my eyes and tried to go back to sleep, but the phone rang again. I cursed to myself and picked up the phone without looking at the screen. "Hello."

"Hey, I won't be there until tomorrow," the familiar female voice said.

I opened my eyes, looked at the ceiling and then at the other side of the bed. I sat up, rubbed my head and tried to jump start my brain. "Who's this?"

"Julia."

"Julia...uhm...what time is it?"

"It's nine o'clock."

"What?" I jumped up out of bed. "Oh man, I'm sorry, I was suppose..."

"Where you asleep?"

"I had a late night. I'm sorry about the car. You can take a cab or..."

"I said I won't be there until tomorrow."

I sighed. "What...why?"

"Work. You know I'm..."

"Fine. Call me and I'll have a car pick you up."

"What's wrong with you?" she asked.

"Nothing. What time will you be here?"

"I'll probably be on the three o'clock."

"Probably?" I sighed. "How long will you be here?" There was silence. "Julia, answer me."

"I have to leave the following day."

"Then why come?"

"Because it's my turn."

"Your turn." I nodded. "You know what Julia, why don't you skip your turn."

"If you're going to be like that, maybe I will."

"Now you're trying to make it seem like I don't want you here."

"That's not what I said."

"No. That's what you implied. I'm your man, not some obligation."

"I don't need this kind of stress right now."

"Neither do I."

"Maybe we should just skip this visit."

"What makes this any different from the last three?"

Click…

"Julia…Julia…" I looked at my screen and all I saw was her name. I tossed the phone onto the bed and went into the bathroom. I leaned on the counter and looked at my reflection in the mirror. It was a dream. A hot dream, but still just a dream. A dream about a woman I can't have, or can I?

Chapter 9
Fiona

Bentley and I have been avoiding people for the past ninety-six hours. We've been binging on Netflix and every take out place in the neighborhood. To the outside world, it looked like I was hiding, but I wasn't. I was processing.

I needed to wrap my head around all the information I received on Thursday. I was officially divorced. I was a divorcee. I looked at myself and I wasn't what I knew divorcees looked like. I didn't look like my Aunt Mildred. When my uncle left her, she reverted into her shell and stopped living. I always felt bad for her. It seemed like my Uncle Sydney had taken her spirit.

Nor was I like my Aunt Stella. When my Uncle Charles left her, she went wild. She packed up all of her things, which was only what fit in two vintage brown Samsonite suitcases, and bought a bus ticket for California. She said, "It's time for me to live." She reinvented herself. It was almost five years before we saw her again, and when we did we barely recognized her. She had cut her hair, changed her wardrobe and showed up with her new husband. A fine, rich, white man. Baby girl had gone "citified" as my nana said, but she was happy and never looked better. I thought she was awesome.

That's the kind of divorcee I decided to become. The kind that kicked divorce's butt, and never looked back.

I got dressed, put Bentley's leash on his collar and decided it was time for a walk. We boarded the elevator and when we reached the lobby, I have to admit taking that first step out was difficult, but I knew I could do it. The past few days, Solomon and Bruce had been very good about taking Bentley out for his potty breaks. But it was time for me to get on with my life.

Bark! Bark! Bark! Bark!

"I know. Give Mommy a second." Ding…Ding… Ding…

Bark! Bark! Bark! Bark!

"Is there a problem, Miss Harris?" Solomon walked over and blocked the elevator door from closing.

Bark! Bark! Bark! Bark!

Bentley started running. "Bentley…"

"I'll get him for you." Solomon took off after Bentley.

I stepped out of the security box and exhaled. I closed my eyes, wrung my neck and exhaled again. Remember Aunt Stella. I stood up straight, put on my sunglasses and walked over to Solomon and Bentley.

"I'll take him, Solomon." I reached for his leash.

"Are you sure? I don't mind taking him out."

I smiled. "Thank you, Solomon. You and the guys have been very helpful. I think it's time for me to get some fresh air."

He smiled. "How about I get you a taxi?"

Bark! Bark! Bark! Bark!

I looked at Bentley. "Thank you, but I think we're going to walk."

He knelt down and rubbed Bentley's neck. "You take good care of your Mommy, okay?"

Bark! Bark! Bark! Bark!

"I know you will." Solomon stood up. "Miss Harris, if you need anything, let us know."

I hugged him. "Thank you, Solomon." I smiled.

"You're welcome." He smiled.

I pulled back and looked at the door. Suddenly a rush of fear came over me, but I shook it off.

"How's the weather today?"

"It's a beautiful day for a walk. Come on. Let me get the door for you." Solomon took my hand and walked me to the door out onto the sidewalk.

I took a deep breath and hesitated. I can do this. I looked at Solomon and he tipped his head and let go of my hand. I looked at Bentley and it looked like he was smiling.

"It's a beautiful day. Let's go." We started walking.

There's nothing like inhaling the smells of New York a mix of exhaust, bodies, food and garbage.

Bentley and I leisurely walked and an hour later I looked up and realized I was near Ty's office.

Bark! Bark! Bark! Bark!

"I agree. I think it would be nice if we paid your Uncle Ty a visit."

I walked into the glass building, boarded the elevator and pressed the button for Ty's office. Bentley and I were fortunate to have the elevator to ourselves. It gave him a chance to lie down as we rode up the twenty plus floors.

When the elevator stopped, Bentley jumped up and stood in front of the door like a body guard. The doors opened and he stepped out, looked around and then back at me. He was really taking his role as my protector seriously.

We walked down the hall to the receptionist desk and stopped.

"Hello, Jake."

"Hi, Miss Harris."

"Is Mr. Wells in?"

"Let me check with Tasha." He pressed a button and I turned my attention to Bentley. "Hi Tasha, Miss Harris is here to see Mr. Wells…okay…okay. Miss Harris…"

I looked up. "Yes…"

"Go in."

"Thank you."

Bentley and I walked down the hall to Ty's office and were greeted half way by Tasha, Ty's assistant.

"Hi Fi." We hugged each other.

"Hi, Tasha."

Bark! Bark! Bark! Bark!

"Hi, Bentley. Come on back. He's finishing up a call."

"I can come back. We were in the neighbor and…"

"Don't be silly." She lowered her voice. "Between us, I need the distraction. He's been snapping at me all morning."

"Really? Is it a case?"

"I think it's personal."

I nodded. "Okay."

"I'll let you deal with him."

"Chicken." I smiled.

"Exactly." She smiled and walked back to her desk.

I walked over to Ty's door, stopped and knocked.

"I said I didn't want to be disturbed unless it was important or…" I pushed the door open and Bentley pushed past me inside. "Bentley…what are you…where's your Mommy?"

I opened the door and walked inside. "You men. You always do things your way." I smiled.

"Fi." He smiled, stood up, walked over and wrapped his arms around me. "What are you doing here?"

We pulled apart, but not before those feelings I felt the other day rose up. Okay, so it wasn't my imagination. There was something there between us, or at least there was for me.

"Bentley and I were out for a walk and…"

"You walked over here?"

"Yes."

"Let's sit down." He placed his hand on the small of my back, ushered us over to the gray suede sofa and we sat down.

"To answer your question, yes, we walked."

"Do you know how far that is?" He looked at my feet. "You walked in those shoes?"

I lifted my foot slightly and looked at my Manolo pumps. "These and a lot of adrenaline."

"Or was it something else?"

"It was probably something else," I laughed. "So what's going on with you? How was your weekend with the lovely Julia?"

He inhaled and then he sighed. "It wasn't."

"What happened?" I kicked his foot.

"She got hung up at work. Then she called back and said she wouldn't be here until Saturday afternoon. So I told her not to come."

"Why would you do that?"

"She pissed me off."

"Ty…"

"This was the third time she cancelled on me."

"You're kidding?"

"Nope. And when I called her out on it, she hung up on me."

"What?"

"Yep. I called her back and she…you don't want to hear this."

He was right, I didn't want to hear about the demise of his relationship, but we're friends and that's what friends do. They listen to their friends lament about their relationships. "Maybe she was having phone problems." I smiled.

"Phone problems, really?" He smiled and shook his head.

Man his mouth is sexy. Those strong full lips are…I bet he kisses like a man with authority and passion. He probably knows how to bring a woman to her knees with his mouth. I felt a flutter in my stomach. "Uhm, give Julia a break."

Bark! Bark! Bark! Bark!

"That's right, Bentley. Your Uncle Ty has been acting like a jerk."

Bark! Bark! Bark! Bark!

"I agree."

"Agree about what?" Ty asked.

I stood up and extended my hand to him. "Get your jacket."

He looked up at me with those warm, sexy brown eyes. "Why?"

"You need some air and Tasha needs a break from you." I smiled.

"I have work to do. I can't just leave."

78

"I think if you don't leave, Tasha is going to stab you with a letter opener. Or worse. She'll staple your tie to your desk while you're wearing it," I teased.

He took my hand, stood up, and adjusted his shirt and tie. "Maybe some lunch would be good."

"Exactly."

❧❧❧❧❧❧❧❧

"I needed this." He sipped his water. "Thanks, Fi."

Bark! Bark! Bark! Bark!

"And you too, Bentley." He smiled.

"That's what friends do." I sipped my water. "So…"

"I think I know what you're going to ask me."

"You do?" I smiled, then put a forkful of chocolate cake into my mouth.

"You want to know what's going on with me and Julia?"

"That's not what I was going to say."

"No?"

"I was going to ask if you knew what you were going to say when you call her?"

"I hadn't planned to call her."

I sat back with my arms folded across my chest. "Really?"

"She hung up on me."

"And you didn't do anything?"

"No. On my last visit I spent more time alone than with her." He sipped his water.

"Uh-huh. And you think not talking is the best solution?" I sipped my iced tea.

"Point made and taken." He sipped more water.

"Enough about my horrible love life. What about you?"

"What about me? I know you can't be talking about a relationship."

"Of course not. How did you spend your first weekend as a free woman?"

"Actually, I've been a free woman since I put Rhys out." I smirked.

"I stand corrected." He smiled.

"Bentley and I spent the weekend at home. This is my first day out."

"Fi, you didn't spend the weekend sulking?" He stole a forkful of my cake. "Hey…"

"What?" He smiled. "So what did you do, sulk?"

Hearing someone else say the words, made me feel like an idiot, but I needed to be honest. "Yes, I did."

"Fi… you…"

"Please, don't chastise me. I know it wasn't healthy, but it was what I needed."

"Okay. So what's your next move?"

"I was thinking about moving."

"Why? You have a great loft."

"Complete with an ex-husband a few floors down."

"Don't let Rhys run you off."

"I wouldn't be moving because of Rhys. It would be so I could start over."

"I understand wanting a fresh start, but a great loft is hard to find."

"You've got a point. Maybe, I'll stay."

"What about the magazines…what did you decide to do?"

"If I sell, what would I do? Those are my babies. I don't think I can just walk away."

"What if I call Fairgate and hear what they have to say? You may not even like the offer.

"True." I finished my cake.

"And if you do, we can always negotiate an offer that works to your advantage."

"That's a thought."

"Don't rule selling out until you know everything."

"Okay. Do it." He squeezed my hand and the heat from his hand traveled the length of my body confirming my feelings. I had fallen for my friend. Or maybe it was Stockholm Syndrome. I looked at him. No, it was lust.

Chapter 10
Ty

My phone had been ringing with that number and annoying ringtone all day. I could have turned the ringer off, but then I might have missed an important call. Instead, I elected to ignore the caller. Talking to Julia wasn't a priority for me. I was tired of her childish behavior and games.

I exited the elevator and walked down the hall to my apartment. I put the key in the lock, opened the door, stepped inside and sighed. It had been a long day filled with tension from work and the thoughts of having to deal with a failing relationship, again. I knew what I needed to do, but I just hadn't done it.

My dad was right. He said I would grow tired of being

involved with a woman I only saw a couple of times a month. I'm not cut out for the distance thing. I like being needed by my girlfriend, making pop visits and having her in my arms and bed whenever I wanted.

What I don't like is being treated as an afterthought and that's how Julia has made me feel. I want to know that my girlfriend wants me around and longs to be with me. I want to see the excitement on her face when she sees me. Call me weak, but I like hearing her giddiness when I call her. Like when I'm with Fi. I shouldn't dread getting a phone call from my girlfriend.

Ring…Ring…Ring…

I pressed the decline call button and walked down the hall.

I laid my phone on the bed screen side up. Then I slipped off my tie and dropped it along with my jacket on the bed. Then my phone started ringing again. I sighed deeply and looked at the screen. Julia. I might as well get this over with. Otherwise, she'll just keep calling.

"Yes." I hoped the sharp tone in my voice was an indication as to how I felt.

"Hey, baby," she purred.

Normally her sexy voice would excite me, but tonight, it just infuriated me even more. She was trying to slink her way back in with a few simple sexy tones.

"What do you want?" I kicked off my shoes.

"I see you're still angry."

"Angry? Julia, we haven't seen each other in almost two months."

"I told you I had to work last weekend."

"It's not about you working, it's about you cancelling at the last minute the last three times."

"I'm sorry."

I shook my head, turned on the speaker and placed the phone on the bed and took off my shirt. "That's what you always say."

"How about I make it up to you. I can catch the next flight out and be at your place in a few hours. I'll do that thing you like and then…"

"No." I was immune to her seductions. Had she offered herself when she called to cancel, I might have considered her offer, but it was too little, too late.

"No?"

"No. Sex can't fix what's wrong with us."

"There's nothing wrong with us. Just because I had to cancel a few visits doesn't mean there's a problem."

"Doesn't it?" I took off my pants. "Who is he?"

"He who? I don't know what you're talking about."

"The dude you're with when you're not with me."

"You're the only man I'm seeing."

"Really?"

"What's that supposed to mean?"

"It means I know your sexual appetite and since we haven't seen each other in over a month, that means some other dude has been..."

"Don't be crass."

"Okay, then I'll be blunt. Who's the dude you're screwing when you're not screwing me?" The silence was thicker than a slab of concrete. "Well..."

"Darryl Green. He's an analyst for Cooper Brandt."

"Were you with him last weekend?" More dead silence. "ANSWER ME!" I started pacing and rubbing my head.

"Yes."

"We're done."

"Just like that?"

"Yes." I started to press the button and end the call.

"Ty..."

"WHAT?!"

"So we're done just like that?"

"Are you finished, because..."

"Fine!" Click.

I looked at the screen of the phone. "Oh well."

❧❧❧❧❧❧❧❧❧

"What happened with you and Julia?" Tasha asked as she walked into my office with the mail and a fresh pot of coffee.

"Why did you ask me that?"

"Because she called and asked me to talk some sense into you."

"Since when did you two get so close?"

"We aren't." She placed the coffee carafe and mail on my desk.

"Thank you." I filled my cup and took a sip. "That's good."

"Thanks. Well..."

"We broke up."

She looked up at the ceiling. "Thank you, Jesus."

I leaned back in my chair and looked at her. "Excuse me?"

"Did I say that out loud?" She sat down in one of the gray leather and brass chairs in front of my desk and crossed her legs. Tasha has beautiful legs and if she were my type, I'd consider mixing business with pleasure. But a good secretary is more difficult to find than the perfect girlfriend.

"Yes, you did." I sipped more coffee.

"I'm sorry. It's just...I never liked that chick. She acts like she's too good for you." She covered her mouth with her hands. "Loose tongue. Trust me Ty, you can do better. Look at you. You aren't my type, but you're very good looking, tall, great job, good sense of humor. You have a slight temper, but I equate that with passion."

"Thanks, I think."

"Trust me, it's a compliment." She poured herself a cup of coffee and took a sip. "So, first things first, you need a new girlfriend."

"I just broke up with Julia."

"I won't hold that bad relationship against you."

"Thanks."

"And you need a woman you can see anytime you want, not only a few days a month."

"Funny, Fiona said something similar." A slight smile rose on my face.

"Now, she would be good for you."

"No." I leaned forward and opened the mail folder and started reading.

"I know you're friends, but who better to..."

"No. Fiona and I are friends and that's all."

She opened her iPad. "You could be friends with benefits." She smirked. "So what do you want me to tell Julia?"

"There's nothing to tell her. I said all I needed to say last night."

"And Fiona?"

"She's my friend."

She smirked and sipped her coffee. "Uh-huh."

Chapter 11
Fiona

"Hey Fi, you busy tonight?" I was surprised to hear from Ty.

"I was thinking about going to the movies."

"Alone?"

"Yes. I need a break from Netflix and I think Bentley would like a little alone time." I laughed.

"Want some company?" Ty asked.

"Uhm, sure. I'll meet…"

"I'll pick you up in half an hour. Maybe we can grab a bite first?"

"Okay." I was hesitant to say yes, considering my new found feelings for Ty.

"I'll see you soon."

"Okay." I pressed the button ending the call and placed my phone on the counter. Then I looked at myself. The jeans and t-shirt didn't seem appropriate. I rushed down to my closet and stared at the sea of clothes looking for something to wear. Then I caught a glimpse of myself in the mirror. What are you doing? It's just Ty.

I took a deep breath and put on my leopard Manolo pumps, and my favorite black Chanel jacket. I put a little product in my hair, added a couple of gold chains and my diamond studs. I went to put my watch on, and my wedding and engagement rings grabbed my attention. I started to take them off, but I couldn't. It was like they were stuck. I twisted the rings and tried to pull them down my finger, but I couldn't.

It had been a month since my divorce and I still couldn't bring myself to let go of the last thing tying me to Rhys. Baby steps.

I put on a little blush, mascara, a red lip and sprayed a little Tom Ford Tobacco Vanilla parfum.

I walked back out to the living room and ran over to answer the phone. "Hello."

"Miss Fiona, Mr. Wells is here. Shall I send him up?" Bruce asked.

"Yes, please. Thank you." I hung up the phone, turned around and Bentley was standing in front of me.

Bark!Bark!Bark!Bark!

"Yes, your Uncle Ty is on his way up. How do I look?"

Bark!Bark!Bark!Bark!

"Thank you, sir." I went down the hall to get my bag and I heard the elevator ding.

Bark!Bark!Bark!Bark!

" Fi..." Ty called out.

"I'm coming." I took one more look in the mirror and exhaled. It's just dinner and a movie with a friend. A friend I happened to have a serious crush on. Get it together girl.

I picked up my bag and walked out to the living room. Bark!Bark!Bark!Bark!

"I'm coming." I walked down the hall into the living room. "Hey, Ty." I walked over, hugged him and it was there, that warm feeling I get in my stomach when I'm around him. Oh man, he smells good.

"Hey, Fi."

We pulled apart and I looked him up and down. I never noticed how hot he looked in casual clothes. "Okay, we should get going. I like to watch the previews."

"I thought we were eating first. I'm starving." He patted his stomach.

"No, the movie starts in an hour. I'll treat you to a hot dog and popcorn."

"That's not dinner."

Bark!Bark!Bark!Bark!

"See, even Bentley agrees with me."

"Would you two stop ganging up on me." I sighed. "Okay, we'll eat first and catch the eight o'clock screening."

Bark!Bark!Bark!Bark!

"Where do you want to eat?" I asked.

"How do you feel about Cuban food?"

"Never had it, but I'm open."

He clapped his hands and smiled. "You're in for a treat." He walked over and pressed the button for the elevator. "Let's go."

I walked over to Bentley, knelt down, lifted his face up and looked at him. "Behave yourself while I'm gone. No partying and no guests."

Bark!Bark!Bark!Bark!

"No. I left you dinner and I turned on your favorite channel."

Bark!Bark!Bark!Bark! He licked my hand.

"You're welcome." I stood up and looked at Ty and he was smiling. "What?"

"Nothing." Ding. We turned in the direction of the elevator. "Let's go." He placed his hand on the small of my back and escorted me to the elevator.

"Night, Bentley."

Bark!Bark!Bark!Bark!

※※※※※※※※

"You tricked me." I smiled.

"I tricked you…how?" He smiled.

"I thought we were going to eat and then go to the movies."

He pointed to himself. "I wasn't the one that kept ordering food."

"I'm pretty sure I didn't eat those croquettes by myself."

"I own up to the croquettes and the churros. But you were the one that jumped up and started dancing." He smiled.

I covered my face with my hands. "Ahhh…I did, didn't I?" I smiled.

"Yep."

"I gotta say, Cuban food is my new favorite. It wasn't what I was expecting. That lamb was incredible." I lowered my hands. "Want some coffee?"

"No, thanks. I should probably get going."

Bark!Bark!Bark!Bark!

"Bentley, I'm sorry. Let me get your leash." I walked over and took Bentley's leash down and locked it onto his collar. "Okay, let's go."

"Want some company?" Ty asked.

I looked up at him. His question caught me off guard.

Bark!Bark!Bark!Bark!

"Okay, seems like it's okay with Bentley."

Ty walked over and pressed the button for the elevator.

A few minutes later, the elevator door opened and we boarded. We looked like that couple on the fifth floor I occasionally see in the lobby with their golden lab. To me they always look like they should be on the cover of a magazine.

I tried not to look at Ty, but I couldn't stave off the thoughts in my head. This was just my friend being nice to me. He probably didn't have anything else to do, or he felt sorry for his newly divorced friend.

The elevator stopped, the door opened and we exited out into the lobby. A rush of feelings came over me. I took a deep breath and continued to the front door.

Bark!Bark!Bark!Bark!

"Okay, we're coming."

"I think Bentley really needs this walk," Ty teased.

"I agree."

We walked out the door and onto the sidewalk with Bentley dragging me.

Ty reached for the leash. "Hand me the leash. At the rate Bentley's going, you'll be on the ground with him dragging you," he teased.

I handed him the leash and watched as he tried to keep up with Bentley. Ty was fast walking as Bentley pulled him to his favorite spot to relieve himself.

I finally caught up to them as Bentley was making his offering.

"I see Bentley has introduced you to his favorite spot," I laughed.

Ty laughed. "We passed three other trees. What is it about this one?"

I shrugged my shoulders. "Haven't got a clue. Here you go." I handed him a plastic bag.

Ty scooped up Bentley's offering, tied the bag and looked for a trash can. He looked up and spotted a trash can a few feet away. He and Bentley walked over to the trash can and then returned to me.

"I think I know why he likes this spot?"

"You do?" I squirted some anti-bacterial gel into the palms of his hands.

"Thanks." He rubbed his hands, turned around and tipped his head towards the window of an art gallery diagonal from the tree. "See that black poodle statue sitting in the window?"

I looked in the direction he mentioned and my mouth turned up into a smile. "I never noticed that."

"I'm pretty sure Bentley has a crush on her...it."

We laughed. "Oh, my God." I knelt down and rubbed Bentley's neck. "Do you have a crush?"

Bark!Bark!Bark!Bark!

"Mommy is sorry she never noticed it...her."

Bark!Bark!Bark!Bark!

"Thank you for forgiving me. But she's not..." I stood up and looked at Ty. "I can't believe my dog has a crush."

"Maybe you should get Bentley a friend."

"I don't know. I've got my hands full with him."

"Then, maybe consider taking him to doggie day care."

I looked shocked at his words. "How do you know so much about dogs?"

"A friend has a dog and you remind me a lot of him. He got his dog when he was going through his sobriety program."

"Oh." I nodded and reached for Bentley's leash.

"I got him." He grabbed my hand and I felt fire transfer to me. It was like I was a teenager on her first date. "Come on, let's head back."

We walked back to my building and I was more confused now than I was the first time my body signaled a change in my feelings for Ty.

I looked at Ty and Bentley as we rode up to my apartment. I wasn't familiar with these feelings I was having for him.

He was my friend, but there was something off balance and I wasn't sure what to do. I was never a very bold woman when it came to men. I've never been the type to ask a guy out. I just never felt comfortable doing that. I think it had to do with the fear of rejection…and leadership. I figure, if a man can't be bold enough to ask me out, then he couldn't be counted on to be bold enough to take the lead in the relationship. Call me old fashioned, but I want a take charge man. A man who's not afraid to take a chance. A man who'll defend me. A man who will love me. I want a badass…a ride or die man. A man who can look at any situation and assure me that we can do whatever it takes to move us along to the next level.

The elevator dinged and stopped. When the door opened Bentley took off running, dragging Ty behind him.

"Bentley…" I cried out as the two of them took off running the length of the loft. "Bentley…"

Bark!…Bark!…Bark!…Bark!…

"Let go of the leash Ty," I called out. Then I heard a

thud. "Oh, my God." I ran down the hall and found Ty lying on the floor tangled up in Bentley's leash with Bentley sitting next to him. I covered my mouth laughing hard. "Are you okay?"

He looked up at me shaking his head.

Bark!…Bark!…Bark!…Bark!…

"Can I get a little help?"

I knelt down to help Ty and tried to stop laughing.

Bark!…Bark!…Bark!…Bark!…

"Bad Bentley." I laughed harder.

Bark!…Bark!…Bark!…Bark!…

I found the end of the leash and unwrapped Ty. He started to sit up and our eyes locked. I started to stand up and Bentley knocked me down on top of Ty. "Bentley…"

Bark!…Bark!…Bark!…Bark!…

"I'm sorry about that." I looked at Ty. "I don't know what has gotten into him."

"That's okay."

I tried to get up but he still had his arms wrapped around me. It was awkward, but also nice. It had been awhile since I was this close to a man I had feelings for.

"Uhm, I better…"

"Fi…"

I looked at him hoping he would say something to break the tension. Or was that lust circling around us?

He gently stroked the side of my face. I closed my eyes and swallowed the jumbo lump in my throat. My heart was racing like a thoroughbred. I knew if I tried to stand up, I'd end up right back where I was. Right now that could be either a blessing or a problem.

He cupped my face in his large soft hands, inched his mouth closer to mine and it felt like I was about to jump out of my skin. I locked eyes with those beautiful dark brown eyes staring back at me and felt drawn to him. It was like I could hear his thoughts or maybe it was just my imagination, because I was so frisky.

"I uhm...I don't think..."

He crushed his mouth against mine in a hard, knee buckling kiss. He pulled me to his chest and we rolled over onto the floor and I ended up lying on my back. This was strange, but not uncomfortable. The weight and feel of Ty's hard, solid body pressed against mine was more exciting than I had imagined. I could feel every muscle in his chest and arms melding against mine. My body was experiencing things it hadn't felt in quite awhile as well as a few new ones I liked. I had no idea Ty was that strong. It was like lying underneath a slab of carved stone.

My hands traveled down his back under his sweater. His skin was so hot. I pulled him deeper into my space and he let out a deep growl. His tongue invaded my mouth, teasing and exciting me. I wrapped my legs around his hips and pulled him closer.

Never removing his mouth from mine, he raised up, took his jacket off and flung it to the side. He lowered his body back on top of mine and pinned me against the floor as our bodies danced. He felt good pressed against me. Then again, as frisky as I was, any man pressed against me would feel good. But this wasn't any man, it was Ty...my friend...my ex-husband's childhood friend...my lawyer. Screw it. My body wanted this.

I needed air, but the only air I could get was whatever I managed to steal from Ty.

I knew we should stop, but I didn't want to. My body really wanted Ty to rip off all of my clothes and use me for wild, hot sex. The kind you enjoy while it's happening, then consciously regret and store in the back of your mind. The kind of sexual experience that would leave me unable to walk for days. The kind of experience I would be ashamed to tell anyone I'd had, but constantly replayed in my mind with a wicked smile.

He grabbed my behind, pressed me against his hips and the feel of his obvious arousal, pressed against my inner thigh. I grabbed his behind and pressed him deeper against me.

I longed to have Ty's lips travel the length of my body tasting every inch of me.

He moved his mouth across my cheek to my ear, gently sucking. Oh, God! What is he doing to me? My breasts were full and it hurt to have his chest pressed against my hard nipples, but I didn't want him to move.

"What do you want to do?" he asked in a tone so seductive my body began to do something I hadn't experienced since the last time Rhys and I had sex.

What do I want him to do? Couldn't he read my mind? I just scripted the next phase of this dance. Including an orgasm so powerful, my body would be left in a state so weak, the only way to revive me, would be with another one just as powerful.

"I uhmm…" I moaned.

"I'll do whatever you want." He moved his mouth along my collarbone, down the apex of my breasts.

"I…I…I wa…wa…want you to…" He eased his hands under the back of my t-shirt and under my bra strap. His large thumb brushed along my hot skin, my breath caught, and my body began to shake. I was on the verge of…I had no idea he had these kind of moves. "Oh, God…"

"Fi…use me," he sang as he nibbled my neck.

Oh man…why did he have to beg. Uhm…the sound of that sexy voice begging was more arousing than seeing him naked. "I uhm…"

He moved his mouth back up to my ear. "Use me," he moaned as he pulled me closer.

There was nothing more sexy than a hot virile man giving permission to be used.

I couldn't think straight. My mind and body were at war and I was picturing Ty and I in a series of positions that would make a hooker blush.

Maybe just for tonight, I could put Jesus in a box in the drawer of my dresser and relinquish my body to Ty.

"I…I…" I knew what I needed to say, but I couldn't make my mouth say the words.

He kissed me, picked up his jacket, stood up and extended his hand to help me stand up. We adjusted our clothes and I couldn't look at him. I felt embarrassed.

Bark!…Bark!…Bark!…Bark!…

Now Bentley comes in. Where was he a few minutes ago when Ty and I were on the floor and in desperate need of an interruption?

"I should go." He turned and started to walk away and I grabbed his hand. He turned to face me. I kissed him hard, hoping he could read between the lines.

He cupped my face in his hands and met my lips with the same amount of passion. He pulled me to him and his hands slid down caressing my behind.

When he removed his mouth from mine, he brushed his thumb along my swollen bottom lip.

I slowly opened my eyes and locked eyes with his. I couldn't believe what was happening.

"I'll do whatever you want, whenever you want."

I didn't know how to answer, because right now, my answer would be, throw me on the bed and make love to me. But I knew what should be said, nothing.

Chapter 12
Ty

"Tasha, will you come in here, please."

"Give me a couple of minutes and I'll be right in."

I can't believe what happened or almost happened the other night. I must have been out of my mind. How could I have let things get out of control like that? Fiona is my best, well ex-best friend's wife…ex-wife. Okay, if I forget about that, seeing Rhys and I are really more like associates now, she's a friend and a client. Talk about unprofessional.

Knock…Knock…Knock

"Come in," I called out. I didn't turn around but heard the door open and close followed by footsteps dragging along the carpet.

"I brought you a cup of coffee."

I turned around. "Thanks." I walked over to the table.

"Man, you look terrible." She sat down. "How much sleep did you get?"

"Not much." I sat down and took a sip of the hot black coffee.

"Maybe I should have made that an espresso," she teased.

"I don't think it would have made a difference." I took another sip. "I need some advice."

"About…" Tasha asked as she opened her iPad.

"There's a woman…"

She looked up and her eyes were wide. "A woman?"

"Yes."

"Please don't tell me you're having second thoughts about breaking up with Julia, because she was not good for you. Our lives have been much quieter since you dumped her."

"Tell me how you really feel."

"I'm just saying, it's been nice not having that…I mean, I thought we agreed it was time for you to find a local girlfriend."

"Are you finished?"

"Yes. So who is this woman?"

"Fiona."

She almost spit out her coffee, choking. "I'm sorry. Did you say Fiona?"

"Yes."

"Your friend Fiona is the reason you look like crap?"

"Yes."

"Damn, who knew?"

"Knew what?"

"That she was capable of putting it on a brother like

that." She crossed her legs. "It's always the quiet ones. Go figure." She smiled and shook her head.

"Fi and I aren't sleeping together."

"But you said she was the reason you didn't get much sleep."

"Sometimes, talking to you is like talking to Jake."

"Look who I'm around all day…you and Jake. Between the two of you, I have heard more guy talk than I care to mention. It's a wonder I don't pee standing up."

"Are you done?"

"Yes." She sipped her coffee. "So what happened that caused Fiona to keep you up all night?"

"We went out to dinner…"

She held her hand up. "Wait a minute. Did you say dinner?"

"Yes."

"So you and Fiona are dating?"

"No. I called to see what she was up to and she said she was heading to the movies. I wasn't doing anything and asked if she wanted company."

"Uh-huh."

"We went to dinner first."

"Where?"

"That Cuban place I like."

"I see, continue."

"Instead of the movies, we ate, danced and went back to her place."

"Uh-huh."

"Then we took Bentley for a walk."

"Very romantic."

"If you call taking a dog out to do his business romantic, then yes."

"Apart from what Bentley did, the after dinner walk was very romantic. What is wrong with you. Didn't you and Julia take romantic walks in D.C.? I know if I was in D.C. that's what I'd do. Walking along the pond by the Lincoln Memorial, sharing a coffee or…"

"I thought this was about me."

"Sorry. Continue." She sipped more coffee.

"When we got back to her place, Bentley took off running with me still holding his leash. I got twisted up in his leash, fell and somehow she ended up on top of me and we almost had sex."

She put her cup down, held up both of her hands and leaned forward. "Hold up. What did you say?"

"We almost had sex."

"You and Fiona…your friend…your client…your ex-best friend's ex-wife…that Fiona?"

I rubbed my head. "Yep."

"How did you go from a walk to sex?"

"Almost sex."

"In order for it have almost been sex, means at some point there had to be physical contact. Was there?"

"Yes."

"What kind?"

"What?"

"What kind? Was there a deep hug, a touch or a kiss that got a little hot? I mean you don't just go from walking a dog, falling down, to sex."

"Almost sex."

"Yeah, yeah, yeah…what happened?"

"She went to help me up and I may have kissed her."

"Now it's my turn to be the lawyer. Did you or did you not kiss your friend?"

"It's not that easy."

"Answer, yes or no?"

"Yes."

"Was there tongue?"

I tried not to look at her, or smile. "Yes."

She stood up and started pacing and wringing her hands. "Where were your hands?

"What?"

"Where were your hands?" she asked again.

"Why does that matter?"

"Just answer me."

"They were sort of everywhere."

"On her behind?"

"Yes." I smiled.

"Her breasts?"

"No."

"Interesting."

"Why?"

"I really thought you were a breast man."

"What?"

"Never mind. So during the course of this hot kiss."

"Who said it was hot?"

"You did by the way your body is telling on you." She looked down at my lap.

"Just get on with it." I brushed my hand in the air.

"It's clear this kiss meant more than you thought. What else happened?"

"I told her I would do whatever she wanted."

"You did what?"

"I left the choice up to her."

"The choice to make love or not."

"Well, more like I told her she could use me."

Her eyes got wide for the second time since this conversation started. "You did what?"

"I told her to use me any way she wanted."

Tasha sat down and looked at me all dreamy eyed. "I wish a man would say that to me. Use him…uhm…then what happened?"

"I started to leave and she kissed me."

"Whoa." She flopped back in her chair. "Uhm… sounds like you had a good time."

"So now what do I do?"

"You're asking me? I haven't had a relationship in over a year."

I almost choked on my coffee. "Excuse me." I wiped my mouth. "I thought you were seeing the investment banker."

"That was a date, not a relationship and he had issues. I'm patient. Back to you. So what are you going to do?"

"I'm not sure."

"That's a lie."

"What?"

"You called me in here because you are at a crossroads."

"Fine. I don't know what to do. I haven't heard from Fi since the other night and I'm scared to call her."

"And you shouldn't."

"Why not?"

"Because you told her to tell you what she wanted to do."

"But she hasn't called."

"Listen to you. Now you see how we women feel." She smiled. "Fiona will call you when she's made up her mind."

Chapter 13
Fiona

"Hi, Ty." I tried to sound calm. I was about to do something that was foreign to me.

"Hi, Fi."

I loved the way he said my name. It sounded like a strong wind cutting through the strings of a harp, with a tail lingering in the air waiting to be captured.

"I was wondering if tonight was a good night for me to settle my debt?"

"Your debt?"

I felt myself get warm all over. I'm a grown woman, but right now I feel like a nervous teenager asking out a boy to the Sadie Hawkins Day Dance.

"I have yet to take you to dinner as a thank you for getting my babies back."

"Oh. Uhm…you don't…"

"I insist." Now I sound like a desperate divorcee looking for company. "I mean, I did promise to take you to dinner as a thank you."

"That you did."

"If tonight's not good or you don't want to, I'll…"

"It's not that."

The silence was deafening. It's like I could hear his brain trying to think up a reason to say no to my invitation.

"Okay, then…I'll talk…"

"It's not that I don't want to go. Are you sure this is what you want?"

"It's just dinner."

"Is it?"

It's as if he was in my head, reading my mind. No, it wasn't just dinner. It was dinner with a heaping side of what the crap was with that kiss and seductive talk. "It's just a client taking her attorney out for a thank you meal."

"If that's what you say. Sure. I'll pick you up at…"

"I'll meet you."

"Where?"

"Peony…say seven o'clock?"

"I'll see you there. Bye."

"Bye." I pressed the button ending the call and sighed deeply. The worst part was over. Now it was on to the next difficult thing, finding something to wear.

I walked into my closet looking for something to wear on my date. DATE. I can't believe I'm about to go on a date. The last time I went on a date…Stop it Fiona Marie Harris. You can do this. It's just Ty…your friend…your attorney. The man you're hoping feels the same way you do and will kiss you like he did the last time.

I shuffled through the racks, but nothing caught my eye. Then I looked at the end of the closet, and spotted a short, black sleeve sticking out of the closet. I walked down to the black sleeve that was beckoning me. I pulled the black Zac Posen dress out of the closet, held it up and looked at it. "I can't wear this."

Bark!…Bark!…Bark!…Bark!

"Really?"

Bark!…Bark!…Bark!…Bark!

"I'm not sure. You don't think it's too simple?" What am I doing? I'm getting fashion advice from my dog. I'm more pathetic than I thought.

I hung the dress on the hook and also pulled out a ladylike orange Oscar de la Renta dress with a full skirt and plunging neckline. I also pulled out a red Victoria Beckham sheath.

I looked at my choices. "I don't want to look like I'm trying too hard. But I also want Ty to know I've decided what I want."

Bark!…Bark!…Bark!…Bark!

"Exactly. I need a man's opinion."

I pulled down the red sheath, put it on and rode the elevator down to the first floor. I exited the elevator and peeped around the corner looking for Solomon.

"Solomon…," I called but he didn't respond. "Solomon…," I called out a little louder and saw him turn around.

"Miss Harris, I'm sorry. Is there a problem?" He walked over to me.

"Not so much a problem, but…okay." I stepped

around, stood up straight and exhaled. "How do I look?"

"Excuse me?"

"How do I look?" I turned around so he could see the dress from all angles.

"You look nice."

"Nice?" My shoulders sank.

"Did I say something wrong?"

"No. It's just…"

He looked at me with a furrowed brow and then he smiled. "Oh, I see. Let me see the dress again." He walked around me and when he came back to the front he said, "You look nice."

"As a man, what do you think."

He laughed.

"I'm sorry." I covered my face with my hands.

"That's okay. I understand. I think you look very nice."

"I have another option. I'll be right back." I rushed upstairs, put on the Oscar and went back downstairs. When I walked around to Solomon's desk he shook his head. "No."

"No? But this is…"

"A very pretty dress, but not for tonight."

"Why not?"

He beckoned for me to step closer. "I assume, you're having dinner with Mr. Wells."

My eyes got wide. "How did…"

"I have three daughters and a wife." He smiled.

"Oh." I smiled.

"I've seen how he looks at your hips and legs when you're together."

"Excuse me." I leaned back.

"Go upstairs and try again."

I went back upstairs and looked at the simple black Zac

Posen dress with the flounce hem and short sleeves. I held it up and looked in the mirror.

Bark!...Bark!...Bark!...Bark!

"Really?"

Bark!...Bark!...Bark!...Bark!

"Okay. I'll wear this one." I put on the black cocktail dress and my leopard Loubo So Kates.

Bark!...Bark!...Bark!...Bark!

"Really?" I looked at myself from all visible sides. I looked at my watch. I had less than an hour to get to the restaurant. I quickly did my makeup and hair, and sprayed some parfum in a few key spots.

I grabbed a black wrap and my favorite Alaia black leather clutch. I stopped in front of the mirror and realized I was missing earrings. I hurried over to my jewelry drawer and spotted the diamond studs Rhys had given me for our fifth wedding anniversary. They were beautiful, but I didn't want to take a fond memory of my ex-husband on my date. I opted for the bold silver and crystal Kenneth Jay Lane oversized floral hoops. I went back to the mirror and inspected myself. PERFECT.

I headed to the elevator, pressed the button and looked at my reflection in the window. Then I remembered something Coco Chanel said, "Before leaving the house, a lady should look in the mirror and remove one accessory." I looked at my left hand and knew it was time. I slipped my wedding band and engagement ring off. Then the elevator dinged. It was time.

Bark!...Bark!...Bark!...Bark!

"Be good. Mommy will see you later."

Bark!...Bark!...Bark!...Bark!

"I will."

I stepped onto the elevator breathing hard. I was on the

verge of passing out. I leaned against the wall of the elevator, praying softly.

The elevator landed and my breath caught. Not only was I running late, but my adrenaline was pumping at a rapid speed. I lifted myself up, exhaled, fluffed out my hair with my hand, brushed my dress and exited the elevator.

I started toward the lobby and stopped at the corner. I took a deep breath, continued around the corner and spotted Solomon.

"WOW!" He had a huge smile on his face. He walked over and circled me. "Much, much, better."

"Really?" I smiled.

He stood in front of me. "Bruce," he called out.

"Yes."

"Come here."

Bruce walked over and stopped in front of him. "Yes, sir."

"I need your opinion on something."

"Okay, what?"

Solomon stood to the side and left me to face Bruce. "Damn!" He quickly covered his mouth. "I'm sorry."

Solomon and I both smiled.

"That's okay."

"Miss Harris, you look incredible." He walked around me. "Wow…I…wow…you…who's the lucky guy?"

"Bruce, that's none of…" Solomon jumped in.

"Now I understand the car," Bruce replied.

"What car?" I asked.

"I was about to call you."

"I didn't…I meant to, but forgot to…"

"The driver said he was here for Miss Harris," Bruce replied.

"I'll go check," Solomon said. He walked out to the curb and spoke to the driver. I tried to stay calm. Solomon returned. "Okay, Miss Harris. Bruce was correct. The car is here for you. Seems, your date arranged for the car." He smiled.

I exhaled. "Okay. I uhm…my feet seem to be stuck." I exhaled again.

"Need a little help?" Solomon asked.

"Yes, please." I smiled.

He walked over, took my elbow and guided me out to the black Maserati.

"Good evening, Miss Harris."

I looked up and immediately recognized the driver. "Good evening Aidan."

"Mr. Wells asked me to give you a lift to dinner."

"Thank you."

"I got this young man," Solomon said.

"Thank you, sir." Aidan walked around and got in the car and strapped himself into his seat.

Solomon opened the door and I climbed into the back seat and sat down. "Thank you, Solomon."

"You're welcome, Miss Harris." He started to close the door and I stopped him.

"Solomon…"

"Yes, Miss Harris…" He looked at me with the compassion of a father sending his baby girl on her first date.

"Would you please check on Bentley in an hour?"

"No problem. Have a good time." He smiled.

"Thank you." I smiled as he closed the door.

Chapter 14
Ty

I looked out the large window at the light filled city, trying to come up with a justifiable reason for cancelling this date. The only excuse I had was fear. Which was strange, because I'm not afraid of anything, and I've had a thing for Fiona for quite some time. I'm sure I'm not the only man in history to have a thing for his best friend's wife. Man, if only I'd met Fiona first, we…

Knock…Knock…Knock…

"Come in." I focused on the door's reflection and saw Tasha.

"Do you know what time it is? I know you don't have far to go, but you don't want Fiona to beat you getting to the restaurant."

I looked at my watch. "I was thinking…"

"No."

"You don't know what I was going to say."

She walked over and stood a few feet away from me in front of the window with her arms folded across the front of her chest. "This view is amazing." She exhaled. "I've been working with you long enough to know how you think."

"Really?"

"Yes. You're thinking if you go on this date and it goes well, things will never be the same between you and Fiona. That you're likely to lose a good friend."

"Reading my mind?"

"Well, I am very good at my job." She smiled. "I have news for you. Your relationship with Fiona stopped being the same the moment you kissed her."

I sighed and wrung out my neck.

"You've been waiting on her to make the next move and now that she has, you're too scared to find out her answer. Am I right?"

"I wouldn't necessarily say that."

"I'm going to give you a little insight into us females. If it was bad news, she wouldn't have invited you to dinner. She would have suggested coffee and told you her answer."

"You think?"

"I know if it were me and I finally made a decision not to get involved with a man I wouldn't ask him to dinner. I would tell him to meet me at Starbuck's. I wouldn't invite him to one of the best restaurants in the city."

"That's you, not Fiona. Fi is…she's…complicated."

"Like most of us." She sighed. "I know you're still reeling from the Julia debacle. However, you cannot let that lapse in judgment…"

"It wasn't a lapse in judgment."

"No, it was blindness."

"Blindness?"

"Yes, you were blinded by the booty and…her other manufactured assets."

I looked at her reflection in the window and her smirk was more devilish than that of a wise woman.

"In spite of the way things ended, I will admit, she uhm…let's just say, I agree with your assessment."

"Don't feel bad. All the way back to Adam, the downfall of every man has always been some tail. If he hadn't succumbed to Eve's temptations, things would have ended a lot differently in the garden."

I looked at her and smiled. "Where do you come up with this stuff?" I walked into my bathroom and brushed my teeth.

"It's the truth. Think about it. Sampson…Delilah… Abraham…Sarah…David…Bathsheba."

I rinsed my mouth, washed my face and splashed on some aftershave. "So, who's my Delilah…Julia or Fiona?" I walked back out to my office, slipped my jacket on and adjusted my shirt sleeves, revealing the gold square cufflinks.

"Isn't it obvious?" Tasha replied.

"No."

"It's both and take off your tie."

"What?"

She walked over, loosened my tie and pulled it off. "This is a date, not a business meeting. I know you know how to dress, but this isn't dinner with that uptight Julia. Relax and let things flow naturally."

"Yes, Mom," I replied.

"Watch it, smart ass." She smiled.

෨෭෨෭෨෭෨෭

I was about to walk into the restaurant when my phone rang with a familiar ringtone. I pulled my phone out of my pocket and looked at the screen to confirm it was the person I thought it was.

I stood to the side of the restaurant door and pressed the accept call button.

"Hey, Dad. What's going on?"

"What's going on with you?" the strong voice asked.

"I'm meeting someone for dinner."

"Dinner or a date?"

"Let me guess, Tasha called you." I put my hand in my trouser pocket.

"No. I called and when she said you weren't there, I asked for details. She told me you were meeting a nice young lady for dinner."

"Somehow that doesn't sound like Tasha."

"You're right. She said you were having dinner with Fiona and it wasn't business."

I felt a smile rise on my face as I cleared my throat. "She did?"

"So, are you finally acting on this thing you have for Fiona?"

"What do you mean, finally?"

"I thought I was clear. Son, I know you've been attracted to Fiona for a while and it was just fate that kept you from…"

"I wouldn't call it fate."

"Okay, poor timing."

I looked at my watch. I didn't want to be standing

outside when Fi got here. "Maybe you're right, but…"

"I raised you to be an honorable man. But I also didn't raise you to be a wimp, but a fighter. I understand why you didn't go after Fiona, but now that she's available, I think you would be a fool not to pursue her."

"Is that supposed to be your version of a pep talk, because if it is…"

"Hear me out, Son. I know you're scared."

"How long did you and Tasha talk?"

"Long enough for me to agree with her about Julia. She wasn't the one for you, and she definitely wouldn't be my choice for a daughter-in-law."

"Hold up, who said anything about a daughter-in-law? Fi and I are simply having dinner."

"Uh-huh."

"Dad, it's only dinner."

"Dinner with your dream girl."

"I have to go."

"Relax, Son. Don't show all your cards."

"What does that mean?"

"It means, don't let her see all of your flaws until later."

"I'm hanging up. I'll call you tomorrow. Bye."

"Good night, Son. Be cool like me."

I shook my head laughing. "Okay, Dad. Bye." I pressed the button, ending the call and went into the restaurant.

Chapter 15
Fiona

The car pulled up in front of the chic Upper Eastside restaurant, and it seemed like my nerves went into over drive. It felt like a team of circus acrobats was practicing in my stomach.

When Aidan got out of the car, in those brief moments, I was seriously considering going back home. What was I thinking? It was too soon for me to be dating. I was newly divorced and the ink was barely dry on my divorce papers.

Aidan opened the door. A strong wind blew into the car sending a chill through me, and I shuddered.

"Ready Miss Harris?" Aidan's strong voice brought me back to reality.

I would never be ready to move forward if I continued to hold on to the past. I couldn't allow myself to continue to be a prisoner to Rhys Walters.

I took Aidan's hand, climbed out of the car, stood up on the curb, adjusted my dress, and exhaled.

I closed my eyes, wrung my neck and looked at the door to the restaurant. All I had to do was take the few steps from the car to the door and the next phase of my life could begin.

"I can do this," I said softly.

"Excuse me?"

I looked at Aidan and smiled. "Nothing." I stepped forward a few paces.

Aidan closed the door. "You look very beautiful."

"Thank you." I stood up straight and continued toward the door. When I reached the door, it magically opened and I stepped inside. I walked over to the hostess station. "Hello, I'm here for the Harris party."

The hostess looked at her iPad and then back at me. "Seems your dinner companion has already arrived."

I started breathing harder. "He has?"

She looked around and leaned in close. "Don't worry. I saw him. He's hot." She winked. "Follow me."

I walked around the tall black lacquered podium. She wasn't walking fast, thank God. It's not like I needed to sprint and even if that were the case, I couldn't, not in these shoes. We continued to the rear corner of the restaurant. I looked up and saw Ty standing up.

We stopped at the table and my eyes traveled the length of him. He looked even better up close. Thank God, he wasn't dressed for a meeting, but a date. The casualness of his unbuttoned white shirt nestled between his black jacket and dark chocolate skin, made him look like an Oreo cookie waiting to be devoured.

"Mr. Wells, your dinner companion is here," said the hostess.

"Thank you," he said.

"Enjoy your meal" she said as she smiled and walked away.

"Thank you." My insides were shaking.

"Hi." He looked me up and down and his eyes sort of lingered on the lower half of my body. Solomon was right.

"Hi," I managed to spit out. Every inch of my body was shaking.

He walked over, pulled my chair out and I sat down. As he pushed my chair in, he kissed my neck and it felt like I'd been injected with liquid heat. Thank God, he didn't kiss me while I was standing, otherwise, I'd be lying face down on the floor.

I watched as he walked around the table to his seat. The way his jacket hugged his broad shoulders and behind was incredible. Rhys wore custom suits, but his didn't fit as nicely as Ty's. Maybe it was my imagination, or maybe it was my newfound attraction to Ty, but the hostess was right, he was hot. I noticed the woman sitting across from us checking him out.

I immediately gave her the evil eye. She needed to direct her attention to her own dinner companion, because the tall drink of chocolate milk was with me.

"What would you like to drink?" he asked.

"Before we order, I need to…"

He reached across the table and covered my hand with his large warm hand. "Let's just enjoy our meal."

I looked up and locked eyes with him. "I need…"

"You look beautiful."

My face felt warm. If it were possible, I'd be blushing. "Thank you. So do you. I'm sorry, I mean…"

"Fi, let's start with dinner and see where the evening goes." He smiled.

"Okay."

He lifted my hand to his mouth, turned it over and pressed those hot, full lips against my palm. The subtleness and gentleness was so sensual, my body instantly betrayed me. My breasts felt full and there was heat somewhere it hadn't been in quite a while. I knew if I tried to stand, I'd fall face down onto the floor.

❧❧❧❧❧❧❧

I looked at myself in the mirror. I couldn't believe I made it through dinner without making an idiot of myself.

I touched up my makeup and went back to the table. As I approached the table, Ty greeted me and helped me with my chair.

"Up for dessert?" he asked.

"None for me." I sipped more wine.

"Please tell me you're not that girl."

"What girl?"

"The girl that skips dessert when she's out, only to go home and eat ice cream," he teased.

"Yes." I covered my face with my hands.

He shook his head and smiled. "I can't believe it."

"What?" I smiled. "I had to make a decision. Wear this dress or decide in advance not to eat the creme brûlée."

"So you chose the dress?"

"Not exactly. I was going to wear something else, but…you don't want to hear this."

"Continue, this is fascinating."

"Stop being sarcastic."

"I'm serious." He rested his elbows on the table and leaned forward. His cologne wafted across the table and filled my nose rendering me a little light headed. I tried to focus on his words and not his lips as he spoke. "I want to know more about how you came to wear this incredible dress tonight." He smiled.

For the second time this evening, I felt my face get warm. Part of me wished I could blush so he could see the effect he was having on me. Although my breasts were doing a good job of that.

I swallowed hard and cleared my throat. "I uhm…in order for me to answer that, I have to talk about something I'm not sure I'm ready to talk about." I sipped the last of my wine.

He nodded. "I see."

"Would you…" the server began to speak.

"We'll take the check, please," Ty interrupted the server and never took his eyes off me.

"I'll return shortly." The server left.

"I thought you wanted dessert?" I asked.

"I want to hear more about your clothing decision." He smiled.

"Really?" I smiled and tilted my head.

"Yes. I want to know what made you choose to wear this dress instead of your other choice. Not that I'm complaining."

Who is this guy, and where has he been the past ten plus years?

"Here you are, sir." The server handed the black leather envelope to Ty.

"Thank you. " He opened the envelope and looked inside.

"What are you doing?"

He reached inside his jacket pocket, pulled out his wallet, placed several crisp one hundred dollar bills inside, and handed the leather envelope back to the server. "Thank you."

"Thank you." The server walked away.

Ty stood up, walked over and helped me stand up. "What was that all about?"

"What?"

We started walking. He casually placed his hand on the small of my back and guided me to the door.

"The check. I invited you to dinner."

We continued out the door and onto the sidewalk. "There's the car." He guided us to the car where Aidan was standing.

"How was dinner Mr. Wells?" Aidan asked.

"Excellent. And yours?"

"I enjoyed the short ribs. Thank you. And you, Miss Harris…how was your meal?"

"It was excellent. Thank you."

I climbed into the car and Ty walked around and got in on the other side. We strapped ourselves in and Aidan pulled out into traffic.

"Where to, Mr. Wells?" Aidan asked.

"Miss Harris' building, unless you would like to go someplace else." He looked at me.

"No. I should get home and check on Bentley. He could be hosting a wild party," I teased.

The car darted in and out of traffic and neither of us said a word during the ride. We pulled up in front of my building and I took a deep breath. We were minutes away from the end of the evening and time for me to say what I had wanted to say at the outset.

"I'll help Miss Harris, Aidan."

"Yes sir."

Ty climbed out, walked around and helped me out of the car. I stood up onto the sidewalk, adjusted my dress as he closed the door. He took my hand and escorted me inside where Solomon and Bruce were still on duty.

"Good evening Miss Harris...Mr. Wells," Solomon said.

"Good evening," we said in unison."

"How is Bentley?"I asked.

"I took him out about thirty minutes ago," Solomon replied.

"Thank you."

We continued to the elevator. The ride was quiet. I couldn't believe neither of us had said more than a handful of words since we left the restaurant.

The elevator stopped, the door opened and I was surprised Bentley wasn't there to greet me.

I placed my wrap and bag on the counter and turned to face Ty. "I need to check on Bentley." I walked down the hall to my bedroom and there in the corner, in his bed, was my roommate.

I took a deep breath and walked back to the living room.

"How's Bentley?"

"Asleep." I walked over to the counter. "Can I get you something?"

Ty walked over and stood in front of me. He was so close I could feel his body heat surrounding me. "What is it you wanted to tell me?"

"What makes you think I wanted to tell you something?"

He stepped closer. "I don't know, maybe it was the way you tried to dictate the evening."

"Dictate?" My face felt hot again.

He stepped closer. "Yes."

"I did no such thing," I smiled and folded my arms in front of my chest.

"You invited me to dinner and then you tried to steal my thunder."

"How did I do that?"

"By trying to pay."

"Okay, but in my defense, I told you I would treat you to dinner if you got my magazines back."

Man, did he smell good. His cologne and natural pheromones mixed together, produced a heady scent that was intoxicating.

"When I go on a date, I pay." He smiled.

"A date."

He stepped closer and there was barely any space between us. My heart was racing and I knew if I inhaled, I might have a wardrobe malfunction.

"A date."

I swallowed hard. "I thought this was a business dinner." I smiled.

"Call it what you will, but I know this is a date. Unless of course, I misread the signals." He eased his hand around my waist and pulled me the rest of the short distant to his chest.

I shook my head. "No you didn't misread it."

"I want this." He gently brushed the side of my face with the back of his large hand.

"Me, too." I wrapped my arms around his neck.

"Are you sure? Because once we go down this road, we

can't turn back. I don't want you to regret this…us."

"I know, and I won't."

He lowered his mouth to mine and gently pressed those sexy full lips against mine. It started out slow and innocent and built into a passionate dance with him taking my mouth hard as his hands traveled down my behind pressing me against him. I parted my lips slightly and he slid his tongue inside my mouth, dancing and mating with mine, arousing me.

He pulled me closer, and I felt how excited he was. I tried to pull back, but I liked the way he held me. It felt nice to be in the arms of a real man. A man, who wasn't afraid to say what he wanted. A man who wanted me in his arms. A man who wanted to kiss me.

Suddenly, he removed his lips from mine and left me heady with a truckload of feelings, and flushed all over.

"I think I should leave." He brushed his large thumb along my swollen bottom lip.

"Okay."

He took my hand and we walked over to the elevator and he pressed the button. He kissed me again while we waited for the elevator.

Ding.

The elevator door opened and we pulled apart. "I'll call you tomorrow?"

"Okay."

He stepped onto the elevator, pressed the button and looked at me. As the door started to close, he stopped it. "Are you sure?"

"Yes." I smiled.

"Come here."

I stepped to him and he crushed his mouth against mine. Then he slipped his hand around my waist and pulled me to his body, kissing me harder. Ding...Ding...Ding...Ding.

Bark!...Bark!...Bark!...Bark!

We pulled apart and looked at Bentley. "I guess that's my cue to leave. Good night."

I sucked on my bottom lip and smiled. "Good night."

The doors closed.

Bark!...Bark!...Bark!...Bark!

I looked at Bentley, "Was that really necessary?"

Bark!...Bark!...Bark!...Bark! Bentley walked over to the elevator, looked at the door and then sat down.

"I wish he would have stayed longer, too."

Bark!...Bark!...Bark!...Bark!

"How was your evening?"

Bark!...Bark!...Bark!...Bark!

"Let's go to bed. Mommy needs to get out of this dress."

Bark!...Bark!...Bark!...Bark! I turned the lights off, picked up my bag and wrap, turned on the alarm, and headed down the hall with Bentley following me.

Chapter 16
Ty

I walked around the corner, not looking up and walked into someone coming around the corner.

"Hey, man, watch where you're...Ty."

I looked up. "Rhys." I started to walk around him.

"What are you doing here so...let me guess, late meeting with my ex?"

"Something like that. Excuse me." I walked around him.

"Oh, I get it. Bro, you're definitely barking up the wrong tree."

I turned around. "Excuse me."

"My ex...Fiona. There's no way she's going...I mean, she's got a nice booty, but she ain't the girl you call for that."

I stepped up to him and got in his face. "Shut up."

"Seems I struck a nerve or you found out the hard way." He smirked.

"Don't talk about her like that."

His smirk turned into a smile. "Don't tell me you're still trying to hit that."

"I said shut up."

"You are." He shook his head. "Well, you may have stood a chance if we hadn't been friends, but I know Fiona. There's no way she's going to hook up with one of my friends."

"Good thing we aren't friends."

I turned to walk away and he grabbed my arm.

"Are you telling me you and Fiona are…"

I broke free of his hold. "Whatever is or isn't going on between me and Fi is none of your business."

"So you are banging my ex." The shock of Fi and I instantly registered on his face. "Go figure. Make a girl rich and you're subject to see all kinds of changes."

My fingers curled up into a fist and my arm raised up. Before I realized it, my fist had connected with his jaw and Rhys was out cold on the floor. The sound of flesh and muscles connecting with the marble floor, bounced off the mahogany walls startling everyone in the lobby.

"What was that?" Solomon said as he hurried around the corner. He looked at Rhys lying on the floor spread eagle and then at me. "Are you okay, Mr. Wells?"

I was rubbing my hand. "I'm fine, but Mr. Walters is going to need help getting up to his apartment."

"What happened?" Solomon asked.

"We had a difference of opinion."

"I don't understand."

"He thought he could say unflattering things about

Miss Harris and I told him to shut up. When he didn't, I shut his mouth for him."

"Good for you." Solomon smiled and patted me on the back. "Are you okay? Do you need some ice or a doctor?"

"I'm fine. Do you need help getting Mr. Walters to his apartment?"

"I guess we should get him upstairs. Can't very well leave him down here devaluing the building," he laughed.

I smiled. "I'll help you."

"No, I'll get one of the guys to help me."

"Are you sure?"

"Yes. You better go in case he wakes up before we get him upstairs. I'll take care of this. Good night."

"Good night." I started to walk away and then stopped and turned around. "Uhm, Solomon, please don't tell Miss Harris what happened."

"She won't hear it from me or the guys."

"Thanks." I reached into my pocket and pulled out a large tip and handed it to him.

He pushed my hand back. "No. We all have been wanting to do what you did for quite a while. Now go before he wakes up."

"Thanks, Solomon. See you later."

I walked out of the building rubbing my hand and got into the car. I closed the door and strapped the seat belt. My hand was throbbing. I couldn't believe I lost control like that. But Rhys deserved it. Implying that Fiona was...I took my phone out of my pocket and pulled up Fiona's number. As much as I didn't want her to know what happened, I had this annoying feeling that I should tell her.

"Mr. Wells, do you need to make a stop before I take you home?"

"No."

I pressed the number and waited for her to answer. "Hello." Her soft, sexy voice was the perfect blend of calm and seduction.

"Hey."

Bark!...Bark!...Bark!...Bark!

"Yes, Bentley, it's your Uncle Ty. Now go sit down." She laughed. "Oh, my God. What have you done to my dog?"

"What can I say...it's a guy thing."

She laughed. "You made it home already?"

"I'm on my way. I ran into an acquaintance."

"I had a good time tonight."

"Me, too. I started to come back."

"You did...why?"

"I wasn't ready for the evening to end."

"You weren't?"

"I think I got cheated with the good night."

She giggled. "Cheated... how so?"

"I only got one kiss."

"Well, it was a first date and I didn't want to appear too eager." She teased.

"Eager? Where you eager to go out with me?"

"Not so much eager, but excited. Did I say that out loud?"

"Yes, you did." I tried to play it cool. "So you were excited to go out with me?"

She sighed softly. "I uhm...a lady never tells her secrets."

This simple flirting was doing something to me. I was feeling things inside I had never experienced from such juvenile conversation. "So you have secrets?"

"Yes, Mr. Wells, I have many secrets."

"Many secrets?" I nodded. "You do know it's my job to learn people's secrets?"

"Well, I'm not telling you mine." She giggled.

The car stopped and I looked out the window. Aidan walked around and opened the door. "Hold on." I climbed out of the car. "Thanks, Aidan."

"When's your dad getting back?"

"He should be back next week."

"Have him call me."

"Yes, sir. Is everything alright?" He closed the door.

The distressed look on his face reminded me of myself when I was on my first job. "No, you've done a good job." I reached into my pocket and pulled out a generous tip. "Here. Thank you for taking care of Miss Harris tonight."

"Thank you, sir."

"I want to talk to your dad about possibly adding her as a client."

"Oh." His shoulders relaxed and his smile returned. "I'll have him call you as soon as he gets back."

"Good night."

"Good night." I walked into my building and put the phone back to my ear. "Where were we?"

"You were trying to learn my secrets."

"That's right." I walked past the concierge, around the corner to the elevator, and pushed the button. "Since you won't tell me your secrets, do you want to have dinner with me tomorrow?" I stepped onto the elevator.

"Dinner...I sort of have a date."

"A date, with who? I mean I know we just decided to..." She started laughing. "Are you messing with me?"

"No. I have plans tomorrow."

"Oh. I understand, then maybe..."

"You could join me."

"Fi, I'm not one of those guys that thinks he and his girl have to be attached at the hip. I know you have a life independent of mine."

"I understand. I just thought you might want to hang out with me and Bentley."

"Your plans are with Bentley?"

"Yes, it's doggie yoga."

"Are you serious?"

"Yes. The vet said it might help with his leg humping problem."

I laughed. "Sure, I'll go with you."

"Afterwards we can grab a bite."

"Sounds like a plan."

"Maybe we can work on a better good night tomorrow."

"Really?"

"Yes. If you play your cards right, you might get two kisses." She teased.

"Two kisses?"

"Yep, two really good kisses. The kind that make your toes curl and your skin feel hot and…"

"Stop it."

"What?"

"Unless you want me to come back, you better stop."

"Can't handle a little flirting?" she teased.

"I might need to do some yoga like Bentley."

She laughed. "Good night."

"Good night." I pressed the button ending the call and headed straight to the bathroom for a cold shower.

Chapter 17
Fiona

At this stage of my life, I thought I would be living the fairytale. A husband, a couple of kids, and a dog. I'd go back to work when the youngest was four. And after getting my multi-task groove going, I'd move up in whatever company I was working.

I wouldn't have expected the only part of that story I would be living would be the dog. And the career has been replaced with my own business, possibly.

Bark!…Bark!…Bark!…Bark!

"That's right Bentley, your Mommy is at a major crossroads in her life."

Ring…Ring…Ring… I rushed over to the counter,

picked up my phone and when I looked at the screen my mouth quickly turned up into a smile. I pressed the answer call button and tried not to sound too eager.

"Hey, there."

"Hey there, yourself."

Bark!…Bark!…Bark!…Bark!

"Bentley says 'Hello.'"

"Tell him I said hello."

"How's your day going?"

"Great. What about you?"

"I'm bored."

"I might be able to help you with that."

"How?"

"I spoke with Fairgate today."

"You did? What did they say?"

"Come over and I'll walk you through everything."

I looked at my watch and then at myself. It was going to take me some time to pull myself together. It wasn't like I could just pop over to Ty's office in what I had on. My leggings, tank top and oversized sweater weren't really appropriate attire for visiting my boyfriend's office.

"Give me an hour. I need to walk Bentley and then I'll head over to your office."

"I'll see you soon. Hungry?"

"I'll pick up something."

"No need, I'll have Tasha order us something."

"Okay, see you soon. Bye."

"Bye."

Bentley and I exited the elevator and walked toward the reception desk and Jake looked up.

"Hi, Fiona." Jake smiled.

Bark!…Bark!…Bark!…Bark!

"Hello to you too, Bentley."

"Behave yourself, Bentley." I smiled. "Hi, Jake. I'm here to see Mr. Wells."

"Go right in. He's expecting you."

"Thank you." I turned and walked down the hall to the last office on the right. I stopped at the door and knocked on the open jamb.

Bark!…Bark!…Bark!…Bark!

"Come in," he called out. His voice is…man, it makes me melt among other things.

I stepped inside and Ty met me in the center of the room. "Hey, babe." He leaned in to kiss me and I backed away.

"I thought this was a business meeting?"

"It is."

"Then we need to keep it professional." I looked at the open door. "What if someone comes in and sees us?"

He walked over and closed the door. Then he walked back and stood in front of me. "Better?"

"Is it locked?"

"Do you plan on taking advantage of me?" he teased.

"No, but I don't want Tasha or anyone else walking in and getting the wrong idea."

He pulled me to his chest, and claimed my mouth in a hard kiss. I completely forgot where I was and let go of Bentley's leash and wrapped my arms around Ty's neck. I was so right about his mouth.

When he released my mouth, I could barely stand up. I slowly opened my eyes and staring back at me were the most beautiful dark brown eyes I had ever seen.

"That's how I expect to be greeted whenever you come to my office."

"Yes, sir."

He smiled. "Hungry?"

I was still a little heady and weak in the knees from that kiss. "Yes." He started to pull away, and I pulled him back. "But first, I'd like another kiss."

"Aren't you a little demanding." He smiled.

"You said tell you what I want." I smiled.

"That I did."

"Well, right now. I want you to kiss me like that again."

He wrapped me in his arms, pulled me close and the muscles of his sculpted chest could be felt against my body. He was broad, solid, and hard. He smelled like he'd been hand dipped in a vat of exotic spices and tobacco. I wasn't sure what scent he was wearing. All I knew is it was like a drug to me, enticing me to act unlike my normal self.

He brushed his large thumb along my swollen bottom lip and I captured it inside my mouth.

"I see someone is also being playful."

He leaned in closer and his hot breath smelled like peppermint. He took my mouth in another hard, passionate kiss. He slid his hands down my behind pressing me against his body. I felt him growing excited and part of me wanted to break away, but the other part wanted him to...

Knock...Knock...Knock

We quickly pulled apart. "Come in," Ty called out.

The door opened and Tasha walked in with a handful of folders. She looked at both of us and smiled. "Uhm, here are the files you requested." She handed the folders to Ty.

"Thank you." He took the folders and walked around his desk. He placed the files on his desk, skimmed the pages and then looked up. "Where's Antwon's brief and the contract for Weaver Pharmaceuticals?"

Tasha folded her arms across her chest and smiled.

"Antwon's secretary said he needed to make a couple of changes, and that she'll bring it up in an hour. And the Weaver contract is in the bottom folder. And that shade of lipstick clashes with your tie."

Ty looked up and locked eyes with Tasha. "What?"

She stepped closer to his desk. "I said, that shade of lipstick on your lips clashes with your tie, but it matches Fiona's dress perfectly." She tilted her head and smiled.

I dropped my head and rubbed my forehead.

Bark!…Bark!…Bark!…Bark!

"That's right, Bentley. Seems Mommy and Uncle Ty were getting busy."

Ty reached into his pocket, pulled out a handkerchief and wiped his mouth. "Is that all, Tasha?"

She turned and started towards the door. "You both look like two teenagers caught making out in the basement."

"Back to work, Tasha," Ty replied.

"Yeah, yeah, yeah…I'll hold your calls and make sure no one disturbs you." She stopped in the doorway and looked back at Ty. "It's about time."

"Tasha…" Ty said sternly.

She closed the door.

"Oh, great."

Ty walked over and wrapped me in his arms. "I'm sorry about that." He pecked me on the lips. "Let's get started."

"Sure." I walked over and joined him at the small conference table in the corner of his office. I sat down and he pushed my chair in then he walked around the table to the chair at the head of the table. "Okay, so give me the bad news."

He smiled. "It's not that bad, but it is as I suspected."

"Meaning?"

"If you sell to Fairgate, you cannot work in any area of

communications for seven years. After which, you can have a small internet presence…a website or an e-zine."

"That's not a surprise. We thought that's what they were going to say. But seven years…that's a little excessive isn't it?"

"Not really. They could have insisted your resting period or non-compete be ten years."

"I think I'll pass."

"Don't you want to know how much they're offering?" Ty asked.

"No."

He patted the black folder. "You sure?"

I bit the corner of my lip and inhaled. I was tempted. "Okay, how much?" Ty passed the folder to me. I took a deep breath, closed my eyes and forced myself to look at the offer. My eyes scanned down and got wider. "Are you kidding me?"

"No. I know, it's a lot of money."

"That's an understatement. Forty five million dollars. Are they serious?"

"I spoke with their chief counsel and he said they are very serious."

"Why did you let me see that?" I stood up and started pacing. "Oh, man. No wonder Rhys was fighting so hard."

"Let me clarify. They offered Rhys more."

I stopped pacing. "What did you say?"

"They offered Rhys more."

"So why the change?"

"They heard about the divorce and thought you were fighting so you could hurt Rhys and prevent him from selling."

"So they have no idea, I'm the one that started those mags?"

"No. Like most people Rhys deals with, they think he's the brains, so to speak."

Those words just made me angrier. "I am part of the reason his company is doing as well as it is."

"So what do you want to do?"

"I'm definitely not selling, unless you think I should?"

"I'm your attorney. I can't…"

"You're also my boyfriend." I sat down. "I want your input."

"As your boyfriend, I'd say take the money, figure out what you want to do and do it. But as your attorney, I can't tell you what to do, I can only advise you."

"Lot of help you are."

"Let me finish." He covered my hand with his. "As your boyfriend that happens to be an attorney, I did a little digging."

"I don't understand." He pulled out another folder and passed it to me. "What's this?"

"After speaking with Fairgate, I made a few calls to some money people, and a branding expert I know."

"Why?"

"Fairgate was basically going to use your mags as the format for their lifestyle division."

"You mean channel." I quickly corrected him.

"No…division. Originally, they were going to start a channel, I mean network, with some branding products. But they shelved that for something much bigger."

"Bigger? I don't understand."

"They want to set up a lifestyle division based on CHIC and DOWNTOWN."

"I still don't understand."

"They want to do a line of housewares, cook books, furniture, home fragrances, body care, cable show, website, the works."

"You're kidding?"

"No. They want to do something similar to Elizabeth Grant."

"What?"

"That's why they want you to be silent for seven years. They figure by the end of your seven years, they will be fully branded with a huge following. And anything you do won't be a threat to them."

"Wow..."

"I thought, if Fairgate could do that with your idea, why couldn't you do that with your idea."

"What?"

"You created CHIC and DOWNTOWN. Why can't you create those same vehicles and become like Elizabeth?"

"Are you serious?" My eyes got wide as I tried to absorb what he was saying.

"Fi, you're smart, stylish, creative...I know you can do this, if you want to. Otherwise, sell. Take the money and do something else." He reached over and grabbed my hand. "Do me a favor. Don't say no because it seems too big. If you say no, let it be because you feel God is leading you in another direction."

That was the first time I heard Ty mention God. I never would have thought...I mean, he didn't seem like a church boy. He definitely didn't seem like a church boy that night we were rolling around the floor close to making love.

"Okay, I'll pray about it."

"Good." His sexy full lips turned up into a beautiful smile.

"When do I need to make a decision?"

"I can probably get you a week."

"I'll need it."

He kissed my hand. "Let's eat."

꧁꧂꧁꧂꧁꧂꧁꧂꧁꧂

A week later…

"Ty…"

"Hi babe, what's going on?"

"Do it."

"Do what?" he asked.

"I'm ready to be like Elizabeth."

"Are you sure?"

"Tell Fairgate I'm not for sale and neither are my babies."

Chapter 18
Ty

Knock...Knock...Knock...

"Come in." I looked up briefly and caught a glimpse of Tasha. "Tasha, set up something with Antwon. I'm not happy with his brief. And then..."

"Ty..."

"Call Brad at Morgan Garrett and set up a lunch for next week."

"Ty…"

"I want to surprise Fi with a spa day at Black Door. Please book the couples package for next Saturday. She's been working so hard…"

"Ty!"

I looked up. "What?"

"Here." She handed me a slip of paper.

"What's this?" I skimmed over the document. "Are you kidding me?"

She sat down in one of the chairs in front of my desk and crossed her legs. "So what happened?"

"This is Rhys trying to get back at me."

"For what?"

"I punched him. Knocked him out actually." I smiled.

"You what?"

"I ran into him in the lobby of Fi's building and we sort of got into it."

"According to that piece of paper, you aren't allowed within two hundred feet of him."

"So I'll avoid him which won't be too difficult, seeing we rarely see each other." I put the piece of paper down and directed my attention back to my work.

"Are you serious?"

"What?"

She leaned back in the chair with her arms folded across her chest. "Where does your girlfriend live?"

I threw my pen down onto my desk. "What the—"

"I see reality just set in."

"I don't believe this. Damn Rhys."

"You and Fiona will figure something out."

I rubbed my forehead. "She doesn't know."

She sat up. "What?"

"I said I didn't tell Fi."

"So she wasn't with you when the incident occurred?"

"No."

"And you didn't tell her because…"

"I didn't want to upset her."

"This is Rhys we're talking about. You do know at some point he was going to tell her and something like this would come from it."

"To be honest, I hadn't given it a second thought. I mean this happened almost six months ago."

"Well, guess what?"

"I know. Now I have to tell her and…"

"Don't worry, she might find it sexy that you were defending her honor."

"Uhm, Fi has a slight temper."

Tasha's eyes got wide and she shook her head smiling. "Oh, man."

"What?" I asked.

"My mind just went someplace it shouldn't."

"What are you talking about?"

She had a devious look on her face. "I was just thinking you two must have an incredible sex life with all that passion and…"

"We aren't sleeping together."

She almost fell out of her chair. "I'm sorry, it sounded like you said you and Fiona aren't sleeping together."

"You heard correct."

"Are you having a problem? Do I need to get you a doctor's appointment?"

"No. We're both fine."

"Uh-huh. Where is my boss and what have you done with him?"

"I'm here."

"Let me get this straight. The man I have worked with for the past seven years who has seen more women naked in his life than a gynecologist, isn't sleeping with his hot girlfriend." She closed her eyes and shook her head. "What's going on?"

"I wanted to do something different this time."

"No sex is very different." She sat back in her chair. "How long have you and Fiona been together?"

"Almost six months."

"Uh-huh…I'm surprised you aren't bouncing off the walls."

"Trust me, it hasn't been easy. I've taken more cold showers than I can count. I was thinking about getting a walk-in freezer and sleeping in it." I laughed.

She looked at me and shook her head. "Well, this will be interesting." She opened her iPad. "So the rest of your afternoon——"

"What did you mean by that?"

"It means, you're a guy, and I don't know many guys who are able to give up sex cold turkey."

"I wouldn't say it was cold turkey."

"You wouldn't?"

"No, I just…"

I stood up, put my hands in my pockets, sighed and walked over to the window. The city was full of life. "I have been wanting someone like Fiona for quite a while. She's the kind of woman I could see spending the rest of my life with. But I don't want to become blinded by the booty."

Tasha laughed at me. "I'm not into women, but even I have to admit, I'm in awe of Fiona's butt. I spend six days a week at the gym, trying to get my butt to look like hers."

"Way more information than I needed to know." I walked back to the chair and sat down. "So in order for me to stand a chance at going the distance with this relationship, I have to do things differently."

"And you think a couples spa day is wise?"

"I thought it would be a good treat for her."

"And both of you half naked walking around the spa wouldn't be tempting?"

"Cancel the couples package and make it just for her. Thanks."

"If you're serious about going the distance with Fiona, I'll help you."

"Help me?"

"Yes. First thing you need to do is clean up this mess with Rhys."

I sighed. "File a Restraining order and make the distance five hundred feet."

"That's what I'm talking about." She smiled.

❧❧❧❧❧❧❧❧

I stood in the doorway watching Fiona at work. I don't think I've ever seen her this happy. I could feel the creative energy bouncing off the walls. It's intriguing watching her move and commanding her team.

When she turned around, our eyes locked and her beautiful full lips turned up into a wide smile. She signaled for me to come to her and like a love sick puppy, I hurried over to her side and she took my hand in hers.

"We'll pick this up in the morning." The small creative army left her office in a single file line. "Carlos, will you close the door and hold all my calls, please."

"Yes, Fiona."

"Thank you."

Carlos closed the door and Fiona quickly wrapped her arms around my neck and crushed her lips against mine. Her aggressiveness startled me, but I liked it. I eased my hands around her tiny waist, and pulled her to my chest. She pushed her tongue past my lips inside my mouth, kissing me hard.

Her commanding behavior was exciting and sexy. I slid my hands down her back, cupped her ass and pressed her closer against my body. Those dangerous curves melding with my body created a heat that clouded my mind. I was growing more excited with every stroke of her tongue. Her parfum mesmerized me. She smelled like a garden of spicy flowers waiting to be picked.

She let out a sexy moan, and I was ready to throw her on the sofa and bury myself deep in between those beautiful thick mocha thighs.

She pulled back and her eyes slowly opened. God, she was beautiful. She cupped my face in her delicate hands and I lowered my forehead to hers and whispered," That's how I expect to be kissed when you come to my office."

"You do?"

"Yes." She pecked my lips, took my hand and led me over to the sofa and we sat down.

"So what's going on?"

Bark!…Bark!…Bark!…Bark! Bentley trotted over to me and looked up.

"Hey, Bentley." I rubbed his neck.

"I think he's jealous of me," she teased, as she got deep into my side and wrapped her arms around me.

"Why do you say that?" I kissed her forehead and rubbed her shoulder.

"He gets excited when he hears me talking to you on the phone. And when you leave, he gets a little sad."

"You're kidding." I laughed.

"No. Look at him."

I looked down and Bentley was snuggled against my leg. This felt comfortable. Like a family. We looked like we should be on the cover of one of her magazines.

"I think it's a guy thing."

"A guy thing, please." She laughed.

"I'm hungry. What about you?"

"Starving."

"How about I treat you to dinner?"

"I'd love to, but I have a lot of work to get done."

"But you have to eat."

"I know, but I have to prepare for the investors meeting in a couple of days."

"I understand, but you also have to take care of yourself."

"I know."

"You need a palate cleanser. We'll grab a little dinner and get some fresh air, come back and…"

"Or, we could go back to my place after dinner." She looked up at me smiling.

"I like the sound of that." I lifted her chin and kissed her. "Maybe we could watch a movie or something?"

"Or something?"

"Yeah. Maybe you could show me how you expect to be kissed after dinner."

"Maybe."

Chapter 19
Fiona

"So why haven't you tried to make a move on me?"

The wine in Ty's mouth came flying out like a fountain. He reached for his napkin and wiped his mouth. "What did you say?"

I refilled his glass with the Pinot Noir we were sharing. "We have been together a few months, and it's been nice, but I was wondering why you hadn't..."

"I uhm..."

"Is there a problem I should be aware of?" I sipped my wine.

"What is it with people asking me that question?"

"So there is a problem?" She propped her elbow on the table and rested her chin in her palm.

"No, there isn't a problem."

"Then why haven't you…"

"Why haven't you?" he quickly retorted.

"It's the man's place to make the first move."

"Says who?" He sipped his wine.

"I…"

"I could ask you the same thing."

"What?"

"Is there something wrong with you?" He smiled.

"Apart from being nervous about having only been with…"

He looked at me and I couldn't quite describe the look on his face. It was part shock, confusion and a whole lot of awe.

"Wait a minute. You've only…"

I folded my arms in front of me. "Yes, the only man I've been with is Rhys. There I said it."

His mouth dropped open and I swear I could see his tonsils. "I uhm…wow…I never would have…I mean I thought…I don't know what I thought."

I took a long sip of wine hoping I'd have a suitable comment that didn't make me sound pathetic. "You know what, let's talk about something else. Want to watch a movie or…"

I started to walk around the counter and Ty rushed over and blocked my path. I turned to go in the other direction and…

Bark!…Bark!…Bark!…Bark!

"Really, Bentley?"

Bark!…Bark!…Bark!…Bark!

I turned back around and came face to face with Ty.

He grabbed me by the arms and I tried not to look at him.

"You've only been with one man?"

I couldn't look at him. For some reason, I felt shame. It wasn't like I couldn't...or there hadn't been any offers. I had made a decision to wait until marriage. "Can we talk about something else?" I turned my face so he couldn't see the tears threatening to come.

"Fi..." He gently turned my head back to him and stroked the side of my face. "You have nothing to be ashamed of."

"Tell that to Rhys." I tried to smile. "I can't believe I said that out loud."

"What?"

I tossed my head back hoping for an answer that wouldn't embarrass me any more than I already was. Why couldn't I just keep my mouth shut. Things were going well with me and Ty. So what if I'm as frisky as my over sexed dog.

I sighed and lowered my head. Staring back at me looking even more sexy, was the man I just basically invited, no begged, to make love to me. And if I'm being honest with myself, it wouldn't be love making. I desperately wanted him to do something my selfish ex-husband failed to do, sexually satisfy me. I sucked on the corner of my bottom lip and came clean. "Rhys wasn't...let's just say I expected much more, but was disappointed quite frequently." He lowered his hands and leaned against the counter.

"I'm speechless."

I rubbed my forehead. "Well, I wish I was." I sipped some more wine. "I thought our sex life was normal, until my girlfriends had a little too much wine and decided to overshare."

"You lost me."

"Never mix a group of women, a couple of bottles of

Pinot Noir and pizza together. Trust me, you'll hear things you never expected to hear."

"How rough could a little girl talk get? I'm sure I've heard worse in the locker room."

I sipped more wine. "Trust me, you haven't. I know more about my friends' boyfriends and lovers than I care to." He folded his arms across his large chest and the cotton of his shirt fighting with his biceps distracted me.

"Remember something?"

"Huh…"

"You disappeared."

I disappeared alright. I was on fantasy island where Ty and I were having wild, hot sex and running around naked.

"I'm sorry. What did you say?"

"You were telling me about girl talk."

"Forget what I said."

He stepped closer and the heat emanating from his body and his cologne was overwhelming. If this were a cartoon, the powerful scent would be a vibrant magenta seductively swimming its way up my nose infiltrating my body. My head was full of erotic thoughts starring Ty.

"No, let's talk about this." He stepped closer, slipped his hand around my waist and pulled me to him.

"Ty, really, we…"

"Shhh…you asked me a question."

"Which I shouldn't have."

He pecked me on the lips. "I told you to tell me what you want and that extends to what the next step is."

"Can we please…"

"No."

"Fine." I huffed and folded my arms in front of my chest.

"Are you ready to take that step?"

"We don't have to."

"That's not what I asked."

"Ty, we…"

"Fiona."

The way he said my name, made my blood boil. It was powerful, commanding and intoxicating. I think if I'd had ten percent less good sense, I'd have pushed him down on the floor and had my way with him.

I was shaking all over and desperately wanted him in a way I never wanted Rhys.

"Yes."

"Yes, you're ready to take the next step?"

I swallowed the desire I had. "Yes and no. Why are you smiling?"

"I'm thinking about something Rhys said."

I started to step back and he pulled me back. "Excuse me?"

"Now it's my turn to be embarrassed. A few months ago, I bumped into Rhys in the lobby and he…we sort of got into it."

"What do you mean?"

"He said some things about you…"

"About me?"

"He said you would never sleep with me because he and I were friends, or used to be."

"Is that why you…"

"Yes and no."

"Please explain."

"I haven't pushed you to go further because I felt it was too soon."

"We've been together six months. At what point will it

not be too soon?" I broke free of his hold.

"Fi…" He reached out and grabbed me.

"I never would have thought you'd be scared of Rhys."

"I'm not scared of Rhys or anyone else." He said it so fiercely. The bite in his words was scary and sexy.

"Then why haven't you made love to me or at least given me the opportunity to say no?"

"I honestly didn't think you were ready."

"Ready? Ty, I'm so damn frisky, I thought about greeting you at the elevator in stockings, a suspender and heels."

"No knickers?"

"Nope."

"Really?" He smiled.

It was difficult to resist his charm and stay angry. He wrapped me in his arms. "Please don't let Rhys…"

"Shut up."

"Excuse me?"

"I said, be quiet. I'm not afraid of Rhys or that restraining order he filed."

"What restraining order?"

"The one he filed after I knocked him out."

"Knocked him out…when…why?"

He sighed. "I told you, he said some things about you I didn't like."

"What did he say?"

"He said although you had a nice booty…which he was wrong."

"Excuse me?"

"You have a beautiful round behind that should be classed as a great work of art. When God sculpted your behind, he used His best tools." He eased his hands down and squeezed my behind.

"Thank you." My face felt hot.

"Anyway, he said you weren't the girl to call for a booty call."

"That trifling piece of…"

"Then he said he knew we weren't sleeping together, because you would never sleep with one of his friends. He pissed me off, so I punched him."

My eyes got wide and I covered my mouth with my hands. "You didn't?"

"He landed on the floor and was out cold."

"What?" I smiled.

"Solomon thanked me. He said he and the guys had been wanting to do that for quite some time."

I grabbed the sides of his face and kissed him. "It's nice having a man who doesn't mind sticking up for me."

He pulled me closer. "You're my girlfriend and I won't have you disrespected." His confession made me want him even more. "But defending your honor came at a price. Rhys filed a restraining order against me."

"So that's why you haven't made a move on me."

"I haven't made a move, because I really thought it was too soon. When we take that step, I want you to have a clear head."

"My head is clear."

"Babe, I know that's what you think, but your situation isn't like mine. I'm coming off of a break up. You're coming out of a marriage."

"I know that, but I'm…"

"Hot in the pants," he teased, "and have only been with one man."

I sighed. "So you want to wait?"

"I want you to be sure. I'm not going anywhere."

"Your little friend…"

"Little?" His eyes got wide.

I smiled. "I stand corrected." I kissed him.

"Thank you."

"So what are we going to do about Rhys's restraining order?"

"I filed my own."

"What?"

"I filed my own. I think he'll find it a little difficult coming and going when I'm here." He smiled.

"You didn't?" I smiled.

"I told you, I ain't scared of nobody."

"A man willing to go to jail for my honor. That's sexy."

He took my mouth in a kiss that left me barely able to stand or breathe.

Chapter 20
Ty

"Hey Sexy."

"Sexy? I never really thought of myself as sexy," Fiona giggled.

"In my eyes you are." She rolled her eyes. "What was that?"

"What?"

"The eyes. Why are you rolling those beautiful brown eyes?"

"Sexy…really? You must mean…"
"You."
Bark!…Bark!…Bark!…Bark!
"That's right Bentley. Your Mommy is sexy."

"Would you stop it." She giggled again. "Okay… okay…I'm sexy."

Bark!…Bark!…Bark!…Bark!

"That's right, Bentley. She finally sees what we see." I smiled.

"Oh, my God." She smiled.

"There's that smile I wanted to see."

She seemed to smile wider. "How's Chicago?"

"Challenging."

"When are you getting back?"

"Miss me?"

"Actually, Bentley wanted to know."

"So Bentley misses me and not you?"

She shrugged her shoulders. "Eh."

"Eh? Way to assault my ego."

"Did I hurt your feelings?" she teased.

"At least Bentley misses me."

She laughed. "When are you coming home?"

"Considering only Bentley misses me…I might stay away a little longer."

"And he'll be very sad," she pouted.

"Maybe we can work out a custody arrangement and…"

She laughed. "Stop it. What am I going to do with you?"

"I've got some ideas."

"So do I," she said followed by a wicked smile.

"Really?" I raised an eyebrow at her response. "What kind?"

"That's for me to know and you to find out in due time."

"Miss Harris, is that a proposition?"

"It might be a promise."

I wanted to climb through the phone and kiss those

sexy lips as my hands caressed her gorgeous ass. My mind filled with sinfully salacious thoughts of Fiona and I rolling around the bed naked teasing each other before I buried myself deep inside those smooth thick thighs.

Watching her mouth as she flirted and teased me sent a jolt to my core. I tried not to give in to what I was feeling or thinking. I was trying to take things slow and follow her lead, but it was becoming more and more difficult, especially with her flirting like this.

"A promise? That's uhm…" I nodded.

"A promise."

I stood up and walked over to the window and looked out onto the city. "A promise is…"

"Filled with a lot of possibilities."

I cleared my throat. "I think we need to change the subject because even if we wanted to act on your promise, we can't."

"Why not?" She tilted her head and sucked on the corner of her bottom lip.

"Fi, stop."

She exhaled and raised her eyebrow. Earlier in the conversation, I thought she was oblivious to what she was doing. But when she did that, I knew she was well aware of what she was doing. She knew she was exciting me.

"You asked if I missed you, but I don't recall you saying anything about missing me, unless of course you don't."

Was she kidding? Right now every inch of me missed her. "My missing you goes without asking."

"It does?"

I cleared my throat. "Baby, you have no idea how much I miss you."

"Do you really?" she hummed.

"Yes, I do."

"So, if I were there what would you do?"

No she didn't. I looked at the image on the screen, because this didn't sound like my sassy, slightly shy, but funny girlfriend. This sounded like the saucy woman from my dreams. The temptress that had been invading my dreams and thoughts since Fiona entered my life over ten years ago.

This was the sexy vixen I had been measuring all other women against. The one I knew I couldn't have because she was married to my then best friend. The one I had had several different ways in my mind. The one I knew that if I did get the opportunity to have in my bed, in my arms, under me, wrapped around me, I would never let go. The one who when I closed my eyes, I could smell her parfum, and hear how she would sound as I tasted every one of her erogenous zones.

Now this very sexy, vixen, my girlfriend, is asking me what I would do to her if she were here.

"If you were here, I would..."

Bark!...Bark!...Bark!...Bark!

Saved by the bark.

"Calm down, Bentley." Fi cast her eyes down. "Hold on someone wants to say hi." She turned the phone on to Bentley. "See your Uncle Ty."

Bark!...Bark!...Bark!...Bark!

"Hey, buddy. You taking care of your Mommy for me?"

Bark!...Bark!...Bark!...Bark!

"Thank you. Good boy."

Bark!...Bark!...Bark!...Bark! Then Bentley walked away.

"I told you he misses you." Fiona smiled.

"At least I know someone misses me."

"Yeah, yeah, yeah...how are negotiations going?"

"It's a little stressful, but I think we'll get everything we want. How…"

"When will you be back?"

"Friday."

She nodded. "Want a ride?"

"Aidan is picking me up."

"I figured as much, but I thought I'd come with him."

"Because you miss me." I smiled.

"No, because Bentley does," she teased.

"Okay, smarty." Her smile is beautiful. "Want to have dinner when I get back?"

"Sure. I'll…"

"I meant Bentley."

"Oh, okay." She laughed.

I laughed. "Meet me at…"

"Your place."

I nodded. "Okay."

"I gotta go. Call me when you land and I'll pick up dinner. Bye, Baby."

"Bye, sexy."

Her beautiful face had been replaced with a page of apps. That woman is way more than I expected.

I scrolled through the contacts and pressed the name for the number I needed to call.

"Tiberius Wells office, Tasha speaking, how may I help you?"

"Hey, Tasha."

"Hey, boss. How's everything going?"

"Stressful, but on track."

"I'll update your schedule within the hour."

"Fine. Thanks. Uhm, I need you to send Fi some flowers."

"Consider it done. What do you want the card to say?"

"Miss me?"

"Excuse me?"

"Send her one of those floral hat boxes with a card that says, 'Miss me?'"

"You two are strange. Anything else?"

"Get a box of treats for Bentley and send them before the flowers. And have the card say, 'Miss you, Buddy.'"

"You know what? I'm not going to even pretend to understand what you're doing."

"Thank you. Please make sure the dog treats are delivered first."

"Consider it done."

Chapter 21
Fiona

I can do this...I can do this...I shouldn't do this.

Ding. The elevator stopped. I opened my eyes and looked straight ahead as the chrome elevator doors opened. I stepped out and stood still, staring down the hall at the door in the middle of the hall on the right hand side.

I wanted to leave, but I couldn't because the concierge had already announced me. I exhaled, clutched the handle on the woven bag and started walking down the hall.

I can do this…I can do this…I can do this.

This felt like the longest walk of my life. I knocked on the door, took a deep breath and waited for the door to open.

I looked around because I didn't want anyone to see me standing out here. I didn't want anyone else to know I was here. I wanted my presence here to be a secret.

The door opened and standing there was my boyfriend. Man, he looks good. No matter what he's wearing, he always looks good. Look at him. He's been flying most of the afternoon after a full morning of meetings, and he still manages to look like he just stepped off the cover of a magazine. He was wearing tailored charcoal trousers and a crisp white shirt. Sexy and classic.

"Give me that." He reached for the dark woven bag, ushered me inside and closed the door. I followed him into the large, open living space. I like Ty's apartment. It reminds me of my place, but his is a little more sleek and contemporary. "Where's your body guard?" He looked over his shoulder and smiled.

"Your best friend is at the spa. I treated him to a day of pampering, and decided to let him stay over because he was having such a good time." I smiled.

"Oh."

"He sends his thanks for the treats."

He placed the bag on the counter, and I placed my jacket and bag on the stool. Ty walked over, leaned me against the white marble counter, wrapped his hands around my waist, and glided his tongue along my bottom lip. My heart began to race as I anticipated his lips on mine.

His hands slid down the small of my back, gently caressing my behind, and I felt flushed and excited.

He moved his mouth along my cheek to my ear, and I let out a soft moan as he traced my ear with the tip of his tongue. This was new. I don't know what kind of case he was on in Chicago, but it seems like he came back with a few new tricks. He squeezed my behind and pulled me deeper into his space. I couldn't believe he was already having a physical reaction. Nor could I believe I was on the verge of one of my own, and he hadn't even kissed me

"I missed you," he whispered followed by a kiss on my neck.

"So you say," I teased.

He kissed my neck again. "You smell good."

"Are you going to kiss me?"

He looked up and, locked eyes with me. Oh man, that sexy stare made my stomach jump and another part of my body tingle.

"Hungry?"

That was an open ended statement if ever I heard one. Not only was I hungry for food, my body was hungry for him as well.

"Yes."

"Let's eat."

He walked away and left me panting like a lioness in heat. But that's what I was. A female cat in heat and in desperate need to be sated by the king of the jungle.

I can't believe he walked away like that. We haven't seen each other in over two weeks and all I get is a kiss on the neck? A nice kiss, but I was expecting more, like a little lip to lip connection.

I walked down the hall to the restroom and stared at my reflection in the mirror. I needed to settle down, enjoy dinner, and be grateful for this time with my boyfriend. A man that is playful and cares about me. So what if he didn't kiss me after having not seen him in a couple of weeks? I'll cut him a little slack, because he's probably still jet lagged.

I washed my hands and walked back down the hall. I

walked around the corner and the mood had been changed in a matter of minutes. The candles seemed to have appeared out of nowhere. The upbeat jazz that was playing when I arrived had been replaced with something a little more romantic and sexy.

"I wasn't gone long enough for you to do all of this." I smiled.

Ty walked over, took my hand, pulled me to his chest, and gently pressed his lips against mine. My hands found their way around his neck and I gave in to the kiss and the atmosphere. I opened my lips a little and he pushed his warm tongue inside my mouth, kissing me harder and deeper. I missed kissing him. Seeing him on my phone satisfied my visual desire, but it did nothing for the physical connection. He slid his hands down my back, grabbed my behind and pressed me against his hard body. His hands and heat were doing a good job of arousing me. I was so turned on. I wouldn't have objected to skipping dinner and going straight to dessert.

He pulled back and brushed his large finger along my swollen bottom lip.

"Did you miss me?"

I swallowed hard. "Yes."

"Much better. Let's eat."

We pulled apart and he escorted me to my seat at the table and kissed my neck. He walked around, sat down, took my hand and said grace.

"Impressive, Mr. Wells." I sipped some wine.

"Thank you, but I can't take all the credit. It was a team effort." He smiled.

"A team?"

"You brought the food, and I got the wine."

"I thought you meant the setting was a team effort."

"No, that was a matter of strategically placing the candles so I could light them quickly." He smiled and sipped his wine.

"Uh-huh."

ഐ഍ഐ഍ഐ഍ഐ഍ഐ഍

"That was good." He wiped his mouth and I brushed my foot along his leg. "What's going on?" He smiled.

"What are you talking about?" I sipped my wine.

"You've been very playful and flirty the past few days, plus you've been a little handsy tonight."

"Have I?" I smiled and raised my eyebrow.

"Not that I'm complaining, but a brother can only handle so much teasing."

"You think I'm teasing you?"

He stood up and took both plates into the kitchen. "Either that, or you want something, but aren't quite sure how to ask me for it."

I got up, walked into the kitchen and rested my hands on the counter. I cast my eyes on his tight behind as he loaded the dishwasher. That is a well sculpted behind. It's like looking at two perfectly round balls. Tight is an understatement. I know he works out, but man, I wonder what the rest of him looks like.

"What could I possibly be afraid to ask you for?"

"I don't know, you tell me." He closed the dishwasher door and turned to face me.

"To quote you. I'm not afraid of anyone."

He wiped his hands on the thick white kitchen towel,

folded it and placed it on the counter. Then without hesitation, he walked around and stood next to me. My heart started to race and it felt like all the air had been sucked out of the room. He stepped closer and a huge lump landed in my throat.

He gently stroked my arm with his large, strong index finger. I expected the tip to be rough, but it was soft and warm and glided along my skin with just enough tension to take my breath.

"You aren't, huh?"

I exhaled. "No."

He stepped closer and I could feel his hot breath on my neck causing my skin to pebble. I closed my eyes, exhaled, and tried not to fall down.

"What do you want?" he whispered.

I knew what I wanted, but I couldn't bring myself to answer him. I licked my lips and swallowed hard. He stroked my arm again and it was like a match striking the side of a box, igniting a fire. I was on fire.

I opened my mouth to speak, but all I could do was moan.

He stepped closer and began to nuzzle my neck. "Talk to me. Tell me what you want." As he uttered the words my body and mind began to war.

"I…I…I should leave."

"Is that what you want?" he whispered.

I closed my eyes and tried to visualize an answer, but my mind was blank. He covered my hand with his large soft hand and the heat transfer was overwhelming.

I pulled my hand back. "It's late. I should go."

"If that's what you want to do."

I swallowed again. "Yes, it is."

"I'll call the car."

"No need, I'll take a taxi."

"Let me get my jacket and I'll walk you downstairs."

"You don't have to, I can…"

"I'll be right back."

He disappeared down the hall and for the first time since we finished dinner I was able to breathe. What is wrong with me? I came over here tonight to…what was I thinking? I'm not a seductress. I'm a newly divorced, horny woman who's only been with one man who never really schooled me in the art of physical love. But even bad water can be missed.

I heard the heavy footsteps walking back towards me, and my heart began to race again. I turned in the direction of the footsteps.

"Really Ty, I can have the doorman get me a taxi."

"Nonsense. I'm escorting you downstairs."

"You aren't angry with me?"

He picked up my jacket and helped me slip it on. Every move he made seemed to be amplified.

"Why would I be angry with you?"

"Because I was flirting with you and…"

He pecked my lips. "Fiona, I told you I would follow your lead. When you're ready, we'll take the next step."

"But…" He handed me my bag. "Thank you."

He picked up his keys and guided me out the door. He locked the door, took my hand in his and escorted me to the elevator. I know he said he wasn't upset, but the plastered smile on his face said otherwise. I thought I was ready to take the next step, but I guess I wasn't.

The elevator stopped and we walked around the corner to the lobby. We continued to the front door and parked at the curb was the black Maserati and a familiar face.

"Good evening, Aidan," Ty said.

"Good evening, Mr. Wells…Miss Harris."

"Good evening, Aidan," I replied.

"Aidan, would you please see Miss Harris home and call me once you've arrived."

"Yes, sir."

"I'll help her into the car." Aidan walked around the car and Ty opened the door. "Here you go, babe."

I climbed into the back seat. "Are you sure you're not upset?"

Ty hovered over the open car door. "Fi, I'm not upset." He leaned in, pressed his lips against mine and slowly pulled back. "Call me when you get home."

"I will."

He closed the door and patted the roof.

We pulled out into ongoing traffic and I looked out the window and Ty was still standing on the sidewalk. I blinked and another car was behind us blocking my view.

What had I done?

Chapter 22
Ty

Maybe it was for the best that Fi and I didn't take that step yet. Although, I have to admit, I was excited about finally having her in my bed. My body really would have appreciated the release. I can't believe I've been celibate this long. Counting the last time with Julia, the break before getting with Fi…it's been longer than I want to say out loud.

Ding…Ding…Ding…Ding…

What the…since when did the concierge start letting people up unannounced…oh, it's probably for the guy down the hall. It wouldn't be the first time one of his twisted chicks mixed up the apartment numbers. I've told him to make sure his dates understand the difference between one and two.

I walked over to the front door, looked out the peephole and all I saw was black hair. I cautiously opened the door prepared to be nice to the dimwit who didn't know the difference between one and two.

I exhaled, opened the door and, "I think you want… Fi? What are you doing here? Is everything alright?"

"Everything is fine. May I come in?"

"Sure." I stepped to the side and she walked inside swinging that gorgeous ass to a rhythm clearly only she could hear. I poked my head out the door and looked down the hall. I closed the door and followed her inside with my eyes fixed on those dangerous curves. "I just put you in a car a little while ago. What's going on?"

She placed her bag on the counter, walked over and crushed her mouth against mine. She kissed me so hard, my body immediately reacted. She wrapped her hands around my neck and pushed her tongue passed my lips inside my mouth like a bullet train. This aggressive Fiona was sexy and definitely not the woman I had put in a car earlier this evening. She backed me up against the wall and kissed me harder. I slipped my hands around her waist and pressed her body against mine enjoying her gyrations. I was so aroused, I could barely contain myself. I wanted to take her right there on the counter. She dove her warm silky tongue deeper inside, ferociously mating with mine, pushing me closer to the edge.

I was confused, excited and aroused like I had never been before behind a kiss. Fi had never kissed me with this much passion and heat. I slid my hands down her back, squeezed her ass and she let out a deep moan. Man, that ass should be on display in a museum. I've often wondered what it looked like without anything covering it. In my mind I pictured smooth, firm, mocha skin covering a curved piece of body perfection.

My hands slid further down under the layers of fabric until I found skin. My fingers traveled up her thighs and I got a surprise. Was she wearing what I thought she was wearing? I grazed her legs again to confirm my thoughts. Seemed she remembered what I said I liked. I loved the feel of a woman's legs in silk stockings brushing against my skin.

She pulled back, licked her swollen lips and smiled. She looked sexy as hell. She took off her, tossed it onto the sofa, inhaled and dragged her finger along the top of her breasts and, "Uhmm…" she hummed.

I don't remember her dress being that low in the front. Nor did her breasts seem that large. I closed my eyes and when I opened them, the image hadn't changed. She was still there flirting without speaking.

She licked her lips again and stepped to me. "I was thinking, maybe I should take a cue from Bentley and go on a sleepover."

I tried not to let the surprise of her words register on my face. She turned around and started walking down the hall swinging that gorgeous ass. I blinked and noticed a few paces into her walk, she had opened her dress. My mouth dropped open and a few more paces, the black and white wrap dress was on the floor. I looked up and walking towards my bedroom was the woman from my dreams wearing barely-there sexy, black, lace lingerie, complete with a suspender, black stockings and sky-high black red bottom stilettos. This definitely wasn't the woman I put in the car.

I was frozen. I told my brain not to think, but told my body to act. I locked the door, turned the lights off and followed the breadcrumbs the vixen had laid out for me.

When I walked into my bedroom, standing next to the bed, with her back to me and that gorgeous ass greeting me, was the woman I had longed to make love to. Her sweet-spicy scent had miraculously filled my bedroom. From this night on, I would always smell her even when she wasn't here.

I stepped to her and kissed her shoulder.

"Hmmm...." she purred.

"What do you want?" I whispered as I nuzzled her neck. Clearly she had a plan if she came back.

"I want you to love me so hard I feel it every time I think about you."

"Are you sure this is what you want?" I dragged my finger along her arm. "Once we cross that line, we can't go back."

She turned to face me, looked up and her eyes said it all. She was hungry and it wasn't for food. She brushed her hand across the front of my trousers and my breath caught. She stepped closer and whispered, "I know what I want." She stepped back and licked her bottom lip.

I looked at her erect nipples pushing through the black lace of her bra and my mouth began to water.

"Take off your bra." She inhaled, pushed her bra straps down her shoulders, one at a time. Then she reached behind her back, unhooked it and slipped it off.

I tried not to look surprised, but I was in awe of the beautiful weighty orbs before me. The combination of mocha skin and dark chocolate areolas and nipples was incredible. I wanted to take her breasts in my mouth one at a time, but not yet. This dance needed to be a combination of what we both wanted...pleasure, passion, empowerment and a lot of lust.

I met her gaze, and she didn't appear to be ashamed or embarrassed at her near nakedness. This was a side of Fi, I had never seen. The seductress drawing me into her lair. She reached down her smooth thick mocha thigh and started to unhook her stockings.

"No."

Her eyes got wide. "No?"

"Take off my shirt."

She raised an eyebrow, smiled and stepped to me. I was trying not to give in to my desire, but I was desperate to touch her...to possess her. She began unbuttoning my shirt and the intoxicating scent of her parfum traveled up my nose and pulled me deeper into her space.

When she reached the last button, she unbuckled my belt, unbuttoned and eased the zipper down slightly on my trousers, and I let out a deep growl. Then she slipped the tails of my shirt out. The feel of her delicate, hot hand just grazing my skin made my blood boil. I was sure she had no idea how close I was to pushing her down onto the bed and burying myself inside her hard and fast.

She lifted my hand, unhooked the cufflinks one at a time, never losing eye contact with me. She pulled my shirt back and glided her hot hands along the contours of my chest and it felt like I was being scorched with a hot knife blade.

She stepped closer, pressed her breasts against my chest and my entire body got hard. She glided my shirt down my shoulders, off my arms and let it fall to the floor. I was trying to stay in control, but she was making it very difficult. Everything she did pushed my arousal to its breaking point. I had been waiting what feels like a lifetime to be with Fiona and now that it was here, I didn't want to rush.

In every area of our relationship, I had allowed Fiona to call the shots. I didn't want her to feel like I was pushing her. I wanted her to be comfortable with her sensuality and not afraid to express herself sexually.

I suspected there would be a little apprehension and nervousness. I had no idea, when she returned she didn't need any help stepping into her role. I don't know what happened between the time I put her in the car and the time she returned and rang my doorbell. Whatever it was, it caused her to return with a completely different attitude. She may have left as an unsure, timid mouse, but she returned as a seductress eager to call the shots.

She dragged her finger along my abs as she teased my nipples with her warm tongue. This was erotic on a level I never expected from her. She eased her hand down the inside of my trousers, inching closer to the bulge she caused. When her delicate hand slipped inside the elastic waistband, and moved further down, I stopped her. I knew if she touched me, this game of foreplay would be over.

"Don't you want me to…" She looked up at me with those gorgeous big brown eyes, and it was difficult not to give in to her.

"I want you to do whatever you want to do, but I can…"

"I want to undress you."

She slid the zipper on my trousers completely down. Then she eased my trousers down my hips and stopped to cup my ass. Damn, I couldn't believe how excited I was. I swallowed hard and she never took her eyes away from mine. She eased her hands inside the waistband of my underwear. She gently pushed my underwear down freeing my erection. She looked down, then back up and smiled. Her obvious approval excited me even more.

She dragged her finger along my length pushing me closer to the edge. Then she wrapped her hand as best she could around my penis, slowly moving it up and down. *Oh, God*…I gently pulled her hand away and she looked surprised.

"Did I…"

I kissed her. "You first." She looked stunned at my response. "But I need to get a condom."

"I'm on the pill and…"

She had no idea how sexy that statement was. I cupped her face in my hands. "I'm clean. I haven't been with anyone in almost a year. Are you sure?"

"Yes. I want to feel you."

I scooped her up and placed her on the bed. She had no idea how many times I had pictured her right there. I climbed into bed next to her, wrapped my hand around her waist and pulled her to me. She felt good pressed against me. I teased her lips with my tongue, trying to take it slow. She cupped the sides of my face, and pushed her tongue inside making love to my mouth. God, this woman is incredible.

I rolled her onto her back as our tongues danced and my body fought not to go too fast. I cupped her breast, massaging and kneading the weighty orb. I loved the way her skin felt, warm, soft, but firm. I brushed my thumb across her hard nipple and my tongue along its twin and she treated me to a deep moan. Her skin tasted spicy and hot and her cries of pleasure were the perfect soundtrack to this sexy dance. She pressed my head down and I sucked her breast harder. Man she felt good in my mouth.

I eased my hand inside her knickers, slowly teasing her. She began to pant and writhe and my fingers weren't even inside her.

"Off…take them off…" She was pushing on the waistband of her knickers.

I removed my mouth from her breast and slid the delicate black lace knickers down her legs. I dragged my fingers along her hot thighs, inside her heat and she moaned. I took my time, teasing her, watching her come apart.

I stroked her nub and she tensed up. It was like she was trying not to give in to the contractions gathering inside her. She was so tight around my finger, I could feel the little pulses as I massaged her heat. When she could no longer resist, she screamed, "OH, GOD...DON'T STOP."

I did as she requested and she came hard, writhing against the bed, enjoying her orgasm. I wanted to be where my fingers were. It excited me to see her be so responsive. Just as she was coming down, I stroked her nub and, "OH, GOD... OH, GOD...OH...," she cried out, arched up, rolled her eyes back and rode my fingers bucking and convulsing. God, she looked beautiful.

I buried my fingers deeper inside her warmth, and she clutched the sheet, breathing hard, rocking her head from side to side. I slid my fingers back and forth and watched as another orgasm consumed her.

"Ba...Ba...baby...plea...please..." she spit out. I loved the way she sounded on the cusp of ecstasy. I continued making love to her with my fingers and she began to tighten again. "Ba...plea...I..."

"Not yet. Hold on," I begged.

I found it difficult not to share in her release. I took her nipple in between my teeth and she arched up against my mouth.

"Baby, I...I...I can...I need to..." she said in between deep breaths.

I couldn't take it anymore. I was desperate to be inside her. I gently stroked the side of her face, eased up to her ear and whispered, "My turn."

I climbed on top of her, nestled my hips in between her thick thighs and slid inside her heat. Damn, she felt good and better than I had imagined. I pinned her hands against the bed and started to move slow giving her a chance to get use to my size. I looked down and she had a surprised look on her face that quickly changed to a smile. I eased into a rhythm and watched as she got in sync with me.

"I want to touch you," she announced as she wrapped her legs around my waist. I liked the feel of her stockings and suspender rubbing against my skin. It was sexy as hell.

Julia would never oblige my request to keep the stockings and suspender on during sex. She said it was uncomfortable and the stockings were hot. But it excited me. It's a little freaky and wild. Makes it seem like she was so hot for me she came ready to play.

Fiona remembering what I said I liked, meant she cared about my pleasure. In turn, I'm going to give her what she wants.

I let go of her hands and leveraged myself against the bed. When she glided her delicate hands down my back and grabbed my ass, that was like throwing kerosene on a fire. I took off and pushed harder, deeper, and faster and she grew tighter around me.

"God, you feel so good."

She lathed her tongue on my nipple and commanded, "Harder."

I smiled and did as she requested. I lifted her legs and dove deeper, growing even more excited as I watched her breasts bounce. Her perfectly hard nipples taunted me the harder I dove.

I fought with my body not to give in. I crushed my mouth against hers, with my tongue mimicking the rhythm of my body.

I buried myself deeper inside her heat and she grew wilder. Bucking against me, but never removing her mouth from mine.   I felt her tighten and knew another orgasm was on the rise.

"Not yet, baby…please, don't come now."

I lifted her legs higher and pounded harder and faster. I was surprised she was able to take all of me. She dug her nails into my skin, and screamed out, "TY…TY…TY…"

Hearing her call my name was like being shot with unfiltered adrenaline. I dove hard and fast inside her. She wrapped her legs around my waist and the heels of her shoes bore into my skin. God, this was exciting. I was trying to hold on.   She was beautiful, breathing hard on the cusp of another orgasm.

She clutched my ass and pushed me as deep inside her as she could handle. The sound of our bodies slapping against each other was the perfect beat to push us over the edge.

"TY…TY…TY…"

"OH, GOD…FIONA…" The sea of orgasms kept coming. I couldn't hold on any longer. She grabbed my ass and…"FIONA!…" I came so hard I thought I was going to hurt her.

I collapsed on top of her and we melded against the bed wrapped in each other's arms until our bodies stopped shaking.

I couldn't move even if I wanted to. She had drained me, yet I was ready for more.

She wiped the sweat on the side of my face and kissed my shoulder. The gentleness was nice. She whispered, "That was incredible."

I rolled over onto the bed and pulled her to my side, rubbing her back. "I'm glad you came back."

She ran her hand along my abs and kissed my side. "Me, too."

Chapter 23
Fiona

I opened my eyes, looked around the very masculine room, and nothing looked familiar. I attribute the loss of memory to all the wine I had last night. Who am I kidding? I didn't have that much wine. I acted out of pure lust.

I tried to sit up, but I was sore. I looked around the room again and a wicked smile rose on my face. Memories of last night, and how I ended up in this incredibly comfortable king-sized bed, came back to my mind. I gingerly sat up, pulled the sheet across my breasts and raked my hand through my hair. I really needed to pee, but I could barely move.

I heard footsteps coming down the hall and looked at the partially open door. I inhaled, anxious for my eyes to confirm what my mind thought.

When the door opened I saw the reason why I was so sore and unable to move. My very own chocolate sex god. I got a little excited thinking about the things Ty did to me last night and this morning.

"You're awake," the deep sexy voice said as he walked towards the bed holding two large white mugs smiling.

"Please tell me that's coffee." I pulled the sheet tighter across my sore breasts, which was pointless. Not only had Ty seen them, he'd done things to them with his mouth and hands I didn't know was possible. I felt a flutter in my stomach thinking about how he brought me to orgasm merely with his tongue on my breast.

"You wanted coffee? I thought you were a tea drinker."

"I'll take whatever it is." He handed me the cup and the rich aroma infiltrated my nose. "Very funny." I took a few sips and sighed. "This is good."

He leaned down and pressed his lips against mine. "Good morning." He smiled.

"Good morning." I sipped more of the black magic or was Ty the black magic? Ty sat on the side of the bed. "How long have you been up?"

"Not too long." He sipped some coffee. "How did you sleep?"

I sighed, tossed my head back and then forward. "Uhmmm…good. I like your mattress." I smiled and looked around the room. "Nice."

He looked around. "Do you like it?"

"It's very you."

"I'll take that as a compliment." He smiled. "Hungry?"

"Starving." I sipped more coffee.

"You should be." He sipped more coffee.

"What's that supposed to mean?"

"You are…"

"I'm what?" I was nervous to hear his answer. Rhys said I wasn't very good in bed. But after the way my body reacted last night, maybe he was the one that was lousy in bed. I don't recall ever having that many orgasms in one love making session.

"Very aggressive and passionate."

"What?" I felt myself on the verge of panicking and searching for an apology for my poor performance.

He leaned in closer. "I like an aggressive woman." He smiled.

"Oh." I smiled. "You do?"

"It makes things spicy and energetic."

I bit my bottom lip. "I never thought of myself as aggressive."

"I don't have a problem with you telling me what you want." He sipped more coffee. "In or out of bed."

"You don't?" I sipped more coffee.

"No." He inched closer. "I find strong, passionate women very sexy, and you my sweet, are very sexy." He covered my mouth with his and pushed his tongue inside, kissing me hard. I felt myself falling back against the headboard. He pulled the sheet down, palmed my breast, kneading and tweaking my nipple. It wasn't long before the gentle caressing and massaging had turned me on. My hand began to shake as his touch became more aggressive. I never felt like this with Rhys. In fact, I don't recall ever having any kind of intimate encounter with him in the morning. I did good to get a peck on the cheek from him on his way out the door to the office.

This was very arousing. I could barely hold my cup. I managed to place my cup on the table without spilling any coffee, before succumbing to the body shakes.

He kissed me harder as his hand traveled the center of my body. I parted my legs and welcomed his thick fingers. He eased his fingers inside my heat and my eyes got wide. I couldn't believe what he was doing.

He moved his mouth across my cheek and kissed his way down my shoulder and then he brushed his warm tongue around my nipple. *Oh, God*...this man is incredible! He grabbed my nipple between his teeth, sucking and pulling. My nipples were still sore from him playing with them all night and this morning. How was it possible I longed for a repeat performance of his tongue on my nipples and breasts?

I started breathing harder and noticed he was still holding his coffee cup.

"Ba...ba...uhm...I...I need to...uhm...oh God...I..."

"What do you want?" he hummed in that deep, sexy voice that got me naked last night. He sipped more coffee and lathed my nipple with his coffee coated tongue.

"I...want..."

"I want a little chocolate with my coffee. What about you?"

He took my breast in his mouth and continued making love to it. *Holy crap!*...What was he doing to me? "I...I...I uhm...I...oh, man...I uhm..."

His fingers were curled up inside stroking me like he did last night. Thank God, I was sitting, because when he hit my sweet spot, I couldn't move. "Talk to me. Tell me what you want." He kissed my neck.

Talk to him. I couldn't think straight enough to form a simple sentence. He continued stroking my sweet spot. Then he brushed his thumb along my nub and... "Holy Crap!"

"Is that what you want?"

Unexpected Love

I grabbed the sheet and I rode his fingers to an orgasm so powerful it ripped through my body, leaving me drenched. I collapsed against the bed as the pleasure spasms riddled my body. I couldn't open my eyes.

He eased his fingers out, leaving me with the aftershocks of a powerful orgasm.

"You're beautiful when you give in to your pleasure," he whispered followed by a soft peck on my lips.

I felt the bed shift and through the orgasmic haze, I saw him stand up and then heard the water running in the bathroom. A few minutes later, I heard those familiar footsteps coming toward me. I opened my eyes and Ty was standing over me. He pulled the sheet back and helped me get out of bed. Then he helped me put on a robe and walked me to the bathroom.

I felt like a limp doll or a floundering fish, barely able to stand or breathe. We walked into the bathroom and he helped me out of the robe and into the bathtub.

"Relax while I get breakfast."

I sunk down into the tub and let the bubbles and warm water surround me. He kissed me and left.

I was pretty sure this wasn't how the morning after was supposed to go. With all the kitchen counter talk my girlfriends and I have shared, I've never heard any of them mention their lovers or husbands treating them like this. I rested my head against the back of the tub remembering how I got here.

I felt a wide smile rise on my face. I knew he was a good attorney, but I didn't know he was a pit bull at his job. I knew he was a nice guy, but I had no idea he was a badass when he needed to be. And I definitely didn't know he was as skilled a lover as he is. I clenched my legs remembering how he felt inside me.

"Ready to get out?"

I looked in the direction of the voice. "What?"

"You fell asleep." He smiled.

"I did?"

"Yes." He started towards the tub. "Need some help getting out?"

"A little." I braced my hands along the sides, stood up and Ty took my hands.

"Be careful."

I stepped over the side of the tub and placed my feet on the thick black rug. "Thank you."

"You're welcome." He wrapped a thick white towel around my shivering body. "I put a few things I thought you might need on the counter."

"Thank you." I looked over at the black marble bathroom counter and spotted the assortment of toiletries.

"I had your dressed pressed."

"What?"

"I had your dress steamed and it's hanging up in my closet, along with your lingerie."

"You had my lingerie cleaned?"

"My building has an excellent laundry." He winked.

"Thank you." I smiled.

"After breakfast, we'll pick Bentley up before heading over to your place. Now get dressed."

"Okay." He kissed me and I watched him walk out. I felt my mouth turn up into a wicked smile. "What have I done?"

I walked over to the counter, looked at myself in the mirror, and a sea of regret came over me. I had crossed a line I couldn't go back over. I had seduced my boyfriend. Me... sweet, naive Fiona Harris, seduced a man. Not just any man, but my ex-husband's ex-best friend.

Last night, I was sexy and confident. This morning, I'm confused and…what was I thinking? I know what part was doing the thinking. The part of me that wanted to have sex because it had been a long time. I know I shouldn't have spent the night with Ty. It goes against everything I believe. But in my defense, my thinking has been a little off since my marriage started doing a nosedive.

I got dressed and walked out into the living room. It was a lot easier walking in these shoes last night when I was a little tipsy. I walked over to the stove and stopped next to Ty.

"What do you need help with?"

He kissed me. "I have everything under control. Have a seat and I'll bring it over."

"Okay." I walked over to the table and gently sat down. The bath was excellent. However, I was still sore. Ty is much larger than I imagined. Another thing he and Rhys didn't have in common. I'm not complaining, but it's going to take some time for me to get used to his size.

I filled the cup with coffee and took a few sips.

"I hope you like it."

He placed the large white plate on the placemat in front of me. My eyes got wide, and I looked at him as he sat down across from me.

"Did you make this or is there a great restaurant in your building?" I teased.

He put his napkin in his lap. "Yes there's room service, but I made this."

"Wow. My boyfriend is a chef. Maybe I should have you do the food features for me." I smiled.

"I might be persuaded." He kissed my hand and then said grace. "Amen."

"Amen."

"This looks incredible."

"Thanks. Eat up."

დოდოდოდოდოდი

After two helpings of Ty's incredible praline French toast and bacon…hey, I worked up an appetite. I needed to replenish my strength. I helped him tidy up. Then we picked up Bentley and went back to my place.

"So, is there a camera in the elevator?" Ty asked. I sort of had a feeling I knew why he was asking, and the thought of what he wanted to do excited me.

"I'm not sure. Is there one in your building's elevator?" I asked coyly. I didn't look at him, although his hand was very active and a clear answer to my question.

"Yes." He kept looking straight ahead as his hand eased up my thigh.

"Is that why you were so well behaved?" He slid his hot thick finger under the strap of my suspender and my breath caught.

"I wouldn't say I was behaved." He brushed my thigh and I clutched Bentley's leash a little tighter.

"I…I uhm…" He eased his finger further up and along my butt cheek. My heart started racing.

"Were you saying something?" He continued to massage my behind and the effects of his touch were becoming evident in other areas of my body. I was starting to feel warm and tingly all over, and that flutter I felt right before I came the first time, was there. "I love the way this lace feels on your skin." I inhaled trying not to give in to the sensations his finger was causing. I looked up to see how much longer before we got to my floor. "I like it even better when my mouth is sucking on your nipple through the lace." He kept his eyes aimed at the door and squeezed my butt harder.

"I...I..." I grabbed the railing, breathing hard, trying not to fall down.

"Of course, if you were sure there were no cameras, I would be sucking that hard nipple like a ripe sweet berry. Ummm...I can taste it now."

Oh, God....This man is incredible. I almost came behind that statement. I closed my eyes and tried to collect myself. Instead, I pictured him doing what he just said and I got weak in the knees. Last night when he laved his warm, wet tongue on my breast, I came so quickly it scared me.

I looked up. We were almost to my floor. I didn't know how much more of this I could take. Between his words and his hand on my behind, I was so wound up, the least little jolt was likely to push me over the edge.

He stopped squeezing my behind, and started rubbing it. The warm, slightly hard touches were more erotic than him squeezing it. My heart sped up. I could barely breathe. It felt like I was going to pass out.

"Then I would drag my finger along the inside of your hot thick silky thigh all the way up to..."

Ding...Ding...Ding... The elevator stopped and the door opened.

Oh, God...I lifted myself up off the wall of the elevator and stepped out into my loft. "We're home, Bentley."

Bark...Bark...Bark...Bark...

I unhooked his leash. "Go play." I slowly stood up and started taking my coat off when I felt another pair of hands. "Thank you." I slipped my coat off and turned to face Ty. "I need to change."

"Okay."

I went down the hall to my closet and stood there breathing hard. Oh, my God. I couldn't believe I was actually considering getting busy with my boyfriend in the elevator. I went into the bathroom, wet a towel, placed it on my face, and counted to ten. I needed to clear my head.

I changed clothes and went back to join Ty. I quietly walked up behind him, slipped my hands around his waist and kissed his back. He lifted one of my hands up and kissed it. Then he turned around to face me. That beautiful smile was mesmerizing. I pictured those full soft lips traveling the length of my body doing some of the things they did last night.

"I was thinking." He slipped his hands around my waist and pulled me closer, and I could feel the bulge in his pants pressing against my stomach.

"So was I." He smiled and buried his face in my neck and I giggled.

"What do you have planned for this afternoon?"

"I was thinking about running a few errands." He eased his hand under my t-shirt. His hot hand felt good gliding along my skin. "What did you have in mind?" he asked as he cupped my breast in his hand, gently caressing.

"I...I was thinking maybe we could, I don't know, maybe pick up where we left off." He pulled back and looked at me. "Or maybe you could do those things you were talking about in the elevator."

He lowered his hands and locked eyes with me. "Are you asking me to spend the afternoon making love to you?"

I inhaled and owned my request. "Yes. I want you to spend the rest of the day and evening, and possibly tomorrow morning with me." He was stoic and that answered my question. "Never mind. I shouldn't have…"

He grabbed my face in his large hands and kissed me hungrily. His hands moved down my body, and he scooped me up into his arms as I wrapped my legs around his waist. I wrapped my arms around his neck, never taking my mouth away from his.

He walked down the hall to my bedroom and dropped me onto the bed. I raised up on my elbows and watched him take his t-shirt off and my mouth began to water. God, his body is incredible. Chest like finely carved dark brown marble…. arms like sledge hammers…legs like carved stone pillars…an ass so finely sculpted it should be a crime to cover it.

My face felt warm thinking about how he felt inside me. My mouth slowly turned up into a smile, and my body started to ache and throb at the thought of him doing some of the things he did last night.

I sat up, slipped out of my shorts, grabbed the hem of my t-shirt, and started to lift it up.

"No." The vibrato in his tone startled me. It was forceful and sexy. I thought I was directing this production. He did say he would do whatever I wanted.

"No?"

"No." He stepped closer. "Lay down." This was new. Then again, anything I do with Ty will be new considering our brief sexual history. I nervously followed his directive. I have to admit, I like when he takes charge.

He got down on his knees, spread my legs and the rush made my skin prickle, heart race and… *Oh, God!*…was he about to…. Then I felt his mouth on the inside of my thigh. The slow tentative kisses to my skin was…*Oh, God!*…his lips are incredible. Then I felt a familiar warm wet sensation traveling up the inside of my other thigh. *Oh, God!*…The closer his mouth got to my knickers the more excited I got.

The heat of his body and the excitement of him being there was so hot. I closed my eyes while enjoying the sensations from his mouth. That's when I felt a rush of warm air on top of my knickers and...*Holy Crap!*...He pushed my t-shirt up, moved his mouth up and dragged it around my navel before dipping it inside and making love to my navel with his mouth. Jesus...I never suspected I could be aroused there.

He reached under my t-shirt, grabbed one of my breasts and...Okay, so I was hoping he would acquiesce to my request, so I didn't bother to put a bra on. *Good God*...I was trying to breathe. But then that sneaky sex machine slid his finger inside my knickers, hooked it around my nub and...*OH, MY JESUS... WHAT THE*.... I had lost the ability to speak. It was like I was on a rollercoaster. *DAMN!* Every inch of my body was orgasming, if that's even possible. Talk about playing me. Just as my clitoral orgasm was subsiding, he did that thing to my navel with his tongue and it sent me flying. I was still in a fog when he consumed my breast, and I took off again. It's like he was playing a finely orchestrated concerto on my body.

As the last spasm subsided, he stopped. I lay there in a pool of ecstasy, breathing hard. I was spent and beginning to wonder if I could handle twenty four hours of this kind of loving.

He leaned over me, smiling. "My beauty, are you ready for more?"

What woman wouldn't want another taste of that?! I nodded, "Yes."

He slid my knickers down my rubber band legs, slipped my t-shirt over my head, and took my breast in his mouth. It didn't take long for me to reach the edge. The soft, wet, warm feel of his tongue teasing my nipple was just as I remembered from this morning. Between his mouth and hands, I didn't know which was more powerful at this point, and I didn't care. All I wanted was another one of those mind blowing orgasms.

I felt my eyes roll back and my body stiffened. *YES… OH YES…YES…*He'd done it again. This orgasm was more powerful than the last. I tried to open my eyes, but they refused to cooperate. Before my body could get back to a rested state, he was conducting another verse of the orgasm concerto… *HOLY JESUS…WHAT THE…*my body was on fire. This can't be possible. How am I able to come like this? It felt like every muscle was locked and Ty's thick finger was the key.

I was spent and we hadn't even gotten to the main course. He brushed the side of my face and kissed my forehead. "Do you want to stop?" He stroked the side of my arm. "We have all afternoon, tonight and tomorrow." He smiled.

I know I should have said no, but I had yet to get what I really wanted…him. He had served up several amazing orgasms, but I had yet to feel him inside me.

I swallowed. "No."

He kissed me and climbed out of bed. I looked at his thick fingers as he unbuttoned his jeans and slid them down followed by his black boxer briefs. My God, he's huge. I still can't believe I was able to handle all of him. He's magnificent. He climbed on top of me and nestled his hips in between my thighs and slowly slid inside me. We got into a steady rhythm as he rocked back and forth. The waves of pleasure were building and…*HOLY JESUS…*He dove his tongue inside my mouth and started doing something indescribable. I told myself, don't think, just enjoy.

He continued his rhythm and kissing me. He lifted my legs, driving deeper and harder. The sensations were rising as he sped up his rhythm. He lowered his mouth to my nipple and sucked and licked greedily as he drove deeper inside me. The warmth of his mouth on my breast and his deep thrusts sent my body into a tailspin. *Oh, God*…my orgasm was rising. He reached down, stroked my nub and Holy Jesus!…I started thrashing and shaking. Each spasm was more intense than the last. I collapsed and tried to recover, but that wasn't possible.

He grabbed my behind and began to rock inside me. He pulled me against him with my breasts were pressed against his hard chest. My nipples were still very sensitive, but I liked the feel of his skin brushing next to mine.

He started moving faster and deeper touching me like…it was like he was branding me. I started to tremble and, *Oh, God*…I can't believe what he's doing to me.

He lifted my legs higher, pinned my hands down and started pounding deeper and harder. *Oh, God*…I started to tighten and knew I couldn't hold on much longer. I looked at him and he had that same pained look on his face he had last night right before he climaxed. He started moving faster and I could feel him trembling.

"OH, GOD, FI…FIONA…OH, GOD…FIONA…"

His movements became animalistic. He was wild and every push he made just intensified the fire growing inside me. I knew I was close.

He grabbed my nipple between his teeth and, "SWEET BABY JESUS…" Where did that come from? It felt like someone opened the door on an airplane and all the air was sucked out.

I screamed so loud it pushed Ty over the edge and we collapsed on the bed. I couldn't move even if I wanted to, not with two hundred pounds of hot throbbing muscle on top of me breathing hard. I closed my eyes, enjoying the feel of him inside me. Rhys never embraced me like this after sex. He was always in a hurry to get up.

I brushed the beads of sweat on the sides of Ty's face and kissed his shoulder. He raised up and looked at me, then pressed his lips against mine in a sweet kiss.

"I'm glad you asked me to stay." He smiled.

"Me, too."

Chapter 24
Ty

"Tasha, would you come in here...thank you."

I didn't look up when the door opened and closed.

"What are you doing here? You're supposed to be meeting with Morris Ellis."

"I rescheduled my breakfast meeting."

"Why?"

"Because I needed a little more time to…"

"Tiberius Wells, look at me," she said sternly.

I looked up at the woman talking to me like my mother and not the assistant she was hired to be.

"What?"

Her eyes got wide. "You had sex."

"Is that coffee?" I reached for the cup she placed on my desk.

"You aren't even going to deny it." She sat down. "Please tell me you didn't go back to that skank, Julia."

"What….no." I sipped my coffee.

"Oh, my God. It's worse than I thought. You and Fiona had sex."

I sipped some more coffee. "I need you to…"

"Don't you dare ignore me. Dish."

"Excuse me?"

"Tell me everything and don't leave anything out." She sipped her coffee.

"I'm not talking to you about my sex life."

"So you two did have sex." She smirked.

I exhaled. "Yes. Happy?"

"Well?"

"Well, what?"

"How did you go from taking it slow to…," she looked at me, sipped more coffee and continued, "sex all weekend."

"It wasn't all weekend."

"Okay, so you took breaks to eat. However, if I had spent the weekend in bed I'd be exhausted. So how's Fiona?" She smiled.

"What?"

"I'm waiting."

"For…."

"Details. How did you end up spending the weekend in bed, the floor, sofa, counter, shower, against the window, on the balcony…"

"Where do you get this stuff?" I sipped more coffee.

"Are you serious? I've been to your apartment. That place is made for sex."

"What's that supposed to mean?"

"Love you like a big brother. But, you know your place was designed for wild sexy encounters."

"You make it sound like I have a sex den."

"Not hardly. All I'm saying is, you expect me to believe you've never had sex in any of the places I mentioned?"

"I refuse to answer on the…"

"Yeah…yeah…yeah…shame on you taking advantage of her."

"She seduced me."

She almost choked on her coffee. "I'm sorry. What did you say?"

"She seduced me." I sipped more coffee.

Her eyes got wide and she threw a fist into the air. "Way to go Fiona. I knew there was a vixen buried in there. So…"

"So, what?"

"Do you want me to choke you?"

"We need to get you a man." I smiled.

"That's what I've been saying." She shifted in her chair. "So…"

"You aren't going to leave this alone until I tell you, are you?"

"You finally understand how this is going to work. Until I get a man, I'm forced to rely on you and Jake for romance. God, I'm pathetic. So, let's have it."

"When we talked earlier in the week, she suggested we have dinner on Friday when I got back."

"Listen to my girl calling the shots."

I shook my head. "She came over, we flirted a lot and she left."

"Excuse me? Where's the meat? What was the setting? I don't want to hear any of this, she came over, we ate and then had sex all weekend. I want details. Wait a minute, did you say she left?"

"Yes."

"Start from the beginning."

I sighed. "Okay, let me see. She brought dinner, spent most of the evening flirting and when I thought we were headed to a different kind of dessert, she left."

"Uh-huh."

"About a half hour later, she came back." I leaned back in my chair. "She was different, very sexy, aggressive." I smiled. "I have to admit, she caught me by surprise. I never would have...she uhm...," I bit my bottom lip and tried not to smile.

"Better than Julia?"

"I'm not...," I leaned forward and rested my elbows on my desk and rubbed my chin. "I remember something Rhys said shortly after he married Fi. He said he didn't know if he had the patience to deal with a virgin."

"Wait a minute. Fiona has only been with two men, you and Rhys?"

"Yeah and he constantly complained."

"Then why did he..."

"He said she had the body, but didn't know how to use it."

"We're talking about the same woman with the incredible behind?"

"Yeah." I leaned back in my chair. "From what I experienced, not only does she have a dangerous set of curves, she definitely knows how to use them."

"Really?" Tasha smiled.

"I didn't mean for that to come out."

"Now that it has. Fiona or Julia?"

"Definitely, Fiona."

"Really?" She raised her right eyebrow. "She put it on you like that?"

"I used my last muscle relaxer last night." I smiled and I wrung out my back.

"That explains the message from your doctor."

"Yeah, I think I did something to my back."

"Way to go, Fiona."

"Stop it, Tasha."

"What? I knew she'd be good for you."

"You did?"

"Yes. Look at you. You never looked like this, nor did you ever come back worn out from your weekends with prim and proper Julia."

"Julia had her…"

"Please, keep telling yourself things were good between you two."

"What does that mean?"

"It means, Julia didn't appreciate you and clearly she didn't handle her business in bed." She sipped more coffee.

"That's not…"

"Not to brag, but I've been the seductress a few times."

"Like last week." I smirked.

"That was someone scratching an itch."

"I see."

"As I was saying. I've been the seductress and it was very satisfying for both parties."

"What are you talking about?"

She shook her head smiling. "You have no idea what happened to you, do you?"

"Clearly I don't."

She stood up and started pacing. "Let me guess what happened. You said Fiona came over, flirted and then left."

"Yes."

"She left because she was hoping you would make the first move, and when you didn't, she left."

"So you're saying if I had made the first move things would have gone differently? I didn't make the first move because I didn't want her to feel like I was pressuring her."

"Uh-huh. What was she wearing?"

"A wrap dress."

She nodded. "And the shoes?"

"Black red bottom stilettos…"

"When she called you earlier in the week, I bet she was very flirty and suggestive in her conversation."

"How did you…"

"I told you, I've played this game before."

"So I got played."

"No, you got laid. I bet she kissed you so hard you, uhm…let's just say you felt it deep."

I shifted in my chair. "Go on."

"Then she did a little striptease."

"Yes, on the way to the bedroom. How did you…"

She sat down. "There was never any doubt you were going to get the booty. It was a matter of how it was going to be served."

"She did say Bentley was at a sleepover."

"Because she planned to be at one as well."

"She did say something like that." I wiped my mouth.

"You said you told her to tell you when she was ready to take the next step."

"Yes."

"She really wanted you to tell her it was time."

"And I didn't."

"So when she came back, she was determined to make

sure you knew she was ready and in charge."

"But I took the lead."

"Only because she let you." She smiled and shook her head.

"That's not quite true. I told Fi I would do whatever she wanted."

"Oooh, okay…" She nodded. "I see your game."

"What are you talking about?"

"Now I see why you have women falling at your feet. You're good looking, but…"

"What are you talking about?"

"You smooth talking rascal. You never push, you merely guide them where you want them to go. Dude, you are smooth."

I smiled at her because she was sort of telling the truth. I've slept with a few women, but I've never forced myself on them. I've always made sure it was what they wanted to do. "I wouldn't…"

"Please don't play a player."

"You know the saying, don't hate the player, hate the game." I smirked at her statement.

"Exactly, my girl played you."

I sat up and leaned my elbows on the desk. "I did not get played. In fact, when I took her home, I…"

"Let me guess, that's when you blew your back out."

"Not to brag, but yeah."

She smiled and shook her head. "I bet you went above and beyond to make sure she was satisfied." She cocked her head and looked at me. "And from the look on your face, and the need for muscle relaxers, you made that happen multiple times."

"Yes, I did." I have to admit I was proud of my

performance this weekend. I would never tell Tasha she was right, but yes, I never returned from a weekend with Julia feeling this satisfied.

"I have to give my girl credit. For a woman you said has only had two lovers, she played you like a pro." She shook her head smiling. "That little scenario is only played by an experienced seductress. I love it.   She's my hero."

"I can't believe I'm about to ask this. So what do I do next?"

"Enjoy the ride and stock up on muscle relaxers."

Chapter 25
Fiona

Knock...Knock...Knock...

"Come in," the strong deep voice called out.

I pushed the door open and stood still taking in his form. Even hunched over a pile of papers, he was incredible.

He looked up and his bright, sexy smile arrested me. I liked seeing him in a crisp dress shirt, with the sleeves rolled up and his veiny forearms exposed, leading to those large hands and strong fingers. Those are the hands that held me this past weekend. Those are also the hands that did some incredible things to my body, that I will never forget and long to experience again.

"Hey."

"Hey, yourself." He put down his pen, stood up and

walked towards me.

Man, is my boyfriend hot. The way he moves is like a dancer...fluid and sure. Each step he made towards me, reminded me that I had seen him naked walking towards me with the same surety. That I had touched that carved, muscular, chocolate body. That I had tasted that rich dark skin. That I had my mouth on him and...

I closed the door, started walking toward him and my heart began to race. What is going on with me? The way I have been behaving lately is very out of character for me. Not only did I have illicit, hot sex with a man I'm not married to, I initiated it. That's so not me. That's not the woman I know. And what's even worse, I'm here visiting my boyfriend, hoping he might be as frisky as I am. That's a lie. I'm here hoping for a little lunchtime action from him.

I'm not saying I want him to take me on the sofa, or the credenza, or his desk even. Or possibly his desk chair, which could be very interesting and proof those private Pilates classes are worth every penny. But I'm saying I wouldn't be opposed to a taste of his magic touch.

We met in the middle of his office, and he wrapped his arms around me. I can't remember Rhys ever being excited to see me in the middle of the day, and we worked in the same building.

I crushed my lips against his and kissed him hard and long. His hands slid down my back to my behind, and my body began to heat up. Being in his presence was like being in the presence of that sinfully delightful dessert you know you shouldn't eat but can't resist, so eat anyway. I shouldn't be here, but I couldn't stand not to be.

He pulled me closer and every muscle in his chest pressed against mine allowing me to take in his exquisite, intoxicating cologne. I almost forgot what I said about not taking advantage of him in his office. His tongue dove deeper inside my mouth and the way his body began to react, I don't think either of us would have objected to some lunchtime office lovin'.

Standing in the middle of his office trading deep moans, my mind went back to Saturday night and that shower we took. I never knew getting clean could be so dirty. I don't know what it was about Ty, but he seemed to have brought out a side of me I never knew existed. Dare I think of myself as a vixen…seductress? More like desperate and horny divorcee.

I moved my mouth along his jaw to his ear and whispered, "Is that how you like being kissed at work?"

"I like being kissed like that anytime." He kissed my neck and we pulled apart. "Come, let's sit down." He took my hand and led me over to the sofa and we sat down. "So, what brings you over here?"

"I wanted to see you."

His eyes got wide. "You did?"

"Yes."

He pecked my lips. "Are you hungry?"

Hungry? Of course I'm hungry but not for food. I rubbed my hand along the inside of his strong muscular thigh and he spread his legs a little wider.

"I could eat something." I smiled.

He cleared his throat.

I reached up and grabbed his ear between my teeth and inched my hand further up his thigh.

"Fi…don't…"

"I didn't see Tasha at her desk."

"True, but Tasha will be back any moment." He cleared his throat. "You didn't answer my question."

I moved my hand up further and his breath caught. "Which was?"

"Are you hungry?"

Bzzzz…Bzzzz…Bzzzz…

He pressed the button on the phone next to the sofa. "Yes?"

"I'm about to order lunch. Do you want me to order anything for you and Fiona?"

I looked at Ty with wide eyes.

"Where are you ordering from?" he asked.

"You tell me."

"Give us a couple of minutes." He removed his finger from the speaker button.

I sat up. "How did she know I was here? No one was out front when I got here."

"It's Tasha. She knows everything."

"Everything? Does she know about this past weekend?"

"What do you want to eat?"

"Oh, my God, she does. Why did you tell her?"

"I didn't tell her, she told me." He stroked the side of my arm.

"What?"

"She looked at me and pretty much told me how my weekend went."

"Oh, my God. She probably thinks we're in here…" I looked away from him. "Never mind."

"What were you going to say?"

"Forget it." I stood up and walked over to the window. "Order Italian with lots of garlic."

"Eating garlic isn't going to make me not kiss you."

I looked over my shoulder. "It isn't?"

"Nope." He pressed the intercom button on the phone.

"Tasha, we'll take two orders of spaghetti with meat sauce and two orders of meatballs. And an order of garlic knots with extra garlic." He smiled.

"Are you sure you want to do that?" she asked.

"Yes. Thanks."

"I'll let you know when it gets here." Click.

I rubbed my head. "She probably thinks we're in here…"

He walked over, wrapped his hands around my waist, pulled me close, and we touched foreheads. "What?"

"She probably thinks we're in here making out or even worse, having sex."

"Would that be so bad?" He smiled.

I stepped out of his hold. "Are you insane?"

"Come on Fi, isn't that why you came over here?"

I folded my arms in front of my chest pretending to pout. "No."

"No?" He walked back to his desk and sat down.

"Is that it?"

"I'm going to do some more work until lunch gets here."

"I guess I'll go out and talk to Tasha." I started towards the door.

"Okay. Let me know when lunch gets here." He directed his attention to his computer.

"Are you serious?"

"About?"

"Fine." I continued the short distance to the door.

"What do you want?"

"Excuse me?"

"What do you want? Clearly you had something in mind when you came to see me."

"Do I need a reason to see my boyfriend?"

"No, but you do need to explain why you're getting upset."

"I'm not…"

"Come here," he said sternly, not looking at me. The way he uttered those two words was a panty dropper.

I collected myself and stood my ground. "No." I waited for him to get up and come to me, but he didn't. I looked at him and he never took his eyes off of his computer. We were at a stand still. He had me at a disadvantage. I desperately wanted to feel his hands on me and apparently the only way that was going to happen, was for me to walk over to him.

I inhaled and walked over to the desk and waited for him to say something or at least acknowledge my presence.

He stood up and our eyes locked. "What…do…you…want?"

I tried to copy his forceful tone. "Kiss me."

"Is that what you want?"

"No."

He stepped closer and it felt like the heat from his body had absorbed all the cool air in the space. This man in no way resembles the laid back, meek man who would come over to our place and watch the game with my ex-husband. This man was sexy, charismatic, powerful and able to…

"Then what…do you…want?" I felt those few words deep in my core.

If I were being honest with myself, I'd be standing in front of him naked, begging him to throw me on his desk and make me come so hard I passed out.

I inhaled and watched as his eyes got dark looking at the swell of my breast. "I want to feel your mouth and hands all over me. I want to feel your tongue teasing my nipples until I cry out. I want to feel your large strong fingers stroking that tight bundle of nerves that makes me come over and over again." I stepped closer and took a deep breath. "I want you to make love to me like you did the first time."

Without missing a beat he responded. "I can't do that."

"Why not?"

"Because what you want and what I desire to do, aren't things that can be accomplished in the course of a lunch time." He stepped closer and his chest grazed my swollen breasts. A soft moan escaped my mouth. God, this man is incredible. He leaned in to my ear and I started breathing harder. He hadn't said anything or touched me. How was it possible for him to have this kind of effect on me? My body was on fire.

He brushed his finger along my swollen nipple and I almost came. How was that even possible? We were both fully clothed and simply talking. He kissed my ear and his hot, sweet breath traveled the length of my body and hit my core. If he agreed, I'd be naked on that sofa or pressed up against the window. I didn't care if anyone saw us, because I was just that desperate to have him inside me.

I was barely holding on.

He inched closer and whispered, "What you want, requires my undivided attention and several uninterrupted hours. Are you willing to devote the time required to bring your desires to life?"

My body was shaking, and it felt like I would crash at any moment. I swallowed and spit out my answer. "Yes."

He stroked the side of my arm with the tip of his strong finger and a swell of pleasure traveled the length of my body and I fell backwards into the chair in front of his desk, breathing hard. Damn him!

Chapter 26
Ty

The elevator stopped and when the door opened, I was greeted by something I hadn't really expected, but was glad to see.

"Hey, baby," she purred.

I swallowed hard and dared myself not to blink. I thought if I blinked, I'd discover this was an illusion, or even worse, a dream. However, the tightness in my trousers was proof this wasn't a dream. Or was it? Even in my dreams, when Fiona greeted me like this, I had the same physical reaction.

I stepped out of the elevator and looked around the loft at the scene she had set. Unlike the other night at my place, things had been calculated with precision to her advantage.

I tried to contain my excitement, but that was difficult.

I suspected this passionate phase in our relationship would be short lived. So I made a decision to take great care in enjoying every opportunity I was presented.

I have to be honest, I never would have pegged Fiona for the sexy, vixen type. Especially after my conversations with Rhys.

Shortly after he and Fiona were married, he complained about her lack of experience and complacency. If this was complacent, I'd be scared to know what excited was like.

I know we've only slept together once. Well, that's not correct. What we did had nothing to do with sleep, and it really couldn't be classed as once. Not when you spend the entire weekend in bed. Well, that's not exactly correct either. I didn't want Tasha to know she was right about everything. It was bad enough she was on point about Fi and I having sex. She didn't need to have her suspicions confirmed. Although she was right. We had sex all over my apartment on Friday, and pretty much every where Fi desired at hers.

This past weekend was one of the best sexual experiences of my life. Man, that woman has got a magic touch. And the way her body responded to me was incredible.

Looking at her standing before me now in a robe that barely covered her swollen breasts, made it very clear what she wanted to do this evening.

My eyes slowly took in every inch of her and I caught myself before I started drooling like a horny, idiot, teenage boy looking at a nearly naked woman for the first time.

Fi's curves were real unlike Julia's manufactured ones. Fi has the body of a voluptuous woman. Tasha was right, her ass is perfection. It's what great sculptors would travel the world over to see for themselves, then replicate for history. I was a little circumspect about its authenticity, until it was backed up against me. But the way that beautiful, perfectly carved mound of flesh felt in my hands as I squeezed, examined and kissed, confirmed it was one of God's best creations.

The thought of that beautiful ass pressed against me, made me glad I'm the one that gets to enjoy it.

So when I replay my conversations with Rhys about him and Fi, I realize the person that wasn't sexually fulfilled or excited in their relationship wasn't him, but Fiona. It's the only thing that makes sense, because this sexy siren standing before me in no way sounds like the woman Rhys described.

She is more sensual, passionate, sexy, open and erotic than any woman I've been with. I had a difficult time leaving her on Sunday evening. If I hadn't been so exhausted and sore, I would have stayed the night like I did Saturday.

And here she is presenting herself to me again.

"Hey, yourself." I stepped closer. "So, are we eating in or…"

She slowly strutted over and stopped in front of me with her parfum infiltrating the air. I couldn't quite put my finger on the scent, but it had an enticing effect on me. She stepped closer, inhaled and her robe opened a little more almost exposing her nipples. She tilted her head and slowly dragged her tongue along her shiny red bottom lip before sucking on the corner and exhaling again. Damn, this woman is sexy and the power she has over me is profound.

She stepped deeper into the small space separating us and the only thing keeping our skin from touching was the thin silk of her robe and the cotton of my shirt.

She aimed those mesmerizing dark brown eyes at me and that sexy gaze sent a jolt straight to my core. My body and mind were at war. My body said, take her now, screw her plan. But my mind said, it's her party and I'm merely a guest. I must wait to be served.

"I was thinking we could order something in," she purred.

I didn't care if we didn't eat. All I wanted to do was bury myself deep in between those hot thick thighs, and fill my mouth with those supple breasts and hard nipples that were screaming to be set free.

"Really? What did you have in mind?"

"Uhm....I'm not sure. What did you have a taste for?" She eased her finger inside my shirt, dragged it across my nipple, and I let out a deep growl.

"Uhm...what I have a taste for isn't on a takeout menu." My hands slid down her back, under the hem of her short robe connecting with her hot, soft skin.

"It isn't?" she purred.

"No."

"What I have a taste for is something that not only awakens my taste buds, but satisfies my desires."

"Uhmmm...sounds like something I might enjoy as well."

"I'm sure you will."

She stepped out of my hold and started toward the back of the loft. "Coming?" She looked over her shoulder, smiling. I watched as she repeated that stroll she did the other night. The way she tossed those hips was so sensuous and mesmerizing. It was like watching a wave crash against a cliff. Not only was it beautiful to watch, it was awe inspiring the amount of pressure the simple move had.

She continued down the hall with me following her. When I reached the bathroom, I was surprised to see the scene she had laid out. The only light was coming from the sea of candles on the counters surrounding the huge freestanding tub. There was sensuous music bouncing off the walls.

I was impressed and excited. No woman had ever done anything like that for me.

She turned and faced me. "Take off your clothes," she commanded.

I like it when she's strong and forceful. She walked over and leaned against the counter with her hands folded in front of her watching me. I stepped deeper into her lair and showed I knew how to follow orders. It was a toss up to see who was more excited at my strip tease, her or me.

I took the last piece of clothing off and stood next to the large soaking tub waiting for instructions.

"Get into the tub."

Another order I had no problem following. I liked the showers we shared, but I had a feeling I was going to like this even more.

I climbed into the tub and let the warm, scented water cover me. After the trying day I'd had, this was much welcomed. I looked up and noticed she was still leaned up against the counter and still clothed.

"Are you going to join me?" I asked.

She untied her robe, eased it off her shoulders and let it fall to the floor in a puddle around her feet. God, she was beautiful. She stepped out of her slippers, walked over and extended her hand to me, I helped her climb into the tub and sit down.

"Why are you way over there?" I asked. Then I felt her foot on me and I jumped.

"What did you say?" She smiled.

"You don't play fair."

"Who said anything about playing fair?" She inched her soft foot further up my chest. I grabbed her foot and started to massage it. She tossed her head back and exhaled. "That feels good."

"This is a surprise."

"Is it?" I felt her other foot dance along my leg. "So you've never shared a bath?"

I searched my mind for an answer. "I don't believe I have."

"If it takes you that long to answer, then you haven't."

I continued to massage her foot. "I can't believe I'm thinking this. Is this something you…"

"No."

"How did you know what I was going to ask?"

"You were going to ask if this is something Rhys and I did and the answer is no."

I put her foot down and picked up the other one. "So, who have you shared a bath with?"

"No one," she said as she played with the bubbles.

"Really?" I smiled.

"I wasn't kidding. You and Rhys are the only two men I've been with."

"You…don't take this the wrong way, but the way you move in bed…is… it's just…how…"

She shrugged her shoulders. "I don't know."

I looked around the bathroom. "And this…how did you come up with something so not you?"

"What do you mean, not me?"

"This scene looks like something a woman who…no offense, a more experienced woman would do."

She nodded. "I have a vivid imagination." She smiled.

"Vivid is an understatement." I smiled.

"I wish I could take credit for this, but I read it in a blog." She covered her face with her hands and the bubbles parted and revealed her beautiful breasts.

I quickly brought my eyes back to hers. "What?"

"It was a post on ways to keep the steam in your relationship outside of the bed."

"Really?"

She put her foot down and picked up one of mine and proceeded to massage my foot with her delicate hands.

"How's that?"

I sighed. "I see what you mean. I needed this. Uhm... tell me about this blog."

"I'm considering a relationship section for CHIC. So I've been doing a lot of research."

"Was last weekend research or..."

Her mouth turned up into a wicked smile. "Will you be angry if I say yes?"

I thought about it. If being with a magazine editor means I get to be a guinea pig, sign me up. "No."

"Yes and no. I came over with the intention of making love, but I had no idea you were going to react the way you did."

"I see." She continued to massage my foot.

"I came back and decided to try something I read."

"Which was..."

"Take charge. I still can't believe I did that." She smiled.

"Well, you did." I inched my other foot up the inside of her leg. "What else did the post suggest?"

"A bubble bath, a sensuous picnic at home, read a steamy book together..."

"Steamy?" I smirked.

"Okay, it said erotica, but I didn't think we needed to go that far."

"And yet, we're sharing a bubble bath."

"And?"

"I'm just sayin'. Continue."

"Let's see, there was steamy scrabble, twenty questions and truth or dare. Oh, and striptease night."

"I could get with that last one." I smiled.

"Really? So you'd be open to giving me a little strip tease show?"

"I just did." I reminded her.

"That was nice, but it's not what I'm talking about. I want a Magic Mike show, complete with music and costumes."

"You know that works both ways." I raised an eyebrow and smiled.

"Meaning?"

"If, and I'm not saying I'd be your private dancer, but if I were to acquiesce to your suggestion, I would expect the same from you."

"Meaning?" she smiled.

"You know what I mean. If, I become your private dancer, I better get the same from you."

"I'm not saying no, and I'm not saying yes. However, if we chose to play that game, I'm pretty sure I'd have the upper hand."

"Really?" I smiled.

"Let's be real, baby. Have you seen what I'm working with?" She tilted her head and smiled. "I'm just sayin'"

"Point made and taken." She put my foot down. "I want to ask you something."

"Are we adding twenty questions to the mix tonight?" She smiled.

"Maybe." She dragged her foot along my abs and I almost forgot what I wanted to ask her. "If you had it to do all over, would you marry Rhys?"

"Would I have the knowledge I have now?"

"Yes."

"Then I can't give you an answer."

"Why not?"

"Question number two." She smiled. "Because the variables are too vast. I can't say I wouldn't marry Rhys, because the things that drew me to him are still there. In spite of how he deceived me, he's still a charming, charismatic, and attractive man."

"I see."

"Now if you ask me would I marry him if I knew his character as well as I do, the answer would be no."

"That's the same question."

"Not really. There's character and then there's morality. His deceiving me about wanting a family is what really caused the split."

"I don't understand."

"He led me to believe that we were on the same page. When in reality, we never were. He said he married me because he needed a showpiece, someone to make him look respectable and successful. I was merely a piece in the puzzle of his life." She sighed. "But if I hadn't married him, I never would have met you."

"You don't think we would have met without Rhys being part of the mix?"

"Which question is this?"

"I don't know. I lost track. So?"

"What was the question again?"

"Do you think we would have met without Rhys in the mix?"

She tossed her head back, looked up and then returned her gaze to me. "I don't know. Let's say we met without knowing Rhys, what chance is there we would have become friends or been attracted to each other?"

"Interesting."

"We're being honest, right?"

"Yes."

"If I had seen you on the street, at a party or wherever, you would have caught my attention. My immediate reaction would have been, he's attractive, but not my type. If I had the privilege to get to know you, I…" She suddenly stopped. "Can we change the subject?"

"No. I want to continue this. What were you going to say?"

She exhaled. "I didn't keep you as my lawyer, to spite Rhys. I kept you because I felt bad about how Rhys treated you. Our lunches allowed me to see a side of you I had never seen. I," she sucked on the corner of her bottom lip, "I uhm…I realized I kept seeing you because I was attracted to you."

My brow furrowed and I shifted positions. "What?"

"Which is strange to me, because you aren't my type."

"I'm not?"

"No. I've generally been attracted to a much shorter man with fair skin. And I never would date a man so strong."

"I hope there's a compliment coming."

"Here it is. I never would have thought a guy like you would be attracted to me."

"What?"

"When I first met you, I thought, this guy probably has a line of model girlfriends twelve miles long."

"That's what you thought?"

"Yeah. And once I got to know you, I realized you were a nice guy."

"I am."

"But when I saw you in action with my divorce, I saw a side I never knew you had."

"Which was?"

"Badass." She smiled.

"Badass?"

"Oh, yeah. The way you took charge and fought for me was so hot. That afternoon, I didn't see Ty my friend and legal advisor. I saw Tiberius, my badass lawyer and protector."

"I had no idea." I smiled.

"Rhys never treated me like that. I always felt like I had no one on my side."

"I'm sorry, he led me to believe things were a lot different between you two."

"Well, things weren't as they seemed. In or out of bed."

"I see that now."

Chapter 27
Fiona

"Hey, Babe." The deep sexy voice that normally sent a chill through me had a strange heaviness on it.

"What's wrong?"

He sighed deeply. "These negotiations are wearing me down. I didn't expect it to be this difficult. My client was all set to sign the papers for the buyout. However, the seller is stalling. We have been waiting over a month for them to give her an answer," he sighed again. "She's close to walking away."

"She?" I tried not to let that little bit of information effect me. "You didn't say your client was a woman."

"Yes. Mrs. Grant. Wait a minute, are you jealous?"

"What? Please." I felt myself getting a little annoyed. He left our date to go be with some other woman. My man is in Miami with some woman. I know why she won't sign those papers, she's probably seen Ty without a shirt. How dare he walk around without a shirt on. She's probably got him rubbing sunscreen on her. She's probably walking around in something so skimpy, you need a magnifying glass to find it.

"Then, why do you sound like you are?"

"I don't sound any way."

He started to laugh. "Turn your camera on."

"No."

"Fi, turn your camera on."

"Why?"

"I want to see your face."

"No. You just want to see if I'm angry."

"I don't have to see your face to tell me what I already know."

"What's that supposed to mean?"

"Don't you trust me?"

"You, I trust. It's that chick you're down there with that I don't trust."

He laughed again. "Fi, are you serious?"

"Yes."

"Fiona, turn on your camera," he said sternly.

I pressed the button and there he was. That sexy, dark chocolate face and beautiful smile was staring back at me. He didn't look like what I had imagined. I expected he'd be bare chested, in swim trunks and wearing sunglasses.

"Where are you?"

"I'm at my client's house."

"What? I don't understand?" He turned the camera around and started walking. "Who's that behind the counter?" I was referring to the petite woman standing at the stove.

"That's my client, Mrs. Grant."

"Mrs. Grant?"

"Are you familiar with Miss G's Kitchen?"

"Elizabeth Grant? Are you kidding me?" I quickly covered my mouth.

"Hold on." He walked over to the petite woman. "Mrs. Grant, would you please say hello to my girlfriend, Fiona."

"Hello, Dear. I'm so sorry for stealing your young man away from you." She sounded like a grandmother. Very soft spoken. She in no way resembled the woman I pictured Ty was spending the week with.

"Hello, ma'am. I love your custard pie."

"Thank you," she replied.

"I can't believe...I am a huge fan. Oh, my God." I started fanning out.

"Thank you, dear. Now if you'll excuse me, I need to finish this. Good bye."

"Good bye."

"I'll be right back Mrs. Grant."

"Take me off the speaker."

Ty put his earphones in his ears. "Feel better?"

"More like a fool. I'm so sorry. It's just...I...the way you ran out of here, I thought..."

"Fi, I told you I'm in this for the long haul."

"I know. It's just...I hadn't heard from you in a couple of days, and I guess I let my imagination run wild. Forgive me?"

"I don't know."

"What? I said I'm sorry."

"I heard you."

"How can I make it up to you?"

He sighed loudly. "Go to your room."

"Excuse me?"

His voice got low and sexy. "I said, go to your room."

I felt a chill run the length of me. I had a feeling what he was about to ask me to do, and although it was never something I had done, I couldn't believe I was even considering it. I bit the corner of my lip, smiled, and walked down the hall to my room and stopped in front of the bed.

"Okay, now what?"

"Go into your closet and…"

"My closet? Why?"

"Just do it."

I walked into the closet. "Okay. Now, what?"

"I want you to take the suitcase on the top shelf down, fill it and go downstairs."

"What?"

"I said, fill the suitcase and go downstairs. Aidan is waiting to take you to the airport."

"Are you serious?" I was relieved I didn't have to make a decision about baring it all on camera, but disappointed I wasn't offered the option to object or agree.

"Yes. I haven't had you in my arms in a week, and I want to spend an extended weekend with you." He smiled.

"Baby, I don't know. It's…"

Bark!…Bark!…Bark!…Bark!…

"I need a little more time. I have to make arrangements for Bentley and…"

"Bring him if you want."

"What?" My mouth was wide open. "You want both of…where are we…does the hotel accept pets?"

"We'll be staying at Mrs. Grant's."

"What?" I stood in my closet rubbing my forehead. "Baby, this is insane."

"Everything has been taken care of. Now pack your

bag and get that beautiful body down here. And pack a couple of swim suits."

"A swim suit?"

"Yes. It's Florida and the weather is beautiful."

"Are you sure about this?"

"Yes. Get that beautiful body down here."

Bark!…Bark!…Bark!…Bark!…

"Okay. I guess we're on our way. We'll see you in a few hours."

"I can't wait."

Bark!…Bark!…Bark!…Bark!…

"Seems Bentley can't wait either."

"See you soon. Bye."

"Bye."

Chapter 28
Ty

"Will you relax?"

"I can't." I hadn't been this antsy since I was fifteen years old waiting for Keisha Andrews to accept or reject my invitation to Clayton Morris' birthday party. "Maybe this was a bad idea."

"It's a little late to cancel your plans." The petite, mocha woman smiled at me. "I don't think I've ever seen you like this."

"Like what?"

"Nervous." She wiped her hands on her apron, sliced a piece of chocolate layer cake, placed it on the white plate with a fork and put it on the counter in front of me. Then she walked over to the wall-sized refrigerator, pulled out the bottle of milk, filled a glass, walked back to the counter, and placed the tall glass in front of me. "Eat up."

"So, you think this will calm my nerves."

"When hasn't it?" She smiled.

I smiled and put a forkful of the rich chocolate cake into my mouth, savoring the flavors. "This is incredible. You changed the recipe."

"I tweaked it a little." She smiled.

"Whatever you did really brings out the bacon flavor." I put another forkful into my mouth followed by a large sip of milk. "It's good and just what I needed."

"Thank you." She leaned on the counter and stared at me, smiling. "So how long have you and Fiona been doing whatever it is you're doing?"

I smiled and put another forkful of cake into my mouth. "A few months."

"A few months?"

I sipped some more milk. "A little over six months."

"And you're just now telling me?"

"I wasn't sure where it was going."

"And where's it going?"

"I'm not sure."

"That's not true."

"Are you calling me a liar?" I ate some more cake.

"No. I'm saying you're not telling me everything."

I wiped my mouth and placed my fork on the side of the plate. "How did you know you were in love?"

She nodded. "Love." She reached across, picked up the fork, scooped up some cake and placed it in her mouth. "You're right, this is good."

"Now who's avoiding the subject?" I smiled.

She wiped her mouth with the bottom of her apron. "It wasn't any one thing. I just knew. I asked God to send me a man that would love me unconditionally and who understood my passions."

"That's kind of broad."

"It's not like I had a list or anything. After coming out of a bad marriage, all I really wanted was a man to love me, who loved God and wanted to share his life with me."

"Sounds a lot like a list," I teased.

"Funny. Are you in love with Fiona?"

"I think so. I mean I haven't felt like this about any other woman." She nodded again.

"You know I've never pushed my beliefs on you."

"I know."

"But I don't want you to confuse sex with love."

My eyes got wide. "What?"

"Sex isn't just something you do, because you were too lazy to plan a good date. It's a binder."

I smiled at her statement. "I know how powerful it is, and we weren't at a loss for something to do."

"Really?" She sipped her water. "You're a grown man. So I can't tell you what to do, but…"

"Are you saying we shouldn't have slept together?"

"No, you shouldn't have." She covered my hands with hers. "I'm not going to chastise you, or make you feel guilty or judge you. Nor am I shocked to hear you're sexually active. I'm not naive and neither are you."

"Do we really have to discuss…"

"Yes. I don't want you to become numb."

"You lost me."

"I know you've slept with a few women."

For the second time in this conversation I smiled at one of her statements. "A few."

"If you don't take a step back, sex will lose its meaning…

its impact…it won't be special and I don't think you want that."

"I hadn't thought about it like that."

"I can say this, because I was a lot like you." She smiled.

"Really?"

"Yes. But one day I realized I wanted more. I wanted love and the soul tie that comes when you're committed to someone."

"Marriage?"

"Yes, marriage. Sex outside of marriage is fine for a while. But sex when paired with marriage is mind blowing."

She turned around and opened the oven door and looked inside. "Come over here and take this pan out for me."

I walked over to the stove and pulled the pan out of the oven. "Where do you want it?"

"On top of the stove." I placed the large pan on the front burner. "Thank you."

"Smells good."

"It's Chester's favorite."

"Not just his." I smiled.

She looked at me smiling. "I know it's yours as well." She basted the prime rib roast and then covered it with foil. "I'll let that rest and when Fiona gets here we'll eat." She directed her attention back to me. "Love is an amazing and confusing gift. But when you mix it with sex outside of marriage, it's easy to get confused."

"I understand what you're saying, but I've never felt like this before."

"If you're so sure it's love…"

"I'm not. I mean I think it's love."

"Are you sure it's not lust?"

"Way to bust my bubble."

"Way to be real and honest." She lifted the lid on a pot

and stirred the contents. "Are you her first relationship since her divorce?"

"Yes."

"Ah-huh."

"What's that supposed to mean?"

"You have had several years to know how you feel about her, but she hasn't."

"And you think I'm her rebound?"

She put the lid on the pot, turned it to simmer and put the wooden spoon on the chrome spoon rest. Then she wiped her hands on the bottom of her apron.

"Let's sit down." We walked over to the table and sat down. She reached over and took my hands in hers. "As a woman that has been where Fiona is, I think you need to be careful."

"I understand, but, things are different with Fiona."

"You are very charismatic, a trait you inherited from your father. But you need to slow things down."

"We've only slept together once."

She looked at me with a raised eyebrow. "Once, really?"

"Okay, maybe it was one weekend."

"Tiberius."

I stood up and started pacing. "In my defense, she seduced me."

"Really?"

I held my hands up. "Honest."

"Uh huh. You expect me to believe you did nothing to lead her on?"

"No. I told her I would follow her lead."

"And she led you to bed."

I smiled and rubbed my chin. "In a manner of speaking. Yes, she did."

"Well, she won't be leading you while you're under my roof."

"I know."

"Then why did you insist she come visit?"

"I miss her."

She smiled. "You miss her."

"Don't look at me that way."

"What way?"

"The way that says…man, what have I done?" I wiped my face with my hands.

"I know how easy it is to think you might be in love when the sex is incredible."

"What?!" My eyes got wider than the freeway. I couldn't believe she said that.

"Don't sound so surprised."

"Are you speaking from experience?"

"Yes, I am."

"With…"

"No. I tried to seduce Chester and he refused me."

I didn't think it was possible for my mouth to open any wider, but it was. "What? You're kidding, right?"

"No. I tried on several occasions to seduce him, but he said I needed to keep a clear head and sex out of my feelings. In fact, it was almost a year before we went from friends to more than friends."

"When was that? Because I remember…"

"You didn't meet me until a couple of months after Chester and I started getting serious. He told me he wouldn't sleep with me, and I told him I didn't want to meet you until I knew this thing between us had legs."

"I didn't know."

"Once we were sure, is when things changed."

"How?"

"He introduced you to me and I became reacquainted with God. I had a similar talk with my mother. She reminded me of who I was and although the urge to be intimate with Chester was still there, I didn't let it control me. I think if he hadn't insisted we not be intimate, things wouldn't have worked out."

"So, I made a mistake."

"I'm not going to say that, nor am I judging you. I'm saying you need to take a few steps back and really get to know the woman you've been fantasizing about for more than ten years."

I nodded. "I know you're right."

"You need to take it slow."

"It's been over six months. How much slower can I take it."

"She's only been single a few months. Give her some time. Give yourself some time. This is the longest relationship you've been involved in for quite a while."

"What if she doesn't feel the same?"

"Then let her go. Either way, you need to take it slow. Just like you let her decide to sleep with you, let the next phase in your relationship be her decision."

Ring…Ring…Ring…Ring…

I pressed the answer call button. "Hey, babe…how was your flight?…how did Bentley do?…good…I'll see you when you get here." I pressed the button and ended the call.

"I take it our houseguests are on the way."

"Yes."

She stood up. "I'm going to freshen up and wake Chester." She reached up and kissed me on the cheek. "Think about what I said."

"Yes, ma'am."

I stood in the open doorway watching as the black Mercedes sedan approached the front door. When the car stopped in front of the door, I stepped down the short flight of aged brick steps, and opened the rear passenger car door.

"Hey, baby." I leaned in to kiss her.

Bark!…Bark!…Bark!…Bark!

"Hi, Bentley. Thank you for escorting my girl." I patted him on the head and helped Fiona out of the car. Once she stood up, I wrapped my arms around her waist and crushed my mouth against hers. I missed kissing her. She wrapped her hands around my neck and pulled me closer to her.

She opened her mouth slightly and I threaded my tongue inside her mouth, kissing her hard. I pulled her closer and my body began to respond to having her in my arms. I leaned her against the car, kissing her harder.

Bark!…Bark!…Bark!…Bark!

We pulled apart. "Seems someone wants to get out of the car."

"How did he do on the flight?" I asked, as I helped Bentley out of the car.

"Remarkably well. But why wouldn't he? A private jet? Baby, you didn't have to do that."

"I know, but how else was I going to see you two." I closed the door and handed her Bentley's leash. "Evan, please see to it that Miss Harris' bags are delivered to her room."

"Yes, sir."

"Thank you."

"Come on. I want to show you around."

Unexpected Love

We walked inside and Fiona looked around. "This is beautiful. I love these high ceilings. And the plaster on the walls is amazing. I love how she's mixed antiques with modern pieces. It's eclectic but cozy. This is pretty much how I expected Mrs. Grant's home to look. It feels very warm and inviting."

We continued into the living room and her eyes got wide. "I think this is the best part of the house." We stood in there looking out the wall of windows on to the lake.

"Are you kidding me? I could sit here all day staring at that view."

"Well, if that's what you want to do, then do it." I kissed her.

"I think I'm going to need more than a few days."

"Let's go into the kitchen." I led her into the kitchen with Bentley following us. "And here we have the hub of her empire."

Fi's mouth dropped open as she looked around the large white kitchen. The centerpiece was a massive white, marble-topped island with a sink and cook top and stools at one end. Behind it were two large Viking ranges and a custom hood. The refrigerator was the length of the wall.

"Ty, this is gorgeous." She walked over and leaned against the counter. "I can't believe I'm standing in the kitchen I've seen on television numerous times."

I slipped my arm around her waist and smiled. "This isn't where the show is taped."

"It's not?"

"No. This is the model for the set. She had the set designed to look like this because it was…you know, I'm not exactly sure why. Ask her when you meet her."

"How do I look?" She turned to face me.

"Incredible." I kissed her.

"Stop it. Someone could see us."

"I haven't seen my girlfriend in a week. I'm kissing you as often as I can while you're here." I pulled her close and crushed my mouth against hers. It wasn't long before she wrapped her arms around my neck and gave in to my kiss. I pulled her closer as my hands slid further down her back, squeezing her ass. I felt myself starting to get excited.

She pulled back and whispered, "Maybe we can pick up where we left off the other night."

Chapter 29
Fiona

"Tiberius..." the female voice called as she approached us. "This must be Fiona."

Bark!...Bark!...Bark!...Bark!...

Bentley trotted over and stopped in front of me.

"Calm down, boy. Mommy's fine." Bentley stood his ground next to me. "I'm sorry about that. He's very protective."

"That's all right, dear." The petite, mocha colored woman with a sassy short bob approached Bentley. "Aren't you a handsome protector?" she smiled.

Bark!...Bark!...Bark!...Bark!... He smiled and rubbed her leg.

"Bentley, stop," I pulled his leash back. "I'm sorry. I

wouldn't have brought him, but Ty insisted."

"That's all right. Elizabeth Grant." She extended her hand to me. "Welcome to the manor."

"Fiona Harris. It's an honor to meet you."

"Tiberius has told me a lot about you But I'm sure there's still more to discover. Let's have a seat in the living room."

We all walked into the living room. I sat next to Ty with Bentley sitting on the floor next to my foot. I sat up straight and stiff trying not to let my nerves show. I couldn't believe I was in the presence of my business mentor. Okay, she didn't know that's how I viewed her, but I planned on soaking up as much information from her over the next few days as possible.

I looked around the open living space. The cream and brown palate was very soothing. The space had a very Latin feel with stone, plaster and amazing oversized furniture and plants. You could feel the history and warmth surrounding you. "Your home is incredible."

"Thank you," Elizabeth replied.

"And that view," I turned to the window, smiling.

"I love sitting here staring at the view," Elizabeth replied. "This is my spot early in the morning. It's perfect for meditating and getting centered before starting my day."

"That's what I told Ty I would do if I lived here."

"Well, you are welcome to do so while you're here."

"Thank you." It seemed like I couldn't stop smiling.

"Where is everyone?" a strong male voice called out. It had a similar vibrato to Ty's.

"We're in the living room, Honey."

The footsteps got louder as they approached the living room. I looked up in the direction of the footsteps and voice, ready to meet the man behind the woman. I had read numerous stories about Elizabeth Grant, and knew her husband was her partner. He was also the one she credited for encouraging her to start her company.

I looked down at Bentley briefly and when I looked up, a tall, dark-skinned man wearing a white shirt and tan trousers, stopped at the back of the sofa and kissed Elizabeth on the shoulder. "Mi Amore, I'm starving."

I looked at Ty and then back at the older gentleman. The resemblance was remarkable. Same strong jawline, smooth dark skin, broad shoulders, dark dancing eyes and that smile. I found myself staring. Bentley stood up and looked at Ty and then at the older man.

Bark!Bark!Bark!Bark!

"I agree," I said.

"You agree to what?" Elizabeth asked.

Ty rubbed my back. "You okay, babe?"

"I'm sorry. It's…it's just, the resemblance is remarkable."

Elizabeth looked at the older gentleman, then they both looked at Ty.

"Well, it should be, considering he's my son," the older gentleman said. He walked over and extended his hand to me. "Chester Wells."

"Excuse me?"

The older gentleman looked at his wife and then back at me. "I see my son failed to tell you about us," he replied.

I looked at Ty with my mouth open wide enough for the boat that was docked outside to fit inside. "Excuse me." I rushed down the hall to the front door and outside.

I started walking. I had no idea where I was going. All I knew was I needed air and to be away from Ty. Because right now, I was ready to knock him out.

Bark!Bark!Bark!Bark! Bark!Bark!Bark!Bark!

I turned around and running after me was my true best

friend along with the man I was currently very angry with.

"FIONA!…FIONA!…FIONA!…"

I stopped walking for two reasons, maybe three… Bentley, I left my phone and bag, and I really wasn't sure where I was. Damn, Ty! I kept my eyes focused on Bentley.

Bark!Bark!Bark!Bark!

He stopped in front of me, breathing hard. I bent down and rubbed his neck as he licked my hands. "Mommy is so sorry she brought you down here. As soon as I can figure out where we are and how to get us home, we're leaving."

Ty finally made it to us.

"Fiona…I…I should have told you."

I stood up and Bentley stood between us. "You're right. You should have told me. What the crap! Why would you invite…your parents!…Ty how could you?" I was so angry nothing I said made any sense. "Oh, and not only are they your parents, your mother is a freakin' icon!"

"I wouldn't say that," he smirked.

"Is that supposed to be funny?" He stepped closer and reached for my arms. I stepped back. "Don't touch me."

"I'm sorry."

"Sorry? Is that all?"

"What do you want from me?"

"How about the truth?"

"I didn't lie to you."

"You said you had a client emergency."

"That's correct. I'm my parents' attorney."

"Why didn't you just tell me you were coming to see your family?"

"It's complicated."

"Un-complicate it, or I'm leaving."

He wiped his face with his hands. "My dad met and

married Elizabeth a few years after my mother died."

"What is all of this?" I pointed to the vast estate with a driveway it would have taken me a good fifteen minutes to walk to get to the curb.

"You mean the house?"

"Where I come from this isn't a house, but a mansion."

"What's the problem?"

"This explains a lot."

"What are you talking about?"

"The apartment, the car and driver, the private plane I came here on, why didn't you…"

He stepped to me and rubbed my arms. "I'm sorry. I should have told you. But I didn't know how to tell you about my parents." He stepped closer. "Forgive me?"

"Ty, this changes everything."

"How…I'm still the same man that…," he sighed. "I'm the same person I was before you met my parents." He stepped closer. "Forgive me?"

I folded my arms in front of my chest. "Maybe."

Bark!…Bark!…Bark!…Bark!… Bentley trotted over and rubbed Ty's leg.

"Seems Bentley's forgiven me." He smiled.

"That or he's feeling a little frisky." We laughed.

"Let's hope it's the first one." He kissed me. "We good?"

"For now, but if you lie to me…"

"I didn't lie."

"You know what I mean."

"I'm sorry. Let's go back to the house, and later I'll do my best to answer your questions."

ಬಬಬಬಬಬಬ

"Fiona and I are going to take a walk while you two finish up in the kitchen," Elizabeth announced. "Come on, Fiona."

"Ty, watch Bentley."

"Bring him with us dear. It's a nice evening and he might like some air," Elizabeth replied.

"Come on, Bentley." I picked up his leash and we followed Elizabeth outside. "You're right, it's a beautiful night." I looked at the clear, star-filled sky.

"I take it my son is in a little trouble?" She smiled.

"A little." I smiled.

"Tell me, why did you accept his invitation?"

"I missed him."

"He said you and I have something in common."

"Oh?"

"Actually we have a few things in common."

"We do?"

"I met Chester shortly after my divorce. And he encouraged me to start my own business."

"I read that somewhere."

"I told Tiberius he needs to take things slow with you, because this is all new for you."

"Thank you, but I don't…"

"Hear me out. When I met Chester, I hadn't been divorced that long. My ex-husband was the only man I had been intimate with as well as the only man to break my heart."

"I see the commonalities." I nodded.

"So when this handsome, charming and compassionate man entered my world and treated me like a queen, I was overwhelmed. It didn't take long for me to realize my feelings for him were deep. I was eager to move our relationship further, but he said no. He wanted us to really get to know each other. In fact, he told me to go date and if the feelings were still there, he would lock it down." She laughed. "God, I love that man."

"Wow."

"I'm no saint, but I had a weak moment or twelve." We laughed. "But he was strong. I don't need to know the details about your relationship with my son. But I know that you shouldn't rush love before it's time."

"Are you saying we shouldn't have slept together?"

"You're adults and quite capable of making your own decisions. Just be sure you're prepared to deal with the consequences."

"We used protection."

"I'm glad to know that. However, I'm not just talking about the physical consequences, but the emotional ones."

"I don't understand."

"It's very easy to confuse love and great sex."

My face felt warm. I couldn't believe she said that. "Excuse me?"

"Did I shock you?"

"A little."

"You'll find I don't mix words. I say what I mean and I mean what I say." We made a slight turn and were headed back to the house. "I know what you're going through now."

"You do?"

"Yes. It's like you've been given a new lease on life, and you're eager to do all the things you feel you missed out on during your marriage. Am I right?"

I smiled. "Yes."

"I also know how charming my son is. He will never push you to do anything, however..."

I rubbed the back of my neck. "I think I know what you're saying."

"I don't need or want details about your relationship. I

will caution you not to move too fast. Take some time and get to know this Fiona. This is a woman you've never been."

"I never thought about it like that."

"Once Chester and I decided to escalate our relationship, he wanted to introduce me to his son, and I refused. I didn't want to become attached unless I knew I was going to be a permanent fixture in Tiberius' life."

"I see."

"I'm not sure why he wanted us to meet, but I'm glad he did. I see a lot of me in you."

"That's a high compliment. I hope I can accomplish at least half of what you have."

"That's sweet and easy to do. Whatever you need help with, you just let me know, and I'll do my best to help you."

"Thank you."

"I also apologize for my son's lack of judgment in how you came to be here."

"Meeting you on the phone was shock enough, but being here and seeing all of this…"

"Honey, this is just our home."

"But I never knew Ty was…I had no idea he came from…"

"Such good stock?" She smiled.

I smiled. "I knew he was a compassionate man, but this…in all the years I've known him, he never said anything about you."

"That's interesting."

"I mean, he's mentioned or referenced his parents, but he never mentioned that you were his mother."

She smiled. "To him, we're just Mom and Dad."

I smiled and sucked on my bottom lip. "I also didn't know he was so passionate."

"I don't need to hear…" She started to cover her ears and I grabbed her forearm and laughed.

"I'm sorry, this isn't about sex."

"Oh," she sighed and lowered her hands. "I may be blunt and open, but I don't need to hear details about my son's sex life."

I smiled. "I'm sorry. I mean he's very passionate when it comes to his clients. I was privy to that side of him during my divorce negotiations. He appears to be very cool and laid back, when in reality, he's a fighter. That's one of the things that attracted me to him."

"His father is the same way." She smiled.

"He's a great motivator. And I like his commanding side. He has great strength."

"Are we still talking about his work or…" She smiled.

I bit my bottom lip, smiled and tilted my head. "Uhm…"

"Tiberius said you recently started your own company."

"Yes. I'm doing something similar to…now I understand why he told me not to sell."

"I don't understand."

"There was a company that wanted to buy my magazines and turn them into a lifestyle brand. Ty said if they could do that with my idea, why couldn't I? I thought about what he said, and now I'm doing something I never thought I could."

"That's how God works."

"Ty said something similar."

"He did?" She raised her eyebrows.

"Yes. He told me not to sell because it seemed overwhelming, but only if I thought that was where God was leading me."

"Interesting." She smiled.

"Yeah."

"We better head back. I think Chester and Tiberius should have everything cleaned up by now."

"So you're the reason he knows so much about food."

"Yes. I use him and Chester as guinea pigs quite often. And when we're on family vacations, we make it a point to sample the local cuisine."

"Now things are starting to make sense."

"I'm glad."

Elizabeth's words kept bouncing off the walls of my mind as we headed back to the house.

We stepped inside and Ty and his father were sitting at the kitchen counter.

"How was your walk, sweetheart?" Chester asked.

Elizabeth walked over and wrapped her arms around his waist and he kissed her. "It was nice. I needed to walk off dinner."

Bark!…Bark!…Bark!…Bark!…

"Seems Bentley enjoyed it as well," Chester commented.

"He's a city dog, so this is exciting for him," I replied and patted his head.

"We're turning in. We'll see you two in the morning. How about we take the boat out tomorrow?" Chester asked.

"What do you say, babe?" Ty asked me.

"Sounds like fun."

"Then it's settled. We'll leave after breakfast. You two get some sleep. Good night," Chester said.

Elizabeth walked over, cupped Ty's face in her petite hands. "It's so good to have you home." She kissed him on the forehead then she hugged me. "Don't stay up too late."

"Yes, ma'am," Ty replied.

"Son, lock up when you turn in," Chester said after he

hugged Ty.

"Yes, sir."

"Good night, Fiona." He hugged me and it surprised me.

"Good night," I replied.

Bark!…Bark!…Bark!…Bark!…

"Good night to you too, Bentley." He patted him on the head.

Chester and Elizabeth walked out hand in hand. "Tiberius, remember what I said," Elizabeth called out.

"Yes, ma'am."

Bark!…Bark!…Bark!…Bark!…

"What was that about?" I asked.

"She was reminding me about the house rule."

"Which is?"

He stood up, wrapped his arms around my waist and pulled me close. "Separate rooms." He kissed me. "So no sneaking into my room once my parents are sleep." He smiled.

"I believe she was reminding you, not me." I smiled.

"Me?" He pulled me closer. "She knows I'm a saint."

"A saint? Uh-huh." I threaded my arms around his neck. "If that was you being saintly the other weekend, I don't know if I can handle your un-saintly side."

He kissed me. "Trust me. You can handle all sides of me."

"Yeah, yeah, yeah." I smiled.

"How was your walk with my mom?"

I sighed. "It was nice. We uhm…we have a lot in common. Thanks."

"Come on, let's sit down."

We walked into the living room and sat on the sofa, staring at the view. "Man, that view is even more incredible at night." We snuggled in the center of the sofa with Bentley nestled next to my feet.

"So, how was your walk?" He gently rubbed my back.

"It was nice. She shared some things about her life and…she's amazing. She offered to mentor me."

"She did?" His surprise seemed genuine.

"Yes. She said I could call her anytime for advice. She strongly suggested we slow things down. Her reason is I need to get to know myself, because I've never been this person before."

"Meaning?"

"I've never been divorced. Or run my own business." I sat up, wrung my hands and looked at him. "Nor have I uhm…"

He gently stroked the side of my arm. "Is this about us sleeping together?"

I sighed. "Yeah. I don't know what came over me." I tossed my head back, closed, my eyes and searched my mind for the right words. When I lowered my head and looked into those warm, sexy brown eyes, I felt peace about my answer.

"Do you regret what happened?"

I covered his hands. "No, I don't regret it. However, I know that was out of character for me. I don't know what happened. Somewhere I forgot who I was and what I believed." He shifted on the sofa and turned to face me. "Rhys really messed me up. He had me questioning my sexual confidence."

"You lost me."

"Things with Rhys weren't as they seemed. He was my first love, and I think I put up with a lot because I was blinded by infatuation. Then he deceived me, and I questioned my judgment, as well as my attractiveness."

"What?"

I felt a surprise tear stream down my cheek. Ty reached over and gently wiped it away with the ball of his thumb.

"I'm not stupid. I saw how Rhys looked at other women. If he wasn't cheating, it was just a matter of time until he did."

His brow furrowed. "So you slept with me to get back at Rhys."

"No. I slept with you because I wanted to."

"That's not how it sounds."

I rubbed my forehead. "I'm not saying this right."

"I don't believe you are."

I took a deep breath and started over. "Rhys and I never…let's just say, in all the years I was with Rhys, sex was never like it was with you. I'm not saying he was bad, but I didn't know I could have or should have expected more."

The tension in Ty's brow seemed to soften after my confession. "You didn't?"

I shook my head. "No. And if it hadn't been for my giving in to my inhibitions, I never would have known I could have more."

He sat up straighter. "So, you aren't upset we had sex?"

"No. But after talking with your mom, I understand what she was saying. Although we've been together a few months, I'm still a little vulnerable. I can't afford to let my body rule me." I sighed and looked at him. Ty isn't Rhys. His character is unquestionable and I don't think he would lie to me or hurt me. "I care about you, a lot. But I need to make sure my feelings are real and not part of the euphoria from…"

He gently kissed me. The swift manner in which he kissed me, caught me by surprise. When he pulled back, he brushed the back of his hand along my cheek and a chill ran the length of my body.

"I told you I would follow your lead. If that means we step back, then so be it."

"Are you sure? Because I'm not sure when…"

"I'm sure. Grant it, it's going to be a little difficult not sharing my bed with this incredible body, but I will." He kissed me.

"Thank you."

"Funny, I was going to suggest we slow things down."

My eyes got wide. "What?"

He stroked the side of my arm. "My mother pretty much gave me the same lecture, but not as nice." He smiled. "She told me I need to make sure I'm not your rebound."

"You're not my rebound."

Chapter 30
Ty

"I'm not?" I may not be having sex tonight, but I just got something better. The possibility of Fi forever.

"No. I like you a lot and I'm having fun getting to know you. Now I need to get to know myself," she confessed. "I need to find that girl that I was before Rhys. I'm a little older now, but I need to relocate those values she had, because I liked them."

"So we're starting over."

"In a manner of speaking."

I nodded and smiled. "This could be hot."

"Really?"

"Yes. It's like we have a clean slate."

"We do. I like that. I'm Fiona Harris again and I like her."

"So do I." I kissed her again.

"I meant what I said. I have very strong feelings for you. And I'm excited to see where this goes."

"Me, too."

"I guess this puts a monkey wrench into our plans for the weekend."

I brushed the side of her arm. "This is Miami. There's plenty to do."

"Are you sure? Because Bentley and I could go home and when you…"

I crushed my lips against hers and she fell back onto the sofa. I fell on top of her and wrapped my arms around her. She threaded her hands around my neck, and pulled me closer to her. She opened her mouth and I slid my tongue inside, dancing and mating with hers. She moaned into my mouth and I kissed her harder. I know we just agreed to slow things down, but maybe this was our version of slow.

She slid her hands down my back and then I felt her hot hands on my ass, pulling me deeper into her space. I moved my mouth along her cheek to her neck and she moaned again. It seemed like our bodies had forgotten the conversation we just had. My hand traveled up the side of her body and cupped her breast. I loved the way her breast felt in my hand. I gently pressed and kneaded the firm flesh and she moaned again.

I moved my mouth back to hers and kissed her. She wrapped her legs around my hips and pulled me deeper into her space and kissed me harder. Trading deep, hard kisses with the moonlight highlighting us was dangerous.

My hand slipped under the bottom of her dress, up her hot silky thigh to the thin lace of her knickers. I eased my hand under the lace and she stopped me. I immediately pulled back and stood up.

"Uhm…" I adjusted my clothes and looked down at her. She looked like a sensual dessert begging to be devoured.

She sat up and covered her mouth. "Oh, my God. I can't believe we…how are we…"

"Come on. I'll walk you to your room." I extended my hand to help her up. She stood up, adjusted her clothes and my mother's words were bouncing off the sides of my head.

I turned the light off and walked back to the sofa and Fi was fluffing the pillows. "How's that?"

"What are you doing?"

"I don't want your mother to know what we were doing."

I laughed. "Are you serious? We didn't do anything."

"But we almost did."

"But we didn't."

"But…"

"Babe, relax. Take a deep breath."

She nodded. "Okay."

"Come on. Let's go to bed." I took her hand and started walking out of the living room. "Come on, Bentley," I called and he trotted beside us. "Babe, I have to ask you something."

"What?"

"What kind of swim suits did you bring?" I checked the lock on the front door.

"Excuse me?"

I set the alarm and took Fiona's hand. "Did you bring bikinis or one-pieces?"

Her brow was furrowed. "A couple of one piece suits, why?"

I sighed loudly. "Thank you, God."

"Why?"

"Seeing things are a little different now, I don't think I can handle seeing you in a bikini and not be able to take it off."

Her eyes got wide and she stopped walking. "What?"

I turned and faced her. "I'm being honest. Now that we aren't sleeping together, I don't need any temptations." I smiled.

"I see. And, what about me?" She smiled.

"Excuse me?"

"What about me? What's your suit look like? Are you a Speedo guy or a trunks guy."

I smiled. "I'm definitely a trunks guy."

"Tight or baggy?"

"Excuse me?"

"Are you short and tight or long and baggy?"

I stepped closer and she seemed a little anxious. "I'm definitely not the baggy guy." She swallowed hard after my reply. "However, I'll make an exception for you."

"Is it warm or is it me?" She smiled.

"It's you. Any more questions?"

"No, I think we've covered everything."

"Good." We walked up the stairs and down the hall to the second to the last door and stopped. "Here you are, my lady." I opened the door and Bentley walked inside.

Bark...Bark...Bark...Bark...

"Good night, Bentley." I redirected my attention to Fiona. "Do you need anything?"

"No, I think I'll be fine."

She looked up and those sexy brown eyes seemed to be begging me to forget about my mother's rule. But I had my eye on the bigger prize, a life with Fiona.

"Okay, I'll see you in the morning."

"Where's your room?"

"I'm down there." I pointed towards the end of the hall.

"That far." She sucked on the corner of her lip.

"Yes."

She sighed. "I should turn in."

"Me, too. Goodnight." I started to walk away.

"I don't get a kiss?"

I turned around, stopped and looked at her. Man, she looked good. I could take her inside, make love to her and in the morning, I could sneak back to my room and no one would be the wiser.

Look at her. I don't think I've ever seen her look this tempting before. That thin white cotton dress is leaving very little to my imagination. Not that I need a reminder of what Fiona's dangerously sexy body looks like. I felt my pants getting tight again and my mouth remembered what her soft skin tasted like.

I swallowed hard. I walked back, stopped in front of her and locked eyes with her. She had no idea what I was wrestling with.

I kissed her on the forehead and stepped back. "Good night." Then I lifted my cement laden feet and walked down the hall.

☙☙☙☙☙☙☙

"Good morning, Dad." I yawned as I walked into the kitchen. "Excuse me."

He looked up. "I didn't expect to see you for a couple of hours." He filled a mug with coffee and placed it on the counter in front of an empty stool.

I walked over and sat on the stool where the large white mug was. I took a couple of sips. "This is good."

"Thank you. Want a muffin?" He pushed the plate of zucchini walnut muffins in front of me. I reached for a plate, picked up a muffin and broke it in half. I put one half on the plate and started eating the other. "Mom changed her recipe."

"I made these," my dad said proudly.

The surprise instantly registered on my face. "You're kidding." I took another bite.

"No. Every now and then your mother let's me into the kitchen."

"Well, these are good." I sipped more coffee. "I thought you said we were taking the boat out?"

"We are. I just didn't think you'd be up this early. Your mother is still sleeping. And I was sure you would have convinced Fiona to break your mother's rule." He smiled.

I smiled and swallowed another bite of muffin. "We almost did."

"Don't let your mother hear that."

I wiped my mouth. "I'm not stupid."

"You're a grown man, and I'm not going to tell you what to do, but I've been where you are and…"

"Mom told me everything."

"She did?" His raised eyebrows clearly registered his shock.

"Yes, and she also spoke to Fi. Last night, before things…well, we decided to slow things down."

"Thank God." He sipped his coffee.

"What?" I popped a piece of muffin into my mouth.

"Did I say that out loud?" He smiled.

"Yes, you did."

He topped off my coffee. "It's just ever since you told

me you were seeing Fiona, I was afraid you were going to rush things."

"You said it was about time I acted on my feelings for Fiona."

"That is correct. But I didn't think things would escalate as they have."

"I didn't either, but...I see this going the distance. That's why I told her I would follow her lead."

"Is this love?"

"I believe so. I mean, how did you know you were in love?"

"I can't really explain it. For me it wasn't like I saw a unicorn and knew she was the one." He laughed. "It was a feeling and a surety. Both times, I felt something different, but the feeling was the same."

"Not really helping, Dad."

"I'm sorry, Son. But as my dad said, when it's right, you know. Is that why you invited her here? Are you trying to figure out if it's love or lust?"

My eyes got wide and I almost choked on my coffee. "Yes." I wiped my mouth. "I wanted you and Mom to meet her."

"I knew something was up."

"Why do you say that?"

"Son, not for nothing, but most of your relationships don't really last more than a couple of months."

"That's not true."

"You're right. Julia lasted a little longer than the others."

"You make it seem like I have commitment issues."

"I know better. I also know you are exactly where you've wanted to be, and that's why I'm glad you two are slowing things down."

"Fiona and I agreed to start over."

"This should be interesting."

"How so?"

"This is love we're talking about. You've never been in love. This isn't getting pissed and walking away. This is getting pissed and working through the issue."

"I don't know how we're going to do this. Last night after we agreed to slow things down, we almost had sex on the sofa, but we didn't because we remembered Mom's words. What happens when we go home and there are no house rules?"

"You have rules. The ones you two set. While Fiona is here, take some time and establish rules for your relationship. But don't make it so stifling where you feel like prisoners. Just set some boundaries you're both comfortable with."

"Boundaries…I like that."

"Know your limitations. I knew a woman who had come from a very intense sexual background. She was a new Christian and was determined to have a new start. She met a man she saw a future with, but she wrestled with her urges. They came up with a simple plan. No kissing."

"Excuse me?" My eyes got wide.

"I know it sounds extreme, but she said it was the only way she could be in the relationship with a clear head. For her, sex was a sedative. It blocked out clear reasoning, and she wanted to be sure about her feelings for him."

"I don't know if we need to be that extreme." I sipped more coffee.

"Maybe not, but you need to figure out what your boundaries are. Once you do, you can be in this relationship with a clear head." He popped a piece of muffin into his mouth and chewed it. "I like Fiona, and I think you and she could have a great future. But you both need to have clear heads."

"Yes, sir."

"I know things are bad between you and Rhys, but I think you should talk to him about Fiona."

"Why?"

"Son, it's the right thing to do. You don't want a cloud hanging over your head. Put an end to this fight. It's senseless."

"He started it."

"And you're going to finish it."

Chapter 31
Fiona

"When will you be back?" I sounded like a lovesick teenager, pining after her boyfriend.

"Hopefully, I'll be back by the end of next week."

"What?!" I quickly covered my mouth, but I was a little late. My response was drenched in my true feelings.

I missed Ty and my feelings were magnified by our new dating rules. I was trying to keep a level head and not think about what happened the last time he'd been gone for an extended period.

I felt flushed and warm in a few places thinking about that weekend. I closed my eyes and remembered how his large hands felt traveling the length of my body. How his full sexy lips felt kissing the insides of my thighs. How his tongue felt teasing my nipple and those fingers…God, I miss those fingers. How is it possible for me to be so frisky? It's not like I was a virgin. Then again, considering how pathetic my sex life was with Rhys, I might as well have been.

Ty did things to me that weekend I never thought I would get to experience. Although, when my girlfriends would overshare, I did get jealous hearing the details of their sex lives. If they knew about me and Ty, they would be the jealous ones.

"Fi…Fi…"

I sat back in the chair with my eyes closed remembering every detail of that weekend and…

"Fiona!"

My eyes popped open and I sat up. "I'm sorry. What did you say?" I was glad he couldn't see me. I looked up and caught my reflection in the mirror. My face wasn't doing a very good job of hiding my thoughts. In a matter of seconds, I'd gone from shocked to excited.

"I said I hope to be home by the end of next week."

"Oh." I sighed.

"What's that?"

"What?"

"I detect something in your voice."

"There's nothing in my voice."

"I'm sorry, babe, but this case is…"

"Is it the case?" Oh crap, that wasn't supposed to slip out.

"What's that supposed to mean?"

"Nothing, never mind."

"Fiona, what's the problem?"

"Nothing."

"Fiona."

The way he said my name, sent a jolt straight to my core. I was trying to forget I shouldn't have been having thoughts about him I couldn't act on. But the way he said my name when he was being forceful was so hot. It made me want to forget about our rule and repeat our lustful weekend.

"Yes."

"Why does it sound like you're angry with me?"

I sighed. "I can't help but think maybe you're glad to be away."

"Why would you say that?"

"Because, never mind."

"Clearly there's something you want to say."

"Fine." I stood up and started pacing. "I can't help but think you're trying to avoid me."

"Why would I be avoiding you?"

"Because as soon as you got back from visiting your parents, you left. You did a drive by kiss and…" He started laughing. "What's so funny?"

"You."

"Me?"

"I've never seen this side of you."

"What side is that?"

"I miss you, too."

"So you think I miss you?"

"Turn your camera on."

"No." Even if I didn't look a mess, I wasn't about to give him the satisfaction of being right. I knew the truth was written all over my face.

"Fiona," he said sternly. "Turn on your camera."

"Fine." So what if I looked like something Bentley picked up behind a bush in the park. If he'd given me advance notice this was going to be a video call, I would have gotten all glamorous. I pressed the camera icon and there he was.

Damn him. Why couldn't he look like crap? Why did

he have to look so good? He knows I love seeing him in a white shirt. Look at him all sexy and debonair.

"Hi." The warm tone of his words entered my head and traveled the length of my body, igniting the flame I was trying to ignore.

"Hi." I tried to pout.

"You know that only makes you look sexier."

"Stop it." I was trying hard not to smile, but he knew exactly how to get to me.

"Man, I miss those lips." He bit his bottom lip and shook his head.

"Stop it."

"And those eyes. I see those beautiful eyes and lips every time I close my eyes."

I was trying not to let his words effect me, just like I was trying not to let his eyes and that sexy smile get to me. But it was pointless. I had become something I thought I'd be with Rhys. I had become smitten.

I know it sounds childish and old-fashioned, but I liked the power Ty had over me. I liked that he could see me, even when I couldn't see myself. I liked that we had connected in a way I didn't think was possible.

And as much as I didn't want to admit it, I had completely fallen for him. That's why I was so angry. Sure, part of me was angry about our new dating arrangement. Which was strange because we only slept together once. Okay, it was one really amazing weekend. Even when I was married, we never spent a weekend in bed. Not even in the very early days of our marriage.

It was incredible being desired. Seeing my lover's eyes warm and his voice hitch as a result of his desire for me. His body language spoke volumes. I knew if Ty were here with me, we would have abandoned that rule and been on the sofa, the floor, the counter, or somewhere, making love until neither of us had the energy to move.

"Do you want to come for a visit?"

A visit…is he insane? I'm standing here trying not to turn this call into one that would require $3.99 every five minutes and he's suggesting an in-person meeting. Yes, I miss him, but if we're going to date without sex, then we need a cooling off period.

I sighed and forced myself to give the right answer. Not the answer I wanted, but the one that would keep us on track. "I would love to. But, I can't."

"I thought we resolved…"

"We did."

"Then what's the problem?"

"Mercer."

"Who's Mercer?"

"My brother."

"Your brother?"

"You forgot my brother's coming to town."

"Oh Crap! I'm sorry. I did. When?"

"He'll be here in a couple of days."

He sighed deeply. "How long will he be in town?"

"About a week."

"I can't promise I'll be there, but…"

"Don't worry. I'll explain." I tried to hide my disappointment, but I wasn't doing a very good job.

"Babe, I'm sorry. I'll try my best to get home, but…"

I felt a tear waiting for an opportunity to roll down my face. I couldn't sniffle, because then that lowly tear would escape and send a wave of guilt aimed directly at Ty.

"Honey, really, it's okay."

"No, it isn't. I promised you I'd be there." He sighed. "Uhmm...I'm going to try." I dabbed at the corner of my eye. "Please don't cry."

"I'm not crying." I patted the corner of my eye. "Stupid allergies." I sniffled. "How's the case going?"

"I can't talk about it."

"Okay, so what do you want to talk about?"

"You."

"Me?"

"Yes. How's my girl doing apart from my disappointing her?"

I smiled slightly. "Baby, you didn't disappoint me. You can't help it that you have to work. I told you, Mercer will understand."

"I know, but..."

"Guess who called me?" We were desperately in need of a subject change.

"I'm drawing a blank. Who?"

"Elizabeth."

"My mother?"

"Yes. She suggested we have a weekly accountability call."

"Really?" I saw his face light up. This was much better than the guilty face I was looking at.

"Yes. She said it would help me stay on track. She said it's very easy to lose focus when you don't have anyone to answer to."

"Is that all?"

"Yes, why?"

"Nothing. I just...that's good."

"I know. I still can't believe she's helping me." I smiled.

"You can't?"

"No. I know it's probably because of you, but…"

"This is all you."

"It's because I'm your girlfriend."

"Girlfriend, huh?" His sexy smile was back.

"What?"

"I think that's the first time I've heard you refer to yourself as my girlfriend."

"No, it isn't." I protested vehemently.

"Yes, it is."

"Anyway. I'm sure Elizabeth is just being nice because of you."

"Trust me, Babe. Mom is doing this because she likes you. There have been a few women to reach out to her and she's turned them down. If she's reaching out to you, it's not because you're my girlfriend, but because she sees your potential."

"If that's what you think."

"That's what I know."

"Well, she gave me homework and…"

"Listen to you." He smirked.

"That's the other reason why I can't come for a visit."

"Well, if you change your mind, I'll…"

"I won't." I was very confident in my decision not to go see him.

"Okay then, I'll talk to you later. Goodnight."

"Goodnight."

Click…he was gone.

Bark!…Bark!…Bark!…Bark!

I looked down at Bentley. "I know, I miss him, too."

Chapter 32
Ty

I can't believe I let her down. I made a promise to myself, not to treat Fiona like Rhys did. He rarely kept his word and I remember hearing the pain in her voice when we would have lunch. Now here I am, letting her down, like Rhys did.

I looked at my schedule, it was tight. These negotiations were moving like honey flowing in snow…not at all. My client made a decent offer. However it's being rejected on all points. I thought if I came for a face to face, I could move things along. But it's been one obstacle after another.

I pressed the other frequently called number and after the third ring, "Hello?"

"Tasha."

"Do you know what time it is?" she barked.

"It's early."

"For who?"

I looked at my watch. "I know you weren't sleeping."

"I wasn't, but…"

"Put the phone down," the deep voice asked.

"Uhm, did I interrupt something?" I asked.

"Hold on." A few moments passed then she returned to the phone. "What do you want?" she asked brusquely.

"I can call back if you're in the middle of something."

"Not that it's any of your business, but I'm not. What do you want?"

"Uhm…I…"

"Well, spit it out. I've got a hot man in my bed resting up for the next round."

I was shocked. "I didn't know you were seeing anyone."

"It's not what you…I know you didn't call to inquire about my sex life."

"I thought you…I mean, you said…"

"I'm off the clock and…"

"As my assistant you're supposed to be at my beck and call."

"Beck and Call is an honor reserved for your wife, if you had one."

"You're my work wife," I teased.

"Exactly…work. I'm on my time and that of the hot man waiting for me. What do you want?" Her annoyance with me was obvious.

"I need you to call Felix and…"

"What did you do?"

"What makes you think…"

"Tiberius Wells, you have ten seconds to tell me what you did, otherwise, I'm going to hang up and…"

"I forgot I promised Fi I would take her and her brother to dinner on Friday."

"I see."

"I let her down and…"

"Please stop talking."

"Excuse me."

"Please stop talking. Fiona isn't that stuck up skank Julia or any of those other snooty chicks you've dated. She's a smart, unpretentious woman. She can't be bought with jewelry every time you think you messed up."

"But I…"

"Do you want my help?"

I sighed. She was right. Fi was different. I think I intentionally dated women who were the opposite of her, so I wouldn't have to remember I wasn't with the woman I really wanted.

"Yes, I want your help."

"Send a note."

"A note?"

"Yes, a note. Not an email or a text, but a note. A nice card would be better. But your apology needs to be handwritten."

"You lost me." I started pacing.

She sighed loudly. "A note says you really feel bad about missing dinner. Don't get me wrong, jewelry has its place. However, this is one of those rare times where a handwritten note will be more valuable than emerald earrings."

"How did you know I was…"

"I over heard you talking to your jeweler. Save the earrings for her birthday or when you really need to apologize."

"I'll add the note to some flowers."

"Agh! What am I going to do with you?"

"I know exactly what to do with you," the deep voice said.

"I bet you do." She giggled.

"Come back to bed, sweetness."

"Go back to…uhm, I'll figure this out," I replied.

"Ty, listen to me. Go down to the gift shop. Pick out the funniest card you can find. Write a heartfelt apology. Nothing long and drawn out. If you're at a loss, simply say, 'Sorry'. Then send it overnight mail. Trust me. She'll love it."

"Good night, Tasha."

"I'm starting without you," the deep voice called out.

She moaned. "Trust me, Ty."

"We'll talk in the morning. Good night."

"Oh, it's definitely going to be good. Bye."

The line was dead. A simple note. Tasha must be out of her mind. I'm not doing that.

☙☙☙☙☙☙☙☙

Bzzz…Bzzz…Bzzz… I reached inside my pocket, pulled out my phone and pressed the Ignore Call button. I placed my phone face down on the table.

"I apologize for that. Where were we?" I asked the older gentleman with salt and pepper hair, square jaw, and ten thousand dollar suit.

We had been going over these same three points for the past twelve days. I was tired and was willing to walk away. However, my client really wanted this company, so I was stuck here.

"You were about to offer me three percent more," Mr. Over-confident replied.

I wanted to reach across the table and wring his neck. Three percent. I was stuck in a stuffy Chicago board room, with a man unwilling to budge, and not at home with my girlfriend in my arms, over three percent. Truthfully, I could have given him the three percent. I was authorized to increase the offer to six percent, but I refused to give in. This company needed help and the only person interested in saving it in the past four years, was my client.

I leaned back in my chair and looked at his face. These kinds of negotiations were like playing high stakes poker. There was only one winning hand, and I was holding it. "Three percent…I'll need to talk to my client." I stood up and picked up my phone. "Give me a moment."

"Take your time," my opponent said with a smirk. "Use the conference room. I'll give you a few minutes."

"Thank you."

He stood up, walked out and closed the door. I turned to the window admiring the beautiful skyline. I scrolled through the calls received and pressed the number that I ignored earlier.

"Hello."

"Hey," the sultry voice sang.

"I'm sorry I couldn't take your call earlier. I was in a meeting."

"I figured as much. How's it…I'm sorry. I forgot, you can't talk about it."

I smiled. "No, I can't. How's your day going?"

"It was dragging, and then I received an envelope from my lawyer."

"You did."

"Yes. He said my boyfriend asked him to send it to me."

"Really? What was in it?"

"A card with a basset hound barking his apologies as he danced."

"Seems like your boyfriend has a great sense of humor." I teased.

"I don't know about that." She laughed.

"I'm glad I could brighten your day."

"Thank you, but you didn't need to apologize. I told you I understood."

This woman is incredible. "I know, but I wanted you to know how horrible I felt about cancelling on you this weekend."

"I told you I…I know your not being here is because of work."

"I know you understand, but…since we agreed to slow things down, I don't…"

"Not so much slow, but…"

"Let me finish." I inhaled, hoping for the right words. "We agreed to not so much take a step back, but to go in a different direction. Just because we aren't having sex, doesn't mean I…" I eased my hand into my pocket and stared out into the sea of high rise buildings. "I told you, I'd do whatever you want."

"And I appreciate that. I don't want you…please forget what I said. I wasn't…"

"Fi, I'm not playing the short game. I'm in this for the long haul."

"You are?" The surprise in her voice was evident.

"Yes." I sensed my time alone in the conference room was coming to an end. I looked over my shoulder and saw my negotiation opponent lurking near the door. "When I get back, we'll talk."

"I think that would be good."

I knew how I felt, but I didn't want to have that conversation over the phone. I wanted to be looking into those beautiful dark brown eyes when I said what I needed to say.

"I have to go."

"Okay. Oh…"

"What?"

"Would you do me a favor?"

"Depends."

"Are you serious?" Her eyes got wide.

"Yes. Are you asking as my client or my girlfriend?" The look on her face was priceless. "Well…"

"As my lawyer…"

"So my client is asking for a favor?" I smirked.

"Yes."

"No, I will not bring you back a deep dish pizza." I smiled.

"What?"

"Isn't that what you were going to ask me?"

"What…no."

"Okay, what can I do for my favorite client?"

"Would you please tell my boyfriend, I understand he has to work and I'm not angry. Also, let him know I love the card. I have it on my desk. However, Bentley has a crush on the girl dog on the cover." She laughed.

"What?"

"He's been staring at the card all morning."

"You're kidding?" I laughed.

"I'm serious." She sighed. "I have to get back to work."

"Me, too."

"Bye."

"Bye."

The line was dead and the screen was replaced with a picture of Fiona. I looked at my watch, and sent a text.

Ty: You were right
Tasha: About what?
Ty: The card
Tasha: Really…
Ty: Thanks
Tasha: You're welcome and thanks for the spa day
Ty: You deserve it
Tasha: Yes I do. Can I get back to my real job and not your relationship coach?
Ty: Yes

Chapter 33
Fiona

"Hey, Peanut," the deep familiar voice said.

"Where are you?"

"The lobby of your building."

"I thought you weren't due until later this afternoon."

"I got in early."

"No kidding," I replied sarcastically.

"Where are you?"

"Coming down the street. I should be there in five minutes."

"Okay."

I took a deep breath and looked at Bentley. "You're

about to meet your Uncle Mercer."

Bark!…Bark!…Bark!…Bark!

"I know you're excited." I rubbed his neck, looked up and caught Aidan's reflection in the rearview mirror. His smile and bright eyes spoke volumes. "You probably think I'm a little nuts."

His smile got wider. "No, ma'am. I think it's nice. My sister got a dog when her husband died."

"I'm sorry."

"Thank you. She said it really helped her heal."

I continued to rub Bentley's neck. "Huh, I never looked at it like that." I looked at Bentley and he appeared to be smiling. "Is that what you're doing?" I smiled.

Bark!…Bark!…Bark!…Bark!

"I think he thinks he's human."

"In his mind, he is." Aidan smiled.

"Mommy loves you." He yawned. "Now I need you to behave yourself and no trying to hump Uncle Mercer's leg."

Bark!…Bark!…Bark!…Bark!

"We're here, ma'am," Aidan said as he parked the car.

I looked at Bentley and lifted his face. "Behave yourself."

Bark!…Bark!…Bark!…Bark!

Aidan opened the door and Bentley climbed out and stood next to him. I took Aidan's hand, climbed out of the car and stepped onto the sidewalk. "Thank you." I took a deep breath.

"You're welcome." He handed me Bentley's leash. "I'll get your bags and meet you inside."

"Thank you." I looked down at Bentley. "Come on, let's go."

I walked inside following Bentley and looked around the lobby, searching for my big brother. I looked to the left and spotted Mercer in the corner on the phone. Although he had his back to me, I'd recognize that physique anywhere. Tall, broad shoulders, and a voice that carries no matter how hard he tries to speak softly.

I walked toward him and signaled Solomon and Bruce not to let on that I was standing behind him.

I cleared my throat and poked him on the back. "Excuse me, I think I might know you."

He turned around and his bright smile almost blinded me. "I'll have to call you back." He pressed the button ending the call. He wrapped his arms around me, lifted me up and swirled me around in the lobby like when we were kids.

Bark!Bark!Bark!Bark!

"Mercer, put me down." He placed me back on the ground and I tried to find my balance.

Bark!Bark!Bark!Bark!

Bentley walked over and growled at him.

Mercer bent down to Bentley's level. "Hey there, boy." Bentley tilted his head. "You must be Bentley." Bentley reached his paw out to Mercer. "It's a pleasure to meet you. Your Mommy has told me all about you."

Bark!…Bark!…Bark!…Bark!

"Thank you for looking after her."

Bark!…Bark!…Bark!…Bark!

I looked at Bentley. "What is it with you…some guard dog."

Mercer stood up. "He's a good judge of character." He winked.

"So I've been told."

"Here are your bags Miss Harris," Aidan said as he handed me the two small bags.

"Thank you. Aidan, this is my brother Mercer."

"Nice to meet you. I've heard a lot about you," Aidan replied.

"You have?" Mercer asked.

"Yes. Miss Harris has been talking non-stop about your visit."

He looked at me. "She has?"

"Yes. I'll pick you up in the morning at the regular time or will you be going in later?"

"I'll let you know later this afternoon. Thank you."

"You're welcome. Nice to meet you sir. Enjoy your visit." Aidan walked out to the car.

"Who was that?" Mercer asked.

"Take the bags and let's go upstairs."

We exited the elevator and I let Bentley off his leash.

"I gotta say Peanut, divorce looks good on you."

"You should have seen me a few months ago. It wasn't that pretty." I started taking things out of the bags and placing them on the counter.

Mercer took of his jacket, folded it and placed it on the back of the sofa. "So, things were a little rough." He unbuttoned his cuffs and rolled up his sleeves.

I put the milk in the refrigerator. "A little would be an understatement." I reached into the glass jar, pulled out a treat for Bentley and put it in his mouth. He walked back into the living room and curled up in front of the window, working on his treat.

"I still can't believe you have a dog…and a pit bull, too." He shook his head with a smirk on his face. "When you said you had a dog, I pictured something a little more…ladylike."

I looked at Bentley.

"Truth is, that's what I was looking for. Then this beautiful dog, walked over, looked up and started humping my leg." I laughed. "I knew he was perfect for me."

Mercer looked over at Bentley and then back at me. "So, how is your ex?"

"Fine, I guess. Hungry?"

"I'm good."

"Coffee...wine...I got this amazing merlot, that..."

"I'm fine. I want to know how you're doing?"

I sighed and leaned against the counter. "It was difficult at first, but it's gotten better. The first weekend after I signed the papers, I couldn't leave the loft. But, after spending the weekend feeling sorry for myself, I realized I needed to get on with my life. I didn't want to be one of those women who sulked and kicked herself because her marriage didn't go as she had planned. I was free, and I needed to start acting like it."

"Is this all an act?"

"What does that mean?"

"It means, I don't recognize you. You're nothing like the woman I visited almost two years ago. A car and driver... what's with that?"

"That was Ty's idea."

"Ty...who's Ty?"

I rubbed the back of my neck, trying to avoid eye contact. I was hoping to have this conversation later tonight over a glass of merlot and dinner. "Tiberius. My uhm...my..."

"Tiberius...Tiberius...why does that name sound familiar." He squinted his eyes and looked at me. I could tell he was processing. "Rhys' best friend?"

"Ex-best friend."

"You're taking advice from your ex's friend?"

"They haven't been friends for a while."

"Was this before or after he started giving you advice?"

"This was long before Rhys and I...he used to be our

attorney. I mean, it's all complicated."

"Uncomplicate it."

"Rhys switched lawyers a few years ago. However, I kept Ty as my attorney."

"Uh-huh."

"When I filed for divorce, he took care of everything for me."

"So, let me get this straight. Your ex-husband's ex-best friend handled your divorce?"

"Correct."

"Why would you do such an asinine thing?"

"Excuse me."

"He's playing you."

I was trying not to get angry. I'm sure to anyone not familiar with our situation, they'd think Ty wasn't on my side, but I knew better. If it hadn't been for Ty, I wouldn't have come out the victor.

"I did not get played. Rhys did."

"How, because right now, it doesn't…"

"If it hadn't been for Ty, I wouldn't have received the settlement I did. Nor would I have opened…he's on my side."

"I'm not so sure about that." He stood up with his arms folded in front of his chest. I immediately felt like I was ten years old again, looking up at my big brother, waiting on him to decide whether or not to tell our mother about the trouble I had gotten into at school.

"Trust me. Ty is a good guy. He cares about me and…" I quickly covered my mouth with my hand.

"Is there something going on between you and your lawyer?"

I lowered my head, exhaled, hoping an answer would magically appear in my mind. I raised my head and looked him in the eye. The last time I saw that confused look, was when I told him I was marrying my college crush.

"Yes."

He nodded. "I see." He wiped his mouth with his hands. "What is wrong with you?" His loud voice was bouncing off the walls. "How serious is it?"

How serious? That's a question I really didn't want to answer right now. Especially when I really wasn't sure. However, I knew he wouldn't stop with the questions until I answered him.

I stood firm, clutched the counter and looked up at my brother. "Serious enough that I thought I was pregnant."

"What?!"

The sound of that one word bouncing off the walls sent a chill through me. If I didn't know any better, I think Mercer would have come around the counter and shook me until I was numb.

Bentley ran over to Mercer.

Bark!Bark!Bark!Bark!

"Bentley…Bentley…" I called out.

Bark!Bark!Bark!Bark!

"Bentley, calm down. I'm okay." I leaned down and pulled him close.

Mercer started pacing with his face cupped in his hands. I didn't know whether to move or not.

Bark!Bark!Bark!Bark!

Mercer stopped and bent down to Bentley's level. "I'm sorry, Bentley. I didn't mean to scare you or your Mommy." He patted his head and Bentley went back to his spot by the window. Mercer stood up, exhaled, and looked at me. "So, you and Ty slept together."

I stood up. "It's a little more complicated than that."

"Fi…I'm about two seconds away from finding this dude and…"

"Ty and I are…he didn't take advantage of me, if that's what you're thinking."

"I'm listening."

"We've been seeing each other for a while."

"And how long have you been sleeping together?"

"My sex life is none of…" His furrowed brow and the whites of his balled up knuckles said otherwise. "It was one time."

"I don't understand. You said you and Ty were…"

"We've been seeing each other for a few months."

"Uh-huh."

"But we've only slept together once."

"One time and you thought you were pregnant?"

"It was more like one weekend." I cringed.

He folded his arms across his chest. "Spit it out, Fi."

"I seduced him and we ended up spending the weekend in bed."

"Wait a minute." He held his hand up. "Did you say, you seduced him?"

"Yes."

"You?"

"Yes."

"The girl who took her covenant with God so seriously, she barely kissed a guy. That same girl…I mean woman, seduced a man." The tension in his face was releasing.

"Why is that so hard to believe?" I said with my hands on my hips.

"Because, unless I don't know my sister as well as I thought I did, you would never do that."

I pulled a couple of wine glasses down, opened the bottle of merlot and filled the glasses.

"I'm sorry if you find it difficult to think I could seduce a man." I sipped my wine.

"I didn't say that." He sipped his wine. "I said, I can't believe you did that."

"Well, I did and we spent the weekend making love."

"Without protection? Was he trying to get you pregnant?" He sipped his wine.

"What...no. How absurd."

"Is it? I know brothers that have run that game so they could become the stay at home dad or claim child support." He sipped more wine. "Peanut, you're a rich woman and you need to be careful."

"Thanks, but it's not about the money."

"How do you know?"

"Because he has more than me."

"He's a lawyer who probably does well, but I'm sure he's not..."

"His family."

"His family?"

"His parents...his mother is 'Miss G'."

"Miss who?"

"Miss G...you know Miss G's pies, jams, muffins... Cooking with Miss G."

His eyes got wide. "That's his mother?" I nodded. "You're right. It's definitely not about the money." He sipped more wine. "Okay. So, you two are serious?"

"I think so. He flew me and Bentley down to meet his parents."

"He did?"

"Yes."

"What did he say when you told him you might be pregnant?"

"He doesn't know."

"He doesn't know?" His eyes got wide.

"I was going to tell him, and then I got my period. I figured…"

"Take it from someone that's been on the other side of that situation."

"Excuse me?"

"As I was saying, he needs to know."

"Why? What's to be gained? I'm not pregnant, just stressed."

"Because you need a plan to prevent this from happening again."

"We have a plan…no sex."

He laughed. "Are you serious?" He sipped more wine.

"Yes. We decided to slow things down."

"I'm glad to hear that, but…"

"But what?"

"What happens if you get caught up in a moment and…I've been there, too. Woke up the following morning with a bed buddy. Besides, Sis, are you sure this isn't a rebound thing. It's your first real relationship since the divorce."

"Ty asked me the same thing. He said he'd follow my lead…do whatever I want. If that means sex then he's happy to oblige."

"I'm sure he is."

"If it means taking it slow, he's good with that."

"I understand, but you still need to tell him. If this is as serious as you say, you need to know where it's headed. Lay all of your cards on the table."

Bark!…Bark!…Bark!…Bark!…

"Even Bentley agrees with me."

"Yeah…yeah…yeah…"

Unexpected Love

He walked around the counter, rubbed my shoulders and kissed me on the forehead, like he did when we were kids. "I can't wait to grill this guy."

"Promise me you'll be nice and not judge him."

"I promise not to cause a scene."

He started walking away. "Mercer, promise me."

"I'm going to get a shower. Are we going out or staying in?"

Chapter 34
Ty

I exited the elevator into the dark space. It was a toss up between which was more likely to give me away. My foot when it hit a piece of furniture as I headed on my mission. Or the eruption of the quiet as I disrupted it trying not to be heard. Either way, I was assured I'd fall victim to one of the night wardens.

I looked around and everything was calm. I slipped my jacket off, placed it on the back of the sofa and quietly walked down the hall. I stopped at the white door, took a deep breath and realized I could still escape without being noticed. Instead, I grabbed the brushed steel knob and pushed open the partially opened door.

I stepped inside, pulled the door close, walked over to

the bed and stood next to it, staring down at her. It was like I had stepped into a fairytale, watching the beautiful sleeping princess.

I leaned down, kissed her forehead, then gently pressed my lips against hers. She moved a little. I kissed her again and her eyes slowly opened.

"Hey…" she said with the tails of sleep trailing on the heels of the simple word before turning her full lips up into a smile.

"Hey."

"Is this real or a dream?"

I stroked the side of her face with the back of my hand. "It's real."

"Good, because I'd hate to discover I was dreaming and you weren't here." She brushed the side of my face with her delicate hand. "I must have fallen back asleep after you called."

"Clearly. I was expecting to see you in the living room or downstairs in the lobby."

"I got up, brushed my teeth and I don't remember anything after that." She started to get up.

"Don't." I sat on the side of the bed.

"What time is it?" She yawned.

I looked at my watch. "It's three fifteen."

She sat up, pulled the comforter across her chest, but it didn't help hide her partially covered body from me. Nor did it stop my mind from remembering how she looked the morning after we'd made love here. Her beautiful naked body was engraved in my mind. The way she felt lying next to me wrapped in that same comforter, was a sight burned in my memory forever. If she asked, without hesitation, I'd be in bed next to her, on top of her, inside her.

"I missed you."

"Here I thought the only one that missed me was Bentley." We smiled and looked across the room at the black pit bull.

"Some watch dog. He hasn't budged at all."

I liked how the moonlight bounced off her skin and highlighted her doe shaped eyes and high cheek bones. "Where's your brother?"

"Guest room." She tucked her hair behind her ear.

I nodded. "I should leave. I don't want to get caught walking out of your bedroom." I started to stand up and she grabbed my hand. "What?"

"You're leaving without a proper goodbye kiss."

I brushed the side of her face with my thumb, leaned in and pressed my lips against hers. I was trying to keep it chaste, but how chaste is a drive by kiss at three o'clock in the morning?

I tried to pull back, but she wrapped her hands around the back of my neck and pulled me closer to her. She grabbed my bottom lip sucking and pulling. Then she inched closer, dragged her tongue along my lips and let out a soft moan.

I knew I should leave, but she had lured me in with her mouth. She covered my mouth with hers and drove her tongue inside, stroking, teasing, and exciting me as our tongues danced. She pulled me deeper into her space as she eased back down onto the bed with me pressed against her. Every inch of her body melded against mine. Her hard nipples punched through the thin silk of her gown brushing against my chest.

The spicy floral notes of her parfum permeated my nose and mind, making me a willing follower. My tongue got in sync with hers and our kiss became more aggressive and dangerous.

I eased my hands around her waist and pulled her

closer against my body. My mind said, stop. However, my body wanted something different. My body wanted to feel her skin next to mine. Even clothed, she felt good pressed against me. Memories of that weekend we spent here, wrapped in each other's arms, rolling around the bed and making love flooded my mind.

I reached down and pushed the comforter away. I needed to feel her skin. I slipped the thin straps of her gown down and cupped her breast. The full orb felt good in my hand as I kneaded and pressed it, teasing her hard peak with the tip of my thumb. She let out a soft moan and I continued making love to her breast.

I pushed my knee in between her legs, nestled my hips in between her hot thighs and she pulled me deeper inside. My body was on a mission and completely ignoring our agreement. I moved my mouth down her chin, along her collar bone kissing the delicate skin between her breasts. She let out another moan and I dragged my tongue across her neglected breast. I latched on to her nipple, sucking and pulling.

"Oh, God…" she cried out softly.

I continued making love to her breast and her body began to dance. I needed out of my clothes. I needed to be buried deep inside her. She pulled my shirt out of my pants and her hot hands connected with my skin. *Oh, God…* I missed her touch.

"I want to feel you deep inside me. I don't care what we agreed. I want…"

I moved my mouth up to her ear and kissed her neck. "Is that really what you want?" I kissed her neck again.

In between deep breaths and heavy panting, she replied, "Yes, but…" she sighed.

I raised up and looked at her. This is how I had pictured

her the first night I was in Florida. I tried not to look below her neck, but I couldn't help but look at her beautiful full breasts and how I could bring her to orgasm with my mouth and hands.

I knew what she was going to say. I lowered my head, closed my eyes and when I opened them, I was staring at another beautiful sight. Her gown was pushed up and the beautiful sea of dark curls were staring at me. Enticing me. It would be so easy to bury my fingers deep inside her, stroking her till she cried out.

"I should leave." She climbed out of bed and when she stood up, the gown fell to the floor. I tried not to look, but there she was in all her beautiful nakedness with the moonlight highlighting her curves.

She stepped to me, unbuttoned a couple of buttons on my shirt and kissed my chest. "Do you have to leave?" She kissed me again and I moaned. She kissed my nipple and I growled. "Stay..." she begged.

This was torture. "As much as I don't want to..."

She looked at me with a devilish smile. "I promise to be quiet and we can start our arrangement over in the morning."

I sucked on my bottom lip. You can go the distance. You can be the man she needs. You promised not to give in.

"Please...don't tempt me." I looked around for her robe and found it lying at the end of the bed. I broke out of her hold and picked up her robe. "Here, put this on."

She took the white silk robe out of my hand and took her time, putting it on. Watching her cover her body was just as seductive as watching her undress it.

"Better?" she asked as she licked her lips. She stepped to me and kissed my neck.

"Yes." I wiped my face with my hands. I can do this.

I can go the distance with Fiona. I kissed her forehead. "Walk me out." I took her hand and walked out to the living room.

I looked up and standing in front of the open refrigerator was the other reason why I should have just gone home.

"Fi, why don't you have..." he turned around. "Who's this?"

Chapter 35
Fiona

"Oh Crap!" That's what I said out loud, but in my head, I was screaming something else.

I knew there was no explanation my brother would understand, let alone believe. I let go of Ty's hand and realized I was a grown ass woman who needed to stand up for herself.

I tied the belt on my robe and continued into the living room.

"I know this looks bad," Ty said as he rushed to my defense.

"You think," Mercer said. He slammed the refrigerator door and braced his hands on the counter. "Is someone going to tell me what's going on?"

I looked at Ty and there was no way this didn't look like what it almost was. "Uhm...Ty was..."

I felt Ty's large warm hand ease around my waist pulling me close to him. It was that reassuring feeling that I wasn't in this alone. That we were going to answer this question.

"Clearly, no matter how you look at this, it looks bad." Mercer folded his arms across his chest, breathing hard as he stared at Ty. "I would never do anything to disrespect Fiona," Ty replied.

"Coming out of her bedroom at three in the morning, with her half dressed, sort of contradicts that statement."

Ty walked over to the counter and took his position on the opposite side of the counter across from Mercer. Both looked like they were preparing for battle. The battle in question was my virtue, what was left of it.

"Merc, that's not fair."

"Be quiet, Fi. This is between me and...your... boyfriend." He spit out the word like it was a curse.

"Don't talk to her like that. She's not a child," Ty retorted.

I saw where this was headed and it wasn't going to be good. I rushed over and stood next to Ty. "Babe, leave and let me talk to Mercer." It was like I was talking to two brick walls. Neither of them was looking at me. "Ty, please...I can handle this." I covered his hand and he finally broke eye contact with Mercer.

"Are you sure?"

I looked into his eyes and I hadn't seen that intensity since my last divorce meeting when he kicked Rhys' butt.

I stroked the side of his face. "I'll be fine." I raised up on my tip toes and gently pressed my lips against his. "Go home, and I'll call you later."

He kissed the inside of my palm. "Alright."

He picked up his jacket, walked over and pressed the button for the elevator. I helped him slip his jacket on and then the elevator door opened. He stepped inside, kissed me again and the door closed.

I didn't move immediately. I searched my mind for the right words to say to my brother. I turned around and walked back to the kitchen.

"What the crap, Fiona?! Have you lost your mind?! I don't believe you had some guy up here." He was pacing back and forth. This was the second time in as many days I'd had the privilege of entertaining Angry Mercer.

Mercer has always had a temper, but it seems my new independence was provoking it even more.

"I'm not going to stand here and let you berate or yell at me. I'm a grown woman and I will not be spoken to like that in my home." I exhaled. "If you can't talk to me like a calm adult, I'm going back to bed." He looked like a spoiled pouting child. Breathing hard with his arms folded across his chest. "Well then, I'm going to bed. Good night."

I walked down the hall to my bedroom and slammed the door. I took my robe off, climbed into bed and looked at my phone.

Ty: Are you alright?
Fi: Yes…sorry about my brother.
Ty: I'm sorry…I shouldn't have stopped by.
Fi: It's not your fault…my brother can be an overprotective ass…but I love him.
Ty: How did it go?
Fi: Refused to talk until he calms down.
Ty: I feel really bad. How about brunch?
Fi: When and where?

Ty: Pink Cafe.
Fi: My favorite…see you at 11:30
Ty: What about your brother?
Fi: Don't know if I want him to come.
Ty: Be the bigger person
Fi: Why are you being practical?
Ty: You know I'm right…just like I was right not to…
Fi: Not what? Smile.
Ty: Succumb to your charms. Smile.
Fi: Charms?
Ty: I believe you were trying to seduce me.
Fi: Good night…I mean morning.
Ty: Can't handle the truth…
Fi: I know the truth.
Ty: Which is?
Fi: Booty call?
Ty: It's only a booty call when you get the booty.
Fi: I tried.
Ty: E plus for effort.
Fi: Text me when you get home.
Ty: Can't handle the truth. Smile.
Fi: Good night.
Ty: Good night.

ಌಭಌಭಌಭಌಭಌ

Bentley and I exited the elevator and the aroma of fresh coffee greeted me. I let Bentley off his leash and I walked into the kitchen. I looked up and saw Mercer sitting at the counter reading his Bible and drinking a cup of coffee.

I walked over, filled the white mug and took a sip. "Good coffee."

"Thanks." He didn't look up from his reading. "About last, this morning."

"What about it?"

He closed up his Bible. "How serious are you about Ty?"

I took another sip of coffee and placed my mug on the white marble counter. "Pretty serious."

"I'm not going to apologize for the way I behaved."

"Then we…"

He held up his hand. "Please let me finish."

I sighed and folded my arms across my chest. "Go on."

"I've been the other man."

My eyes got wide at his statement. "What?"

"I've been the other man. I've also been the rebound man. Neither situation was appealing."

"I didn't…why didn't you tell me?"

"It's not something you want your sister to know." He sighed. "The first situation, I was young and fell for her lies. She said she and her husband were having problems and were headed for divorce. The joke was on me. She was only interested in a plaything. When she thought she was pregnant, I freaked out. I wasn't ready to be a father."

"Mercer…what happened?"

"False alarm and a wakeup call for me. I broke things off and never heard from her again."

"And the rebound?"

"I should have known better. She seemed to be ready to move on. When I started talking about a future together, she freaked out and we broke up. That one hurt a lot, because I was invested. I'd met her son and we were getting along. We were doing the whole family thing and then, out of nowhere, she broke it off."

"I'm so sorry."

"She said she needed more time to heal and…well." He wiped his face with his hands. "I'm not telling you to become a nun, although, that would make me very happy," he smirked. "I just don't want you to rush."

"His mother said the same thing."

"What?"

"His mother told me I need to take time to get to know this Fiona."

"She's right."

"I know, but, I've never felt like this before."

"Are you sure it's not the newness and excitement of freedom?" He sipped his coffee.

"That's what I thought, but when Ty said, he'd do whatever I wanted and hasn't pushed me…he's not the one trying to move things faster, it's me."

"I know."

"You know?"

"Any man brave enough to come over for a booty call and…"

"It wasn't a booty call."

"Fi, don't insult my intelligence. It was a booty call. I've been that man as well." He smiled.

"I'm learning a lot about you this morning." I smiled.

"I saw something in his eyes that made me think, he might have been telling me the truth."

"Him you believe, but not your sister."

"It's guy's intuition." He smiled.

"Really?"

"If he hadn't been a stand up guy, he would have hid

until I went back to bed. But he didn't. He faced me like a man."

"Nothing happened."

"I know better than that."

"You do?" I rubbed the back of my neck.

"Yes and if you insist on…please be careful. Not that I wouldn't be excited to become an uncle, but I…"

"I'm on the pill." I exhaled. "I think in the back of my head, I knew I wasn't pregnant, but…I was hoping I was."

"I don't understand."

"One of the reasons Rhys and I divorced is because he lied about wanting children. When I was late, it was like I received confirmation I wasn't the reason why I never got pregnant."

He nodded. "I see. So if you were pregnant, you would have known it wasn't just that he didn't want children, it was that he couldn't have them."

"But it turns out he had a daughter." I felt the tears coming. "And didn't want children with me."

Mercer got up, walked around and wrapped me in a bear hug and the tears came harder.

Bark!…Bark!…Bark!…Bark!

"Your Mommy is fine, Bentley." Mercer rubbed my back and it felt like it did when I was a teenager experiencing my first broken heart. "Let it all out." I cried harder.

After what felt like an eternity, I pulled back and Mercer patted my wet face with the kitchen towel. "Better?" I nodded. "Come on, let's sit down."

"I can't. I have to get dressed. We're meeting Ty in…"

"We have plenty of time. Let's talk."

We walked over to the sofa and sat down. I was dreading this conversation. Mercer looked at me and it was like he was looking into my soul. He had this uncanny ability to read me like a book. "I know what you're going to say."

"You do?"

"You don't think I've really dealt with my divorce and that I'm still healing from Rhys."

"Uh-huh."

"But I'm fine. I just…I've got a lot going on and…"

"You're right. I don't think you've really come to grips with your divorce."

"But I have."

"Hear me out." He rubbed my hand.

"Go ahead."

"Divorce isn't something you just get over, even if it had been a long time coming. You still have some scars you need to deal with."

"I'm fine."

"What was that in the kitchen?"

"Stress."

"Stress?"

"I've got a lot on my mind. In case you forgot, I'm preparing to re-launch my magazines on my own, and it's scary."

"So the tears were about work?"

"Yes. I'm fine."

"If that's what you say."

"If I wasn't, I'd tell you." I stood up. "We need to get ready. We don't want to be late."

Chapter 36
Ty

"Mr. Wells, Mercer Wade is here to see you. He says he knows he doesn't have an appointment, but..." Jake said.

"Where's Tasha?" If ever I needed my gate keeper, it was now.

"Ladies room."

I hesitated to reply. "Send him back. Thank you." I hung up my phone, closed up the file I was working on, and mentally readied myself for my surprise meeting.

I walked over to the door and heard familiar voices engaged in a heated conversation. I opened the door and got a front row seat to the encounter.

"I told you, you cannot see Mr. Wells without an appointment," Tasha announced.

"I understand that. However, he said for me to come back," Mercer replied.

"I don't know who you are, but…"

"Tasha, it's fine."

"Mr. Wells, this man claims…"

"Come in Mercer." He looked at Tasha and smiled as he walked into my office.

"Who is that?" Tasha asked.

"Please hold my calls. Thank you." I walked back into my office and closed the door. "Have a seat." I extended my hand to the sofa for Mercer, and I sat down in the club chair. "This is a surprise."

"For you," Mercer said.

"What can I do for you?"

"How serious are you about my sister?"

"I thought you grilled me sufficiently at brunch." I crossed my legs and leaned back in the chair.

"My sister isn't as strong as she looks."

"I'm very well aware of Fiona's vulnerability."

"I don't think she's fully dealt with her divorce."

"Neither do I."

He looked vexed at my answer. "I'm a lot confused. Why do I get the feeling you two are on a bullet train headed for marriage?"

I bit my bottom lip and nodded my head. "I was expecting that question at brunch."

"So that means you have an answer."

"I wasn't expecting any of this. I was seeing someone when Fiona asked for my help. In fact, it was Fiona that helped me through my breakup."

"So two broken people are in a relationship."

"I wouldn't say we're…how much do you know about Fi and Rhys' marriage?"

"I know I never liked him. I thought he was very selfish, but she insisted she was in love, so I kept my mouth shut. I figured if I said anything, she'd surely marry him."

"And look what happened."

"I didn't say anything and she married him anyway. I thought I was doing what our parents would have done," he sighed. "I basically raised Fi after her dad and our mother died."

"I didn't know that."

"That's why I'm a little over protective."

"Before Rhys and I ended our friendship, he told me things about his marriage and…I never understood why he stayed if he was so unhappy."

"I suspected there was a problem." He eased to the edge of the sofa and clasped his hands.

"I have no proof, but I believe he was cheating on her."

"He what?!" The vein at his temple was beginning to throb. Fi had warned me about his temper. She said apart from her, the other thing we had in common was matching tempers.

"He never came right out and said it, but he hinted at it frequently. Then there was the business. I helped him secure financing and later he dumped my firm."

"Interesting, because Fi asked me to help him."

"I didn't know that. What happened?"

"His plan was good, but," he leaned back against the sofa and crossed one leg over the other, "I don't like him. I got a weird vibe from him." He clasped his hands in his lap. "I figured Fi would wake up and leave him, and I didn't want to be tied to my sister's ex."

"I had no idea you felt that way."

"Fi knows I don't like him. That's why I limited my visits." He sighed. "Fi and I talk daily, but I missed my sister. When I got here and saw her, I knew she was different."

"Different?"

"I sat in front of my computer every day watching my sister convince me that everything in her world was fine."

"And it wasn't."

"No, it wasn't." He exhaled. "So, what are we going to do?"

"I don't understand."

"You and Fi. What's going on? I know what I think is going on, but I'd like to hear it from you."

I shifted in the comfortable gray leather chair. I had an answer. It may not be the one he wanted to hear, it may not even be the one I wanted to hear, but it was an answer.

"When we started meeting for lunch, I think she felt guilty about how Rhys treated me, and this was her way of doing penance. Rhys and I had been drifting apart for quite some time, so when he severed our business relationship, I felt relieved."

"You did?"

"Mine and Rhys' friendship had run its course. We were on different paths. He was looking to be the next Rupert Murdoch and I wasn't trying to be the next F. Lee Bailey."

"But you're on your way." He smirked.

I moved to the edge of my chair and rested my elbows on my knees. "I run a boutique firm with a tight client list."

"Boutique?" He questioned me with a raised eyebrow.

"Compared to other firms, mine is...that's not the point."

"Continue."

"I didn't go searching for wealthy clients, it just happened. However, Rhys has always been about the image...trappings...the money. Fi isn't like that. I negotiated a nice settlement for her."

"She told me."

"I begged her not to sell those magazines, because I saw how passionate she was about them."

"Professionally, I know she admires you. But I can't help but think it's too soon for her to get involved with someone."

"I agree it is. However, I saw something..."

"I know she talks and looks strong, but she's..."

"Strong."

"So you say."

"Clearly, we aren't going to agree on this."

He quickly copied my seated position. "I know my sister."

"And I know my girlfriend." His eyes got wide. It was a bold move making that statement. "I know Fi says I saved her, but the reality is, she saved me."

"She did?"

"She's very charismatic and her energy is infectious. It's a little impossible to resist her." I felt my mouth turning up into a smile. "She uhm...she's...I tried keeping things platonic, but I...I told her I would follow her lead. I'd do whatever she wanted."

"So it's true, she seduced you?"

I looked at him and he was stone faced. "She told you about that?"

"Yes."

"No disrespect, but Fi is a woman who knows what she wants. The weekend we spent to…"

"So the other night, were you giving into to Fi's wishes, because I thought you two had an understanding?"

"Seems she's told you everything."

"Pretty much. So?"

"I know it was foolish of me to stop by, but I hadn't seen her in a couple of weeks and…you know what it's like."

"Exactly. That's why I didn't believe Fi when she said nothing happened."

"I wouldn't say nothing." I rubbed my neck. "We uhm…we…"

He held up his hands. "I don't want to know."

"I thought that's why you came here?"

"I wanted to see if you were willing to be open without Fi by your side."

"I'm not going to talk to you about the details of mine and Fiona's sex life."

His eyes got wide. "Thank you."

"We've agreed to slow things down, but it's a little more difficult than we expected."

"Thus the 3:00am booty call."

"Yeah." I smiled.

"I'll back off and let you and Fi figure things out."

"Thanks."

"But if you hurt my sister, you'll have to deal with me." We stood up and shook hands. "Your assistant."

"Tasha. I'm sorry about…"

"Is she seeing anyone?"

"You're interested in Tasha?" I smiled.

He slipped his hand inside his trouser pocket, rubbed his chin and smiled. "I like her fire."

"I think it's all clear. But be careful."

"Definitely."

"When are you leaving?"
"Depends on Tasha."
I nodded. "Let me see what I can do to help."
"Thanks. I'll owe you one."
"Don't thank me just yet."

Chapter 37
Tasha

"Tasha, do me a favor."

"You know I'm off the clock."

"Are you still in the office?"

"I'm standing at the elevator, which means…"

"You're still on the clock."

"What do you want, Ty?"

"Is that any way to talk to your boss?"

"Excuse me?"

"I think I left an envelope on my desk I needed to give Fi."

"And this is my problem how?"

"You're my assistant and I pay you very well to do just that…assist me."

"Exactly. I'm your assistant, not your girlfriend."

"Client."

I sighed. "What do you want?"

"Check and see if there's an envelope on my desk with her name on it. Please."

"Hold on." I walked down the hall to his office. When I entered, I went straight to his desk. The large manila envelope was sitting in the center of the desk blotter. "I see it."

"I need you to bring it to me at the restaurant."

"What?!"

"Why can't I send a messenger?"

"Fine with me if you want to wait a half hour or longer for one to get there."

"Fine."

"Where are you?"

"Peony."

"Are you serious?"

"Yes."

I looked at my watch. "That's all the way…"

"Aidan is downstairs."

I sighed. "Fine. This will cost you."

"I'll treat you to dinner."

"I don't want to be the third wheel to you and Fi." I picked up the envelope and started toward the elevator. "I'll call you when I get there and you can come out and get it."

"Fi will be upset if you don't join us."

"I'm sure she'll be fine. Bye." I pressed the button ending the call and stepped onto the elevator.

I tossed my head back against the matte chrome wall and rested my behind on the railing. I closed my eyes and asked myself if I really wanted to see William again. Sure we had a good time, and the thought of his magic hands and mouth, made my core shudder, but it really wasn't enough. I wanted more than good sex. I wanted and needed intellectual and emotional stimulation.

The gentle ding of the elevator landing broke the self-deprecating I was doing. I leaned forward, sighed and exited the elevator. I kept my eyes straight ahead, aimed at the glass doors.

"Good evening, Miss Cummings."

I looked in the direction of the deep voice and spotted the young man in a black jacket and white shirt standing at the security desk. "Good night, Gavin."

"Aidan is out front."

"Thank you. I'll see you tomorrow."

I headed out the front door, looked ahead, and spotted Aidan standing next to the black Maserati with the door open.

"Good evening, Miss Cummings." Aidan smiled.

If he was a few years older, I'd take him under my wing and teach him a few things. It could be fun being Mrs. Robinson. "Hello, Aidan. I'm sorry you had to come all the way over here." I smiled.

"It's my pleasure."

"Thank you." I climbed into the back seat of the car, locked my seat belt, tossed my head back, and exhaled.

This is not what I had planned for the evening. I was hoping to go home and forget about William. I don't know why I'm so upset. I went into that brief interlude knowing full well his purpose was to scratch my itch.

I closed my eyes, crossed my legs, and remembered how proficient he was at tending to my itch. A warm sensation traveled the length of my body as I replayed our last encounter. Honestly, I wouldn't have broken things off so soon, but overhearing his phone call pissed me off.

The nerve of him making a date with some other chick right after we'd just…tacky, tasteless, disrespectful. But I only have myself to blame. That's what I get for being blinded by the package. I have to admit, he didn't disappoint. I can't believe he was able to bring me to orgasm that many times. His hands and mouth should be classed as the eighth and ninth wonders of the world.

Maybe I should adopt Ty and Fiona's new dating paradigm. Effective immediately, no sex until marriage.

"We're here," Aidan's deep voice penetrated my thoughts, bringing me back to reality.

"I'm sorry. What did you say?"

"We're here."

I leaned forward and looked out the window. Crap. I really wanted Ty to come out so I wouldn't have to go inside.

Aidan got out, walked around the car and opened the door. I extended my hand and he helped me out onto the curb. I adjusted my clothes and looked around.

"I won't be long."

"No problem." He closed the door and walked back around the car.

I walked up to the door, opened it and stepped inside. I walked over to the hostess station and waited for the young blond woman to hang up the phone.

"Hello. Welcome to Peony," the young woman said. She looked like she should be in her dorm studying, or pre-gaming for a frat party. Instead, she was working.

"Hello. I need to drop something off for Mr. Wells. Can you please ask him…"

"You must be Miss Cummings," she cut me off.

"Yes."

"He said when you arrived I was to take you to the table."

"What the...," I looked around the vestibule, "...fine. Where is he?"

"Right this way."

I held my head high and followed the average height young woman. It was William's fault I had to walk in here and then right back out. If I hadn't been fantasizing about him, I wouldn't have forgotten to call Ty and tell him to be outside when I arrived.

The aromas of the food being served traveled up my nose, making me rethink Ty's offer to join he and Fiona for dinner. I looked to my left and spotted a plate of incredible looking crab cakes. Then a server crossed in front of me with a pork chop that made my mouth water. Maybe dining with Ty and Fiona wouldn't be too bad.

"Here's your table," the hostess said.

I looked at the empty table. "Is this the correct table?"

"I'm sorry. I was told when you arrived to seat you. The rest of your party should be here soon."

I looked at my watch. I probably had time for a plate of crab cakes. "Okay. Would you please have the server bring me an order of crab cakes and a glass of your house chardonnay. Thank you."

"My pleasure," she replied and walked away.

I sat down, placed the black napkin in my lap, and looked around the crowded restaurant. I wasn't happy to be sitting alone, but it beat sitting at home kicking myself about how things had ended with William. Stop it. It wasn't a real relationship, but a situation of convenience.

I rubbed my neck and was glad no one could read my mind. I sipped my water and then it occurred to me, I should invite Aidan inside to join me. At least I'd have a little company until Ty and Fiona arrived.

I took my phone out of my bag and started to dial his number.

"I hope you don't mind, but I changed your wine request."

I looked up in the direction of the uninvited voice. "Excu——" I was sure my eyes were playing a trick on me. "What the…"

He walked around the table and his physique didn't go unnoticed. Even covered in fine wool and silk, it was clear he wasn't lacking in muscle definition. In the brief seconds it took him to walk around the table, I had scanned his body from head to toe, and picked out my favorite rear view.

He casually sat in the chair on the other side of the table. I still couldn't believe the view my eyes were sending to my brain.

"Did you want to finish your call?" The way the words rolled off his thick juicy lips was mesmerizing. And those teeth…his teeth looked like perfectly sculpted piano keys. All aligned and ready to move at his command.

"What?"

"Your call…seems I interrupted your call." He pointed to my phone.

"Oh, I can…" I pressed the home button on my phone and placed it face down on the table. I adjusted my napkin and sat up straight. "Are you following me?"

"In order for me to be following you, I'd have to have been hanging around your office all afternoon." He leaned across the table. "You're fine, but not that fine that I'd miss making money." His breath smelled like cinnamon. Honestly, I didn't hear anything he said, because I was imagining how his lips would feel pressed against mine.

"You do know you can leave."

He winked and leaned back in his seat. "Yes, I could, but then I'd miss out on annoying you." He placed the napkin in his lap.

"What do you want?"

"I saw you and thought I'd come over and speak."

"You've spoken, now you can leave."

"Sir, is this what you asked for?" the sommelier presented him with a dark bottle.

"Yes. Thank you. Please fill both glasses."

I covered my glass with my hand. "I'm not drinking that."

The server appeared on the other side of the table with a plate of crab cakes and another with bone marrow. The smells were incredible. The fresh thyme and garlic were teasing my senses.

"Here's your first course, sir," the server said as he placed the plates on the table.

"Thank you. Unfortunately, it seems my dining companion won't be joining me."

The server looked confused. My mouth was already savoring the flavors and I hadn't taken a bite yet. I looked at the wall of muscles with the sexy smile and then at the crab cakes.

"Since the chef went to so much trouble..." I removed my hand from my glass and the sommelier filled it. "Thank you." I held my glass up to drink and he reached across and grabbed my wrist. When his hand touched my skin, it seemed as if time stopped and I floated outside of my body observing myself.

"We're doing this right."

"What?"

He locked eyes with me and I swear he was looking at my soul. "Here's to a great meal and even better sex." He clinked my glass, released my arm and sipped his wine.

"What did you say?"

"You know the saying. If you look each other in the eye when you clink glasses, you'll be blessed with great sex. And if you don't…" He sipped more wine. "Smooth." He nodded.

I followed his lead and took a sip. He was right. The flavors danced on my tongue. I could taste the apricot, apple, honey and smooth citrus flavors. I took another sip and placed the glass on the table.

"Well…"

"It's okay." I folded my arms across my chest. "What do you want Mercer?"

"You remembered my name?" He smiled.

"Don't be flattered."

"But I am."

"I remember the names of everyone that barges into my office without an appointment."

He bowed his head and said grace, completely ignoring me. He scooped out some bone marrow, placed it on a piece of toast and presented it to me. "Open up."

"What?"

"Woman, open your mouth and eat this."

"I can serve myself."

"I'm sure you can. Think of it as your chance to bite my finger."

The thought of doing him a little physical harm was appealing. I leaned forward, opened my mouth and watched as he placed the toast in my mouth. I bit down and the flavors were just as I imagined. The thyme and garlic were like a savory explosion capturing my tastebuds. He took the remainder and popped it into his mouth. My eyes rolled back into my head savoring the warm, spicy flavors.

"This is good."

"I thought you'd like it." He sipped his wine.

I patted the sides of my mouth. "Very good."

We finished our appetizers and I looked at my watch, noting the time. "Meeting someone?"

"I'm meeting Ty." I sipped more wine and looked at him. The smile on his face told me our meeting up wasn't a coincidence. "What does he owe you?"

"Excuse me?"

"What does Ty owe you?"

"He doesn't owe me anything."

"Uh-huh. So you just happened to be at the same restaurant I was told to deliver an envelope to. Not to mention, I haven't seen Ty yet."

Mercer wiped his mouth, finished off his wine and smiled. "I asked Ty about a spot for dinner and...I can't even say that with a straight face. I asked Ty to help me out."

I looked at him stone faced. I finished the last of my wine and placed my glass back on the table. I patted the sides of my mouth. I folded my napkin and placed it on the table next to my plate. I stood up and so did he.

"I expect the next course to be here when I return from the ladies room."

"Yes, ma'am." He smiled.

Chapter 38
Mercer

I couldn't take my eyes off her. She was even more fascinating than this morning. Her fire and sassiness were refreshing and added to her sexiness. It was exciting being with a woman not trying to please me, but comfortable and confident enough to be herself.

"This has been a pleasant surprise, but it's late." She patted the sides of her mouth and placed her napkin on the table.

"It's not that late."

She picked up her phone and started typing a text. "I don't know what your watch says, but it's late." She smiled.

I stood up, walked to her side of the table and extended my hand to her.

"Dance with me."

Her mouth dropped open. "Are you insane? This isn't a club."

"Haven't you ever done something a little insane?"

"Besides have dinner with a stranger?"

"I'm not going to sit down until you dance with me."

"I hope those are comfortable shoes." She cocked her head to the side. "You're serious?" She looked around the restaurant, then reluctantly took my hand and stood up. "I can't believe I'm doing this."

"Be quiet and enjoy the music."

I slipped my hand around her waist and pulled her to my chest. I took her hand in mine and we swayed to the soulful sounds filling the restaurant. I couldn't believe how fast my heart was racing. I felt like a scared teenaged boy dancing with a girl for the first time. Being this close to her scintillating scent was like an invisible magnet, drawing me closer to her. She smelled like spicy vanilla and tobacco. It was a seductive, sexy scent designed to hypnotize anyone who dared get close to her.

I pulled her close and was surprised there was no resistance. Instead, our bodies synced up seamlessly.

"See, no one is looking at us."

"You're insane," she said softly.

"Could be."

She looked around the restaurant to verify my words. I noticed some more couples started dancing.

"Seems we've started something." She looked up at me and her dark brown eyes pulled me deeper under her spell. "Are you always this spontaneous?"

Her question caught me by surprise. I would never use that word to describe myself...practical...methodical...

focused, but never spontaneous.

"Never."

The look on her face spoke volumes. "You're kidding, right?"

I shook my head. "Nope."

"I don't believe you." She smiled.

"That's not the first word people use to describe me."

"So tell me the word." She tilted her head and sucked on the corner of her bottom lip.

"Shy." I smiled.

She laughed out loud and then rested her forehead on my chest. Once she stopped laughing, she raised her head and directed those beautiful eyes at me. "Who was the idiot that called you shy?"

I tried not to join in her laughter. I clenched my jaw and replied, "My last two girlfriends."

"Really?"

"Just kidding." I smiled.

She stopped moving and stepped out of my hold. "Just kidding?" Her sexy smile was gone and replaced with a stone face. "Settle the check." She picked up her bag and walked towards the front door.

I couldn't believe she was leaving. I stuffed some money into the black leather folder and hurried behind her. When I got outside, I looked straight ahead and noticed the back door of the black Maserati was open. All I saw were Tasha's gorgeous legs. I continued to the car.

"How was dinner, Mr. Wade?" Aidan asked.

"Incredible. And yours?"

"I really enjoyed the crab cakes. Thank you."

"You're welcome." I leaned down and poked my head inside the car. "Can I get a ride?" She removed her bag and crossed her legs. I climbed into the car and sat down.

Aidan closed the door and walked around the car and got in. Once he'd locked his seatbelt, he looked at me in the rearview mirror.

"Where to, Mr. Wade?"

I looked at Tasha and then back at Aidan. "Miss Cummings' building. Thank you." I looked at Tasha and she was looking straight ahead. "I take it you didn't like my joke?"

She didn't respond.

We rode to her building in silence. I couldn't get a read on her. We continued, and arrived shortly at a modern high rise building on the Upper Eastside. "We're here." Aidan got out, and opened my door.

"Thank you. I'll help Miss Cummings." I walked around the back of the car. I opened the rear passenger door, extended my hand to Tasha and helped her exit the car. She walked inside and I followed behind her like a lost puppy, hoping the pretty lady would take me home.

We continued past the concierge and around the corner to the elevator. We stood in silence waiting for the elevator to arrive. I stood behind her, inhaling her mesmerizing scent. I saw her look at my reflection in the chrome doors, but she remained stone faced.

The elevator dinged and we stepped to the side waiting for the doors to open. When the doors opened, no one exited. We entered, she pressed the button for her floor, and we rode up in more silence.

I wasn't sure what was going on. She hadn't said a word since her directive at the restaurant. I have to admit I was baffled. I'd been in negotiations that weren't this complex and unreadable.

The elevator stopped, the doors opened and I hesitated

to exit, but I did. I followed those sexy hips as they walked down the hall, swaying to the rhythm in her head. The slow, confident strides were like a pied piper luring her prey. She had me. I was prepared to do whatever she commanded.

She stopped at the light gray door with four numbers… one zero one four. She took her key out and held it up. That was my signal and instruction. The cold war was over. I walked to the door, inserted the key, turned the knob and pushed the door open. She walked past me, not acknowledging my gentlemanly behavior.

She placed her bag on the end of the white quartz counter and slipped off her jacket. This little dance was fascinating to watch. My eyes followed as those sexy hips continued into the living room. The finely crafted dance left me speechless. She folded her jacket, placed it on the back of the chair, turned around, and placed her hand on her waist.

"So, Mr. Shy guy," she smiled, "are you just going to stand there, or are you going to kiss me?"

Well played. I suppressed my smile. She was definitely a woman I wanted to spend more time with. But I couldn't let her win this round. I'd give in to her later, but not tonight.

I walked over and stopped in front of her. I desperately wanted to possess those full sexy lips. I was trying to stifle my body's reaction to the thought of what those lips would feel like on my body, and how her skin would feel pressed against mine. My mind was full of thoughts about her in my bed. Clearly, she liked being in charge, but I got the feeling she would like being possessed.

I lifted her hand, turned it over and placed her keys in the palm of her hand, and then closed her fingers.

"Good night." I turned around and started toward the door.

"Excuse me?"   I didn't turn around, but kept walking. I opened the door, stepped out into the hall, closed the door and headed toward the elevator. Thank God, it opened immediately. I stepped inside, pressed the lobby button and when the doors closed, I leaned against the back wall and let out a deep sigh. "This is going to be fun."

Chapter 39
Fiona

The heavy footsteps shuffled into the kitchen, followed by a loud yawn. "Good morning, sleepyhead." I looked up and watched as my temporary roommate walked towards the counter. I filled a white mug with coffee and placed it on the placemat.

Mercer walked over and stopped at the counter. He lifted his cup, and took a few hefty sips. "Ahhh...that's good." He leaned down and kissed me on the forehead. "Good morning, Peanut." He took another big sip, placed the mug on the counter and scratched his head.

"Good morning to you, too." I sipped some coffee. "You got home late last night."

He sipped some more coffee. "It didn't seem like it was late. Are those cinnamon walnut muffins?"

"Yes."

His eyes got wide. "I haven't had one of these in a while."

"That's because you haven't been here in a while." I smirked. I knew why he didn't visit much...Rhys. The last time he was here, they got into a fight and Mercer left. Since then, whenever he was in New York, he stayed at a hotel. I didn't agree with his decision, but I was loyal to my husband.

"I know, and I'm sorry about that." Mercer reached over, picked up a muffin, broke off a piece, popped it into his mouth and placed the rest on a small plate. "These are good."

"Thanks."

"How was your evening?" He sipped his coffee.

"Interesting."

"How?" He walked around the counter and sat down.

"I told Ty I thought we might need to take a break."

Mercer's eyes got wide. "You did?"

I sipped more coffee. "If so many people I respect think we're going too fast, then maybe we are."

"So you're making a decision about your relationship based on the opinion of other people's feelings and not your own."

I folded my arms across the center of my chest. "You said..."

"Forget what I said." He sipped more coffee. "What did he say?"

"His patented answer. Whatever I want."

"So what do you want?"

I opened the oven and pulled the frittata out and placed it on the trivet on the counter. "What's that?" he asked.

"Spinach, potato, bacon frittata." I handed him a knife and a plate.

"Are you trying to ply me with good food so I'll forget what we're talking about?" He smiled as he put some frittata on two plates.

"I know better than that." I smiled and took one of the plates. "Thanks."

He took my hand and said grace. I missed this. I missed being with my family. My girlfriends were great, and Ty was incredible, but Merc was family. I was glad to have him here.

"Amen." He put a forkful of frittata into his mouth and chewed. "Oh man, this is good."

"I'm glad you like it." I smiled.

He chewed, swallowed and said, "So you want to take a break from your boyfriend."

"Yes…no…maybe…I'm not sure. My mind says I need to slow things down, but my heart…" I looked at Mercer.

"What does your heart say?" He put another forkful of frittata into his mouth and chewed.

"My mind…"

"I didn't ask what your mind said." He pointed to his heart. "What does your heart say?"

"Merc, it's not that easy."

"Do you love him?" He sipped more coffee.

The answer was simple. My heart and mind were on the same page, but everyone telling us to slow down had me confused.

"The pregnancy scare and his mother and you and…"

"Fiona…" He wiped his mouth and locked eyes with me. "How do you feel about Ty?"

"I think I love him."

"You think?" His eyebrows raised as he put another piece of muffin into his mouth.

"Why are you trying to confuse me?"

"That's not what I'm doing. I want to make sure you're not confusing sex with love."

"I'm not." I ate a little more frittata.

"You're not?" He sipped his coffee. "Sex can be powerful and...I don't want you to wake up and discover you made a mistake."

"Mistake?"

"Like get with someone God didn't want in your life or bed."

"I'm not naive."

"I didn't say you were. Sex is easy. Love takes work and patience."

"So you think I made a mistake."

"I think you had a slip up." He sipped more coffee. "Are you in love with Ty? It's a simple question that requires a 'yes' or 'no' answer."

I shuffled from side to side, sipped more coffee and looked at my big brother. He had always been my protector, my confidant. He was the one I told about my crush on Rhys in college. He's also the only one I called when I decided to divorce Rhys. I knew he could be protective, which was evident the other night when he and Ty almost got into a fight over my virtue or the lack thereof. But all of this was new for me.

"It's complicated."

"No it isn't. That's the excuse you're using because you're afraid of your feelings."

"Really?"

"Yes. Right now, you're more concerned with what people will say because you haven't been divorced that long."

"Maybe."

"Who cares what other people think."

"Even you?"

"Even me. Sure, I wish you had waited a little longer before getting involved again. And God knows, I really wish you hadn't slept with Ty," he smiled, "but you're a grown woman and I can't tell you how to live your life." He sipped more coffee. "So back to my original question. Are you in love with Ty?"

"I think so."

"Then tell him." He put more frittata on his plate. "This is really good."

"So you're okay with me and Ty?" I ate some more frittata.

"I never said I had a problem with Ty. I had a problem with him coming out of your bedroom at three in the morning, and you being naked." He wiped his mouth.

I smiled. "I wasn't naked. I had a robe on." I ate some more frittata.

"Girl, that thing was so thin, I saw parts of you I never want to see again." He sipped some coffee and I laughed at him. "It's not funny. No brother wants to see his sister dressed like that."

I tried to stop laughing. "So you like Ty?"

"I'm not saying we're boys, but he's a decent guy."

"So, if we were married…"

He held his hand up. "Married? Who said anything about marriage?" He put his fork down and looked me in the eye. "Are you two that serious?"

"Yes…no…I'm not sure." I sipped more coffee. "He's said some things that make me think he's headed in that direction."

"Like?"

"Meeting his parents."

"That doesn't…"

"Agreeing to no sex until we're sure where things are headed."

"I see." He nodded. "So I'll ask again. Are you in love with him or do you want to take a break?"

I shrugged my shoulders.

Chapter 40
Ty

"You're welcome. How did it go?...really...she was, but...okay...I won't...we'll talk later. Bye."

Knock...knock...knock...

"Come in." I looked up and saw Tasha walking towards my desk. She placed a small stack of manila folders on the corner of my desk and emptied out the black leather box. She was very quiet, which was unusual for her. I was expecting her to have come in here ranting and raving or worse, threatening to cut off parts of me I really need to father children. I cast my attention back to my work and heard her walking away. "Tasha, would you please call Peony and get me a dinner reservation for tonight. Thank you."

I heard her footsteps stop. "Is that supposed to be a joke?"

"What are you talking about?"

"Peony…"

I looked at her. "I don't understand." I tried not to smile.

She placed her hand on her hip. "Is that how we're going to play it?"

I put my pen down and looked at her. "How was dinner?"

She walked back to my desk, braced her hands on the edge and leaned forward. "Dinner was fine, but then you already knew that."

I could continue to play dumb and see how angry she would become, or I could just admit I had a hand in her plans last night. "Yep."

"You think you're real smart."

"Yep."

"So now you're a match maker."

"On the contrary. I told him going out with you wasn't a good idea."

She leaned back and folded her arms across her chest. "What?"

"I told him I didn't think it was wise, especially after watching the two of you yelling at each other. But he said he liked your fire."

"Really?" Her mouth turned up into a soft smile.

"How was dinner?"

"Like you don't know."

"What's that supposed to mean?"

"I know you spoke with him." She cocked her head to the side.

"Yes, I did."

"And…"

"He said he had a good time."

"And…"

"That's it."

"I know you're not telling me something."

I stood up, walked over to the table, picked up a bottle of water, twisted off the top and sipped. "All he said was he had a good time."

"That's it."

"Yes." I sipped some more water. "Were you expecting more?"

"What…no…I mean…considering how the date…"

"Date?"

I saw something I'd never seen before…fidgeting. She was nervous. "Don't act like you didn't know it was a date."

I smirked. "I know some things."

"Well, I'll be surprised if I hear from him again."

"Huh. Is that what you think?"

"What do you know, Tiberius Wells?" she said as she placed her hands on her hips.

"I know nothing." I held my hands up in a defensive pose.

"Yeah…yeah…yeah…just like I don't know that you want to propose to Fiona."

I spit out the water that was in my mouth. "What?" I wiped my mouth.

"I have to get back to work." She turned and headed toward the door.

"Tasha, if you don't stop walking, you better not stop until you reach the unemployment office." She stopped and turned back around.

"Yes," she said smugly.

"What did you say?"

"I said, I know you want to propose to Fiona."

"Where...how did you...what?"

"Oh, please." She leaned against one of the chairs in front of my desk with her arms folded in front of her chest. "Why else would you fly her down to meet your parents."

"That doesn't..."

"And your jeweler called to say, the ring is ready." She smiled.

"That's...I...uhm...you're way off base."

"Am I?"

"Yes."

"Let's examine the evidence. Since I've been working for you. I have never known you to introduce any woman to your parents, except me, and we don't have that kind of relationship. Second, you waited several months before having sex with her."

"In my defense, I told her I would follow her lead."

"Exactly. You let her call the shots."

"So I wanted to try something different."

"That would be believable, if it weren't for the fact that you have been in love with her for a while."

I wiped my face with my hands. "Is it that obvious?"

"Yep." She pulled the chair out, sat down and crossed her legs. "So, what's the plan?"

I finished my water, walked over to my desk and sat down. "I haven't got a clue. I mean, we haven't really talked about marriage. We've glossed over the subject, but noting too in depth."

"Uh-huh, so it's safe to say you're in love."

"Yeah, I think so."

"You think so?" She rolled her eyes.

"I've never been in love, so…"

She sat up. "You've never been in love."

"Have you?"

"This isn't about me."

"Wait a minute. Miss Cool, Calm and In Charge has been in love." I took some pleasure in knowing that little piece of information. "I want details."

"You may want details, but you aren't getting any. Besides, this is about you." She leaned back in the chair. "So…"

"Wait a minute. You grill me every time I'm with a woman more than a week, and I can't ask…"

"You can, but not now. This is about you and Fiona. What's the plan?"

"Don't have one, because I'm not…"

"Oh, please. You and Fi are made for each other."

"Are we? Just because I love her and the sex is incredible, doesn't mean…"

She leaned forward. "Ask yourself this. If you couldn't have sex with her, would you still feel the same?"

"We aren't sleeping together anymore."

"That's not what I asked. If you physically, couldn't make love to her, how would you feel about her?"

I didn't hesitate. "I'd still feel the same."

"You would?" Her eyes got wide.

"Yes. The sex was mind blowing, but even without it, my feelings wouldn't change. If all I could do was have her in my bed platonically, I'd still feel the same."

She nodded. "If that's your answer, then you need to talk to her."

"I know how I feel, but I'm not sure about her."

"There's only one way to get your…"

"Ask her."

"Exactly."

She stood up, adjusted her clothes and looked at me. "If it's any consolation, I'm pretty sure she feels the same."

"You think so?"

"I bet my life on it." She started towards the door. "If you'll excuse me, I need to make a call to a rather tall, infuriating, sexy man."

Chapter 41
Fiona

I rang the doorbell, took a deep breath and looked around the deserted hall way. In all my visits here, I have never seen anyone else in the hall. It's like there's some unwritten rule, that only one person is allowed in the hall at a time.

The door swung open and it startled me, even though I was expecting it to open.

"Hey, babe." Ty smiled, ushered me inside and then looked around the hall. I guess he was making sure I hadn't violated the one person in the hall at a time rule. He closed the door and helped me with my jacket.

"Hi."

He hung my jacket up in the closet opposite the front door. "Did we have plans tonight that I forgot?"

"No." I started walking down the short path into the large open living space.

"Just thought you'd surprise me?"

"What?"

"I said I like getting surprise visits from you."

"Oh, yeah." I continued walking into the living room.

"Is everything alright?" he asked.

"Yes."

"Are you sure?"

I turned to face him. "Yes, why would you ask me that?"

He slipped his hands inside his pockets. "I don't know, maybe because you stopped by unannounced, which I'm completely fine with." He stepped closer. "But you didn't kiss me."

"Oh, I'm sorry." I stepped to him and gently kissed him on the lips. I started to walk away and he grabbed my hand, pulled me to his chest and crushed his lips against mine. He slid his hands down the small of my back pressing me closer against him.

We agreed no sex, but the way he kissed me made sticking to that agreement a little difficult. I threaded my hands around his neck, sinking deeper into the kiss.

He slid his hands further down, squeezing my behind. I opened my mouth and he slid his warm tongue inside, slowly stroking and teasing me. I moaned and pulled him deeper into my space. One of his hands traveled up the side of my body grazing my breast. I moaned again into his mouth, and my mind filled with a catalog of lustful things I wanted him to do to me.

I was on the verge of losing control. My bag slipped

out of my hand and landed onto the floor, but that didn't stop us from stepping closer to breaking our promise to each other.

His hand slid inside the top of my dress and cupped my breast. The heat of his hand penetrated the lavender lace of my bra and sent a surge of heat to my core. He slipped his hand inside the lace cup of my bra and gently pinched my nipple. *Oh, God…* He's making it difficult for me to do what I came here to do.

He moved his mouth across my cheek and down my neck. His hot breath caused my skin to pebble. His hands were at work torturing me. My body was experiencing things I hadn't felt since that night we shared a bath. Even then, he left me high and dry to go handle a client. A client I later discovered was his mother.

He gently bit my neck and my breath caught as his hand made love to my breast. Oh man, this…this isn't supposed to be happening. I came here to…uhm. I moaned again. I wanted out of my clothes and Ty inside me.

I whispered, "Kiss me." He moved his mouth back to mine and… "Not there."

He pulled back and looked at me hungrily. "Where?"

I stepped back, opened my dress and revealed the lavender lace covered breast he was just teasing with his hand. I pulled the straps down one at a time and I saw his body react. "Here."

"Where?"he asked.

I took his hand and placed the tip of his large index finger on my diamond sharp nipple. "Here."

"Is that what you want?"

I sucked on my bottom lip and nodded, "Yes."

"And then where?"

I guided his finger down the center of my chest stopping

at my navel. "Here."

"And then?"

I was trying to torture him, but instead...

I closed my eyes and tossed my head back. I felt him stepping closer. "I'll do whatever you want." He kissed my neck and then moved his mouth along my collar bone and along the swell of my breast. It was like I was drunk. My head was bobbing from side to side. I swallowed hard, and felt something hot and wet on my nipple and the fog lifted.

I pushed him away and ran down the hall to the powder room. I stood in front of the mirror breathing hard. I slowly raised my eyes and looked at my reflection. I was more ashamed than embarrassed. I'd given in to lust and was about to break a promise I...we made.

I splashed some water on my face, adjusted my clothes, took a deep breath and went back out to the living room.

"Are you okay?"

"Yes." That was a lie. I was far from okay. He walked over and I stepped backwards.

"What's going on? Is this about our agreement?"

I rubbed the back of my neck. "Yes and no."

"I was just..."

"I know, following my lead." I lowered my head and turned away from him.

"Fi, what's going on?" I heard him step closer to me and then his hands eased around my waist. "Talk to me," he said in a soft, sexy tone.

Talk to him. "I think we need to take a break." I spit the words out. I turned around to face him. "I think we need to take a break." The stone face was back.

"Is that what you want?"

He removed his hands from my waist, stepped back

and wiped his mouth with his hands. This calm reaction was definitely not what I was expecting.

"Yes."

We locked eyes. I'm not sure which was worse, the silence or his staring at me.

"Okay."

"What?!" Now I was the one not sure how to react. "I'm sorry, did you hear what I said?"

"You said you wanted to take a break."

"And you're fine with that? Don't you want to know why?"

"No." He walked into the kitchen, opened the cabinet and pulled down a bottle of scotch. He pulled the short glass across the counter, poured about a half inch of the brown liquid and drank it in one swallow.

"No?" I was getting hysterical.

"No."

"Ty, I don't understand you. I said I want to take a break and all you can say is okay."

"Of course I want to know why, but what's the point?" He poured another drink.

"Am I missing something here? Most men would want an answer…a reason, not just say, 'okay'."

"The other night you made your case and I figured we were fine, but…" He sighed. "I told you from the beginning, I would do whatever you wanted. If you want to take it slow, I'll slow things down. If you want me to make love to you. I'll make love to you. If you want to take a break, we'll take a break."

I rubbed my forehead. This was surreal. "Just like that?"

"Fiona, I'm not going to get upset or fight you, because clearly this is something you've wanted to do for a while."

"And you're fine with it?"

"No."

"So if I hadn't run down the hall, would we have made love?"

"If that's what you wanted."

I shook my head. "Why won't you fight me on this?"

"Why should I?"

"I don't know, maybe because this is our relationship we're discussing."

"Our relationship?"

"Yes."

"Huh…" He finished his drink.

"Yes. We're in this together."

"Are we?" He was stone faced.

"Yes."

"We can't be, because I don't want to take a break, but you do."

"Then…"

He stepped to me, gently grabbed my upper arms. "I don't want you to stay in a relationship you don't want to be in." The strong alcohol coated his words as he spoke, burning my eyes.

"That's not what I said."

"It's what you meant, and I'm fine with that."

"But, Ty…"

"Sweetheart, I understand."

But I didn't. I wanted him to fight me, give me his reasons for us not taking this step. "How long?"

"How long what?" he asked.

"How long do we want this to last?"

"You're the only one that can answer that." He kissed

me on the forehead, walked to the closet, pulled out my jacket and handed it to me. "Come on, I'll walk you out."

"You don't have to do that." He helped me slip on my jacket. I turned to face him and I couldn't read his face. He had his stern lawyer face on. He escorted me out and down to the elevator. He pressed the button and the elevator door immediately opened. That was a first. I stepped inside, turned around and looked at Ty. He held the door open with his hand, stepped inside and gently placed his lips against mine and then stepped back.

"Is this what you want?" he asked.

I looked at him and felt tears gathering in my eyes. I didn't want him to see me cry. I nodded my head. He let go of the door and it closed. I leaned against the wall of the elevator and brushed the tear that escaped my right eye.

I closed my eyes during the quick ride to the lobby. When the elevator stopped and the doors opened, I had an epiphany.

"I made a mistake."

The End

EXCERPT FROM

Generational Curse

1

KYLA PROMISED HERSELF SHE WOULD never be like the other women in her family, dating a married man and settling for the pennies he doled out.

She'd always felt she was worth more. She met Eric at a fundraiser. He smiled, she smiled and after the cocktail hour, they found themselves seated next to each other. During dinner they talked and flirted and once the evening was over, he asked for her number. She declined and while getting ready for bed, she reached into her bag for her phone and noticed that she also had someone else's phone.

She called the last number dialed and a vaguely familiar voice said, "I've been waiting for your call. So what time do you want to meet for breakfast so I can get my phone?" They both laughed.

They agreed to meet the following morning for breakfast. Two days later, they met again and included an extra slot for "therapy."

Making love in the morning seemed so decadent. She didn't think anything of it until she received her first black envelope a month later.

Eric said, "I'm tired of hotels. Rent a place and fix it up for us and keep whatever is left."

"I'm not a hooker."

"I didn't mean any disrespect. I want to keep seeing you, but my neighbors are nosey."

"Oh, you're married."

"No, I'm not. I just like my privacy. I like being with you, but—"

"I understand." She dropped her head and quickly began getting dressed. "I don't think this is—"

He noticed the change in her behavior and rushed to reassure her. "I don't want you to think I'm ashamed of you, but I also don't want you to think I'm monopolizing your time. You need your space and so do I. When we get together, it should be on neutral, comfortable ground and not some cold hotel room or a place filled with memories of past lovers."

He wrapped his arms around her pulling her to him, gently stroking her hair, inhaling her neck and gently placing a kiss on her soft shoulder. She turned around trying to read the expression on his face. Looking into his eyes, she wondered how many more love nests he had scattered around the city. She pulled his face close to hers and covering his mouth with hers, kissed him passionately. She slipped her hands inside the front of his pants while sliding her tongue inside his mouth, exciting him to the point of arousal.

She pulled back and whispered, "Once more before we have to go?"

He couldn't resist her. The soft seductive tone of her

voice and the gentle touch of her hand, made him weak and willing to do anything she asked. Kyla knew if there were anyone else, they would have a hard time competing with her.

She got her education in how to manipulate a man by eavesdropping on her aunts' conversations. They were all experts when it came to being with and manipulating married men. She learned how to kiss from her high school boyfriend. And her college boyfriend, her biology professor, schooled her in anatomy and how to physically please a man.

Before getting involved with Eric, she had dated, but she only had two other semi serious relationships. Neither was fulfilling. The first was Thomas Smith. He was cute, but he lacked the drive to satisfy her physically. When they were together she found herself fantasizing about other men. Intellectually he was a genius, but no one really makes love to a person's brain. It was the other part of his body that needed more educating and she knew she wasn't a school teacher.

Then there was Alister Humphrey. The name alone intrigued her. She had never met a black man with such a stuffy name. In the beginning he seemed like the complete package. Model good looks, intelligence and his skills in bed were unbelievable. The first time they made love, the intensity of his being inside her brought tears to her eyes. Not because it was painful, but because she had never felt such pleasure. Alister knew exactly how to read her body. A skill that was the result of his blindness. What he lacked in vision, he more than compensated for in his other senses. But, he was a man and as they all do, he began making demands and that's when she called it quits. Mind blowing sex aside, Kyla was gone.

Her aunts always said, "Don't allow a man to make demands on you. You make the demands on him. Use what you have and any man can be controlled with the sway of your hips and the wink of your eye. And, showing a little cleavage wouldn't hurt either."

If she were going to marry, it would be to Eric. He was everything she wanted. Handsome, well educated, focused, rich and eager to please in and out of bed. But she also learned from her aunts, the wife always got the leftovers and Kyla didn't like leftovers or sloppy seconds. When Eric suggested the apartment, at first she thought, he was ashamed of her. But Eric's response to her kiss and touch convinced her, she was his priority.

She knew she was in charge. She eased her hand further down his pants pleading, "Baby, please make me sing again before sending me off to start the day."

She kissed his neck before dropping the sheet that was caressing her body and walked into the bathroom. He stood still contemplating the repercussions of being late to the office, when he heard the shower running. He looked at his watch and texted his assistant he would be late. He put his phone on the desk, striped, walked into the steam filled bathroom and opened the shower door to a wet and soapy Kyla, smiling.

"Are you ready to sing?" he asked as he leaned her up against the slippery tiled wall. He pressed himself against her and filled his mouth with every inch of her. He lifted her from behind and rode her like a beautiful long legged mare. The harder he rode, the louder she sang. One last trot, and he sang out too. He rested his head on her chest and she had her answer, "no," there was no one else, just her. She reached over and turned the hot water off. They both needed to cool down. "Baby, I'll do whatever you want, just don't leave me," he begged.

She smiled to herself and replied, "Whatever you say baby." He pulled away and she turned the hot water back on and washed him like a newborn baby. Gently stroking every inch of him. He knew there wasn't another woman like her. No woman ever treated him like this. He stood still and let her soft hands wash him clean.

On his way to work, he called her. "You are an amazing woman." She remained silent. "Can I see you tonight?"

She thought for a moment before replying, "Only if you promise to repeat that shower scene."

"Your wish is my command."

Now more than three years later and countless showers and secret meetings, she's still calling the shots.

EXCERPT FROM

A

Southern Gentleman

Chapter 1

Avery walked into the River Grill and knew as she approached the hostess station it was pointless to ask if any of her party were here. Since she and her girlfriends started having these catch up dinners, they'd played with a variety of times to accommodate her friends' schedule, they were always late. Secretly she hoped just once one of them would surprise her and be on time, or even beat her, getting to the restaurant.

"I'm here for the Marshall party," she said to the hostess.

The hostess scanned her iPad, and then cast her eyes back at Avery with a sympathetic smile. "I'm sorry, but you seem to be the first one here."

"Of course I am," Avery said under her breath.

"Excuse me?"

"Nothing."

"Unfortunately, our policy is not to seat you until at least half of your party are present."

"I understand."

"You are more than welcome to have a seat in..."

"The bar." Avery said sarcastically under her breath.

"Excuse me?"

"I'll just wait in the bar. Thank you." Avery smiled.

"I'll let the rest of your party know where to find you." The hostess smiled.

"Thank you."

Avery turned around on her very expensive heels and headed to the bar. She stopped at the bar entrance, looked around and exhaled. She hated sitting in a bar alone. She told herself that any woman sitting in the bar of a luxury hotel full of men at this time of day was probably a hooker, looking to score a wealthy John for the evening, or possibly as a steady gig. She suspected most of the men at the bar thought she was either a new call girl or an old one hoping to catch her last big John.

Avery looked around the bar and categorized all the men she saw. There were the young guns, looking like they should be ordering milk instead of martinis or scotch. Then there were the ones that thought they were good looking and too good for her. That was fine by her. Her last boyfriend was in the latter class…a pretentious player who believed his overly hyped, professionally written biography. And then there were the silver foxes. Loaded with money and little blue pills, searching for a sweet young, thin thing looking for a sugar daddy…or a very discrete call girl. And she was neither.

Avery stood up straight, careened her neck around the line of suits, and spotted an empty seat at the other end of the bar. She took a deep breath and walked towards the empty seat. As she headed towards the bar stool, she began to regret her fashion selection for the evening. She had treated herself to a new dress. A beautiful royal blue Zac Posen fitted cocktail dress, with a deep scoop neckline. She was confident in her decision to buy it. However, if she'd known the only available bar seat meant she had to walk the gauntlet of men to get to it, she would have worn basic black, so she could blend into the crowd.

She exhaled and cursed her girlfriends for putting her through this. She held her head high and started towards the only seat with a partial view of the hostess station. As she walked, her feet began to voice their dislike for the distance she was forcing them to go in five inch Christian Louboutin So Kate heels. The leopard print satin stiletto pumps were beautiful, but definitely not designed to go distance. Not that the distance from the hostess station to the last available seat was that far. But right now to her feet, it felt like she was asking them to run a half marathon in stilettos.

Horrified she might fall, she focused all her attention on walking a straight line. Unfortunately for Avery, that meant not concentrating on her hips. Her mother constantly told her it wasn't appropriate for a woman of her size to sway her hips. It's not like she should be working as the fat lady for the circus. She was only a size ten on her slim days, and a twelve on most others. But her short height emphasized her curves. And when she wore heels, she seemed to bring more attention to her voluptuous figure. Avery wasn't ashamed of her body, but she wasn't quite comfortable with it either. Thanks in part to her mother constantly comparing her to her cousins who were all thin…and married.

Avery figured if she concentrated on the bar stool it would prevent her from toppling over in her heels. Wiggling hips be damned, she was determined to get that seat.

She looked up and noticed a well-dressed gentleman enter the bar from the hotel entrance. He was headed towards her seat. Crap. *If it wouldn't slow me down, I'd take these heels off and run over and plop my butt on that empty stool.*

She tried walking a little faster, keeping her eyes focused on the gentleman she was sure was headed towards the last empty stool. Suddenly he stopped mid stride, reached into his jacket pocket, pulled out his phone, and started talking. She sighed and continued on her destination.

She didn't dare slow down in case there was another unseen

contender for her seat. She turned the corner of the bar and focused on the stool. When she made it to the stool, she felt victorious. Not only had she managed not to fall down, she'd won the seat. She turned the back of the stool around and, "What the Crap!" There was a coat on the seat of the stool. She looked around and there wasn't another empty seat at the bar. Her shoes were definitely not meant for distance walking, and her feet were killing her.

Suddenly, a large, dark chocolate hand, with a beautiful gold Phillippe Patek watch, removed the tan trench coat.

"I was saving you a seat," announced the very handsome gentleman sitting on the stool next to her seat of choice.

"Excuse me?"

"I said, I saved you a seat." He stood up, and Avery's eyes scanned the length of him. He was very tall and handsome. He pulled the stool out a little, and helped her up onto it.

"Thank you." She was shocked and surprised one of these men would do something so chivalrous for a woman who was not a model or a thin beauty like most of the other women in the bar.

She got comfortable on the stool and exhaled. When she sat on seats with cushions smaller than her behind, she was convinced God had a great sense of humor. Her behind barely fit the small but comfortable seat. She crossed her legs and noticed her seat saver looking her up and down. She tried not to fidget as she put her black and gold Chanel clutch on her lap, sat up straight, and sighed.

She knew she couldn't sit at the bar without ordering. Another reason she didn't like waiting at the bar. She was trying to lose ten pounds at her mother's insistence. Her mother convinced those ten pounds and curvy hips, were the reason Avery's last boyfriend broke up with her. Avery felt their break had more to do with his roaming eye and social climbing.

Now that she was seated, she had no choice. She had to order something, or give up her seat and stand by the hostess station to wait for her girlfriends in shoes that hurt her feet. Now she understood why the salesman told her to size up. "Tomorrow, I'm taking these back and sizing up."

"There's nothing lonelier than sitting in a bar alone," said the deep voice next to her.

She really didn't want to talk to him, but felt obligated since he had saved her a seat. "I know what you mean." She raised her hand, to flag the bartender.

"It took me a little while to get his attention, but then I'm a guy, and he'll probably jump at a chance to wait on the most beautiful woman in here."

She smiled and shook her head. *Is this guy for real?* "Your sentiment is nice, however…"

"It's not a line, pretty lady."

When he said pretty lady, it hit her. There was something very distinctive about his voice.

"I'm sorry, what did you say?" She locked eyes with him, hoping it would help her focus on his voice.

"I said, I wasn't giving you a line."

"That's not what you said. You said lady something."

"Pretty lady."

"Yes. That accent…where are you from?"

"Birmingham, Alabama." He turned to face her and extended his hand. "Let me introduce myself. I'm Jeremiah Augustus Logan and you, Pretty Lady, are…"

She smiled and shook his hand, and felt a flush of heat come over her. "That's a lot of name," she replied as she tried to compose herself.

"Where I come from, that's barely enough name."

When he aimed his eyes at her and smiled, Avery almost fell off her stool. It felt like she had just witnessed the birth of the sun. His smile was bright, warm, and friendly. And his beautiful dark eyes sparkled like black diamonds. She wasn't a fan of men with facial hair, but the close cut beard and mustache suited this handsome stranger.

"It's a nice name." She let go of his hand.

"Thank you, pretty lady. And what's yours?"

"I'm sorry. It's Avery. Avery Marshall." She didn't know

why, but she felt compelled to tell him her last name.

"That's a beautiful name for a beautiful lady."

She'd heard that line before, but never with such sincerity. "So, Jeremiah…"

"Pretty lady, if it would make you more comfortable, call me Jay."

Her smile had returned. "I like your name. It's sort of regal." She couldn't believe she was flirting, and doing a pretty good job of it so far.

He stood up straighter and brushed his jacket. "I never had anyone say I was regal. My mom would be proud to know all those charm lessons were worth it." They laughed. "Your laugh is infectious."

Avery rubbed her neck. "Uhm…I see you were wrong."

"About what?"

"The bartender. Seems he's ignoring me as well."

"He has no taste when it comes to women. What would you like to drink?"

"A glass of their house merlot would be fine. Thank you."

"Save my seat." He winked and walked around the bar to the end where the bartender was talking with two pretty and thin brunettes. Jeremiah slipped in between the two women and smiled. "Excuse me, ladies. Sir," the bartender turned around, "the beautiful lady at the end of the bar and I would like two glasses of your house merlot, thank you."

"Coming right up," the bartender replied.

Jeremiah stepped back and started to walk away.

"You should stay here with us," one of the women said to Jeremiah.

He smiled. "Thank you, but that beautiful lady at the end of the bar is waiting on me. Have a good evening, and the next round is on me."

He walked back towards Avery and she carefully examined him. He seemed even taller as he walked towards her. She liked the way he filled out his jacket. She wasn't a fan of double breasted suits on large, muscular men, but on Jeremiah, it looked good. She also noticed he had strong defined thigh muscles by the way the fine, lightweight wool grazed his legs as he walked. She also wasn't big on muscular men, probably because those were the ones who thought she was fat. She couldn't help but notice the way his jacket hugged his tight behind when he had walked around the bar a few minutes ago. He carried himself very well for a man of his size.

By the comment Jeremiah made earlier, he was attracted to her as well. It was that, or he was drunk, or possibly had a vision problem, or maybe that was just his southern charm.

"Do I meet with your approval?" he asked.

"Excuse me?"

"I saw you checking me out. So do I pass?" He spun around and stopped in front of her and smiled.

"Confidence isn't an issue for you, is it?" She smiled.

"Nope." He sat on his stool. "Besides, I'm talking to the sexiest woman in the joint."

The bartender placed both glasses of wine in front of them. "Will there be anything else?" the bartender asked.

"I've been hearing a lot about truffle fries. Do you have those?" Jeremiah asked, his southern accent singing every syllable.

"Yes, sir."

"We'll have an order of truffle fries and the short rib sliders with a little extra barbecue sauce. Unless you want something else?" He looked at Avery.

"No, what you've selected will be fine."

"That will be all, thank you."

Avery lifted her glass to her lips and took a sip. "This is good."

He sipped his wine. I agree. So Miss Avery, why are you sitting in a bar alone?"

She placed her glass on the counter. "I'm meeting friends for dinner, and they can't seem to be on time."

He nodded. "Their tardiness is my blessing."

She smiled. "I like that." She sipped some more wine. "What about you? Why are you alone in a bar?"

"I didn't feel like sitting alone in my room." He sipped some more wine and Avery watched his lips. "If your friends hadn't been late, I wouldn't be here talking to you. I'd probably be playing black jack or solitaire on my phone."

"Somehow I think you would have found another woman to talk to." She sipped more wine.

"I have been in town for two weeks and…"

"Two weeks? Business or pleasure?"

"Now that I've met you, it's both." He smiled.

"Uh-huh, what's your business reason?"

"I'm doing research on a project I'm considering."

"Sounds mysterious." She smiled.

"You have a beautiful smile."

She was beginning to feel a little self-conscious by his compliments. "Thank you."

"What about you?" he asked.

"What about me?"

"Are these girlfriends you're meeting? Or am I going to have to give up my stool to some dude like me with good taste in women?" He smiled.

She laughed. "Your seat, I mean, your stool is safe." Avery was having a good time flirting with Jeremiah.

The bartender walked over and placed their snacks in front of them. "Will there be anything else, sir?"

Jeremiah looked at Avery. "Are we missing anything Miss Avery?"

"No."

"That will be all. Thank you."

"Sure." The bartender replied and left.

Jeremiah reached for Avery's hand, and the rough texture stunned her, but not as much as his bowing his head and saying grace. She felt a jolt in her core. How was it possible she met a nice, southern Christian guy in a Manhattan bar? Those words sounded like the beginning of a bad joke.

"Amen." He picked up a slider, and aimed it at her mouth.

"Okay, ladies first."

She hesitated to open her mouth, but acquiesced. He placed the slider inside and she bit down taking half into her mouth. His large finger grazed her bottom lip sending a heat charge through her body. She covered her mouth with her napkin and chewed. Jeremiah popped the other half of the slider into his mouth and patted his mouth with his napkin.

"That's good," she replied.

"Oh man, that's almost as good as my granddad's prize winning ribs." He popped a couple of fries into his mouth and bobbed his head from side to side. "Worth the hype."

She popped a couple of fries into her mouth, closed her eyes and hummed. "These are my favorite."

"Dangerous." He hummed

"Excuse me?"

"Eating with you is dangerous for me."

Avery's brow furrowed. "Exc—"

He quickly covered her wrist. "No, pretty lady, that's a compliment. For the past couple of weeks, I've been at meals with women who seem to be afraid to eat, let alone enjoy their food. Watching you enjoy your food means you appreciate the talent involved in creating good food. Not to mention, you have incredibly sexy lips."

Her eyes got wide, because she was thinking the same thing about his mouth. "Uhm…I've…"

He looked her up and down, leaned in close and his cologne encircled her making her feel a little light headed. "When you walked in here I couldn't take my eyes off of you. I couldn't believe that not one of these men was waiting for you. The way you moved was mesmerizing. And those hips, girl, you are this southern gentleman's fantasy come to life."

Avery found it hard to breathe. No man had ever said the things to her that Jeremiah had said in the short time they had been talking. His words were powerful and effecting her in a way she had never experienced. She felt flushed all over and very excited. Then he gently brushed her forearm, and she almost climbed out of her skin. Her body started to tremble and she knew standing up wasn't an option.

She reached for her glass, but her hand was shaking too badly. She quickly put her hand back on top of her clutch and tried to calm down. Jeremiah inched closer and now she was really having a problem. He gently brushed her forearm again and her breath caught. "I should probably…"

"Have dinner with me tomorrow?" he whispered.

She swallowed hard and fixed her mouth to answer. Chirp…Chirp…Chirp… She picked up her phone and looked at the screen. "Seems my friends are here." She smiled. "I…uhm…it…"

He stood up, turned the stool, extended his hand to her and helped her climb down onto the floor. She adjusted her dress and his eyes followed every move she made. She turned to face him and he was wearing a huge smile. Instead of feeling self-conscious, she felt a little sassy.

"You didn't answer my question."

Her phone started chirping again and she pressed the Answer Call button. "I'm coming. Bye." She pressed the button ending the call and looked at Jeremiah. "Jeremiah, this has been nice. Enjoy your stay in the city."

"Oh darlin', I can't believe you're leaving me like this." He smiled.

She thought to herself, *neither can I*. And she walked away.

❧❧❧❧❧❧❧

Avery sat at the table listening to her girlfriends go on and on about their husbands and children. This was becoming common at these dinners. Seeing she had neither, she had very little to contribute to the conversation, and realized she was bored. She started to think back to her conversation with Jeremiah and was chastising herself for not saying yes to his dinner invitation. She tried to look in the bar, but their table was across the room and her view to the bar was obstructed.

After dessert, she flagged the server. The sooner she got out of here the better. She'd had her fill of the one-sided girl talk and was in need of fresh air. But first, she'd stroll by the bar and see if Jeremiah might still be there.

The server handed Avery the black leather envelope. "I'll take care of that when you're ready Miss."

"Thank you." She opened the envelope and tried to hide her smile. She lifted the leather folder up and read the slip of paper. *"I know you wanted to say yes to my invitation. I'll meet you tomorrow at seven at the end of the bar in our seats. Dinner with your friends is on me. It's my way of saying thank you. If they hadn't been late, I wouldn't have met you. If you agree to dinner, write your number on the receipt and take my card. Jeremiah."*

"Is there a problem with the check Avery?" Erika asked.

"Apart from you three drinking most of the wine, no," she teased. She wrote her number on the receipt, took Jeremiah's card and handed the leather envelope back to the server. "Thank you, everything was excellent."

"Hope to see you again," the server smiled.

"I'm sure you will," Avery replied.

THE FLING

CHAPTER ONE

"YOU ARE CORDIALLY INVITED TO the wedding of..." I continued reading the invitation and my entire body went numb. I slid down the wall and landed on the cool Moroccan tiled floor and wrapped my arms around my knees. I re-read the thick cream colored card with gorgeous navy blue letterpress text. My mind begged me to stop lying, but it was the truth. My ex-fiancee, the man I gave two years of my life to, was getting married.

How could he do that when I was still grieving? I hadn't even had the ceremonial bonfire for his blue Armani suit that was mixed in with my dry cleaning. I had just got around to tossing out his toothbrush and aftershave.

As much as I refused to believe it was over, this beautiful cream colored card confirmed that we were done. He wasn't coming back. I really didn't think our last fight was going to be our last. I thought he'd just disappear for a few days. But when a few days turned into a couple of weeks, and the weeks turned into months, I realized he was gone.

I should be glad, because now I knew where we stood...where I stood. Now I could stop buying that dreadful carrot apple juice he liked. And the almond butter. Every time I opened the refrigerator and saw that half-full jar, I'd start crying.

I tossed my head back, banging it against the wall, crying harder. I closed my eyes thinking back to the day we met.

I really needed to re-charge my batteries. So, I treated myself to a vacation to Anguilla. My sister, Naya, had backed out at the last minute. She said her boyfriend had a problem with her taking a sisters' trip. I didn't have a man and even if I did, I wasn't going to let him tell me I couldn't spend time with my sister.

When I got to the resort, I immediately changed into something more resort appropriate, and headed to the restaurant. I was starving and that little airplane meal had long worn off. I was sitting outside on the patio enjoying the view, when I spotted a sexy piece of chocolate sitting across the patio. He smiled, I smiled, and that was it. A few minutes later the server appeared.

"Good afternoon, Miss." He placed a tropical fruit concoction with a straw on the table in front of me. "The gentleman," he looked in the direction of the guy I smiled at earlier. "As I was saying. The gentleman would like to know if he may join you."

I looked at Mr. Sexy and then back at the server. "Is this a joke?"

"No, Miss." He looked at him and then back at me. "Mr. Porche…"

"I'm sorry, what did you say?"

"Mr. Porche."

"Please tell me he's not named after a car."

He laughed. "No, Miss. It's por-shay."

"Uh-huh…please tell me that's his last name."

"Yes, it is." The server smiled. "Mr. Porche is very serious about his request."

I looked at Mr. Porche and thought about his offer. It would be nice to have someone to talk to. "He's not some weirdo is he?"

"I don't think so. He's been here a few days and I've yet to see him with a companion."

"Maybe she, or he is tied up in the villa."

"You are very funny, Miss. If you would like, I will tell him you're not interested."

I looked at him again and then back at the server. "It's only lunch, right?"

"Exactly."

I lifted the drink he sent, smiled, and nodded. He stood up, and I felt a jab in my gut. From that moment on, his walk to my table became the scene in every romantic movie…slow, and enticing. The only thing missing was some cheesy music. He was what fine men aspired to be.

I wondered if I stayed here long enough would my skin bronze to that color. I tried to close my mouth, because I could feel the saliva trying to escape, making me look like a drooling fool.

This man was well over six feet. His skin looked like he had just been hand dipped in a vat of rich dark chocolate. The closer he got, the more pronounced his features were. His jaw line was square and solid. His shoulders were broad and wide. He was solid muscle. The fine cotton t-shirt molded itself along his upper body, highlighting his sculpted chest. I swallowed hard as I watched him walk towards me. He held his matching tropical drink up, and the muscle in his bicep looked like he was holding a small melon in the bend of his elbow.

I looked at the server. "Are you sure he meant for you to give me the drink?"

The server smiled. "Yes, Miss."

"My God, he's incredible."

"As you young ladies say, he's hot."

I smiled. "What's your name?"

"I'm Cyrus, Miss."

"Cyrus, even a blind person can see that is a fine, black man."

He finally made his way to my table and stopped. He extended his hand to me and smiled. "Reuben Porche."

I took his large, firm hand in mine and felt a jolt run the length of my body. It was like a magnetic force drawing me to him. "Selena Crawford." I smiled, still shaking his hand.

"Can I have that back?" He teased.

"Oh, I'm sorry." I let go of his hand, staring at the beautiful specimen before me. God, You are an excellent architect and craftsman. He cleared his throat and broke my euphoric excavation of the beautiful man standing before me. "I'm sorry. Please, sit down."

"Thank you." He pulled the chair out and I watched every one of his muscles cooperate as he lowered his body onto the black iron chair.

Reuben wasn't the type of guy that usually approached me. He was the kind my younger sister, Naya, attracted. She was tall and thin like a model. I was what my aunt called petite and curvy with a beautiful face. That was her polite way of saying I was short and fat. I seemed to attract the slightly fluffy guy. Or better put, I got the guy that was in the before picture of the workout ad. Not the after, like Reuben. "Thank you for the drink."

"You're welcome."

I looked around the restaurant. There had to be another woman in here and the server got the instructions mixed up. And because the server made a mistake, Reuben was stuck with me. But the only other woman I saw was a senior citizen. Unless this guy had a major cougar fetish, I was the one he intended the drink for. I looked at his beautiful face and decided to roll with it. If nothing else, this would be a great story to tell. My sister definitely wouldn't believe it. Me, her short, chunky sister, was hit on by a hot guy. I really needed a picture for proof.

"Are you here alone?" What a stupid question. If he wasn't alone, he wouldn't be buying me a drink. Besides,

Cyrus told me he hadn't seen Mr. Tropical Chocolate with anyone.   But, just because Cyrus hadn't seen him with anyone, didn't mean he was alone.

He sipped his drink. "Yes."

I nodded. "Couldn't get a date?" I teased. Bad joke.

"No." He didn't smile.

"I'm sorry. I was just...why are you here alone? I mean, this is a place you come with..." Then my brain caught up to my mouth.   "You know what, it's none of my business."

"My assistant said I needed a vacation."

"Excuse me?"

"It seems the only trips I've been taking have been work-related. Depending on where I was, once I completed my business at the end of the week, I would stay over the weekend."

"That's not a vacation."

"That's what she said." He smiled.

"When was the last time you had a real vacation?"

He looked up and his brow furrowed, then he lowered his face and looked at me. "Seven years ago."

"What?"

"My then-girlfriend wanted to go to Tahiti, so I took her."

"So, let me get this straight. Your last vacation was with your last girlfriend?"

"Not exactly."

"But you said..."

"I said my girlfriend at the time."

"I see."

"Let me explain."

"Really, it's none of my business." I cast my eyes onto the menu. "What do you suggest for lunch?"

He grabbed my hand and a heat charge traveled up my arm. "I haven't really been…she was…we were visiting possible wedding locations."

"Really, I don't need to hear this." I looked back at the menu. "I think I'll have the Chilean Sea Bass or possibly the Nicoise Salad."

"Selena…" I looked at him, and it felt like he was staring at my soul. "I'm not some weirdo. I'm just a work-a-holic."

I wasn't sure if he was lying or not, but he was nice eye candy for lunch. I wasn't in a position to judge, because my dating situation was pretty much the same. There had been a couple of semi-serious relationships, but nothing to send me to Pinterest to set up a wedding board.

"I understand." I sipped my drink and he let go of my hand. "Seems my dating life has been on an extended vacation." We laughed.

He lifted his glass. "Here's to enjoying our vacation." We clinked glasses.

"I second that."

TRACY'S
LIBRARY

THANK YOU so much for taking the time to read my book. Your support means a lot to me. If you enjoyed this book, please recommend it to a friend, family member, a stranger, your book club, your social media posse, favorite bookstore or anyone.

If you haven't done so already, join Tracy's mailing list for free short story and novella downloads and advance notice of new releases and giveaways.

Subscribe to Tracy's Mailing List
www.readtracyreed.com